Taylor's mouth was too dry to pray aloud

She watched as Nick wriggled across the carousel platform and dropped into the center well. A shot pinged against the metal door of the control booth.

"Hell!" Nick snarled. He snatched at the door handle and dove inside. Taylor could no longer see him.

Suddenly the organ wheezed into life with a cheerful rendition of "In the Good Ol' Summertime." The carousel began to turn. Lights blinked. It was like being trapped in a kaleidoscope.

Taylor grabbed the nearest pole and felt herself jerked up. As the horse's pole rose, so did she. As it sank, a bullet struck the pole exactly where her head had been a moment earlier.

The music was loud above the whirring of the motor. Taylor let go and grasped the edge of a chariot and held on as the carousel picked up

She felt the c_____ er out toward the ed_____d her grasp, then ra_____e'd been hit she'd ri_____pun off onto the concrete

Nick mus_ __ve, she thought. She couldn't lose him now.

Dear Reader,

The first horse I ever rode circled majestically on the fine old carousel at our local amusement park. Years later, I realized I'd been perched on a work of art. While many of the great American carousels are long gone, the horses, lions, tigers, pigs—even ostriches and giraffes—that originally graced them have become collectors' items.

Because they are both beautiful and valuable, somebody somewhere is going to steal or fake them to make a dishonest buck.

And where there is a crook, there's a detective—in this case, an inexperienced widow with a fierce determination to solve her first big case all by herself, even if it kills her. And it may.

Not if her new client has his way. He intends to keep his detective safe in his arms, even if he loses the carving school in which he's invested his reputation and his savings.

Although Rounders, Ltd., and the people who inhabit it are strictly figments of my imagination, a number of real carving schools all over the country teach even dangerous klutzes like me to carve carousel animals in the great tradition. You might like to try it yourself.

And now, dear reader, heed the carousel barker's cry and "Climb aboard, climb aboard." I hope you enjoy the ride.

Carolyn McSparren

Books by Carolyn McSparren

HARLEQUIN SUPERROMANCE
725—THE ONLY CHILD
772—IF WISHES WERE HORSES

RIDE A PAINTED PONY
Carolyn McSparren

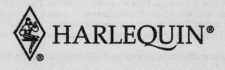

HARLEQUIN®

TORONTO • NEW YORK • LONDON
AMSTERDAM • PARIS • SYDNEY • HAMBURG
STOCKHOLM • ATHENS • TOKYO • MILAN • MADRID
PRAGUE • WARSAW • BUDAPEST • AUCKLAND

ISBN 0-373-70804-1

RIDE A PAINTED PONY

Copyright © 1998 by Carolyn McSparren.

Printed in U.S.A.

For Bess Burgess, who helps me out of plot pickles.

For those wonderful people at Horsin' Around, a school that teaches ordinary folks to carve carousel animals, and who took the time to show me the process. Any technical errors are mine, not theirs.

For those who cherish and seek to preserve the great carousels and carousel animals.

For my husband, George, a left-brain type who still enjoys the ballet and the opera.

PROLOGUE

NICK KENDALL OPENED HIS EYES onto darkness as solid as basalt.

His heart pounded painfully beneath his ribs. For a moment he thought he'd gone blind. As full consciousness returned, he remembered where he was. Lined drapes shut out every vestige of light from the Seattle hotel room. The air conditioner hummed; cold sweat rolled off his chest.

He sat up and drove his fingers through his damp hair. He'd been dreaming, but not the same old nightmare. In the dream with the carousel tickets, he always woke up with a jolt of loss so terrible it filled his throat with bile. No, this dream opened another black hole in his subconscious. This was about the job, about restoring the hippocampus. But why should he be so disturbed about a simple restoration job?

He strained to remember his dream, but it was gone. He lay back with his hands locked behind his head and thought about the work. He rolled over on his side, closed his eyes and brought the image of the hippocampus to his mind. Mentally he slid his hands over the wood, felt the sponginess along its belly, the flakes of turquoise paint on its scales. He felt the joints loosening and the seams opening where the aging glue had failed.

A tingle of disquiet eased up the back of his neck.

His scalp began to prickle.

He squeezed his eyes shut and saw the tiny black-and-white picture that had run with the article—the only article he'd ever seen about that long-gone carousel, toppled by a fierce killer hurricane that buried it and all its animals under tons of New Jersey beach sand. It had been a grand old carousel with three rows of horses—outside row of standers, center row of prancers, inside row of jumpers, and two chariots.

Horses. Only horses.

No ostrich, no pig, no lion. No hippocampus.

Nick sucked in his breath and sat bolt upright. He flung the covers back and padded naked to the chair where he'd dropped his dusty jeans when he'd fallen into bed. He felt around for the desk lamp and flicked it on. He blinked in the sudden light. Three in the morning. Damn.

He pulled on jeans and a sweatshirt, pushed his feet into dust-covered loafers, grabbed the keys to the rental car and left the room.

Fog rolled in off the Puget Sound as he sped through empty streets to the warehouse. He had to know *now*. Dawn lay an eternity away.

Nobody had dug that old hippocampus out of any New Jersey beach. Maybe it was genuine, but from another carousel. Maybe the provenance proving its authenticity had gotten mixed up. Nick tried to think of a reasonable explanation, while part of him stood aside whispering the possibility that he didn't dare admit. That possibility could destroy him and his carefully constructed reputation.

Somebody had been conned. Was it Helmut Eberhardt—the man who'd sold the animal? Pete Marley who'd bought it without checking? With full provenance, the hippocampus could be worth fifty thousand or more. Without it, the hippocampus—genuine or not—was worth half as much.

Nick's stomach churned.

He slid the car to a stop in front of the warehouse and got out. He pulled a set of keys out of his pocket, opened the front door and slammed it behind him. It clanged like the door of a cell.

The hippocampus stood under a spotlight in the center of the room. A round metal pole lanced through its midsection, securing it to a heavy wooden stand. Its fine-boned horse head still lifted towards the sea breeze. Its nostrils seemed to scent the odor of long-abandoned ocean depths. Its teeth fought the bit in its mouth. Front hooves pawed the air as though in a desperate battle against captivity.

Then just behind the withers, the finely carved horse pelt changed to scales as its body morphed from horse to fish. The carving—a mer-horse ready to carry a mermaid princess through gray-green ocean depths—was a perfect blending of horse and fish. It balanced on the lashing split-tail flukes of a whale.

Nick had already stripped the flaking paint from most of the head and neck. He closed his eyes and ran his hands over the raw wood, remembering the eye sockets, the pointed ears, the heavy flat planes of the cheeks. His hands moved down to the fish's body and finally slid beneath the double flukes of the tail.

Yes. Oh, yes. He knew this creature, all right. He should have known it instantly. It wasn't an antique. It was his creation.

He'd carved it twenty years ago. And right now it should be locked up in his storeroom at Rounders—three thousand miles away.

CHAPTER ONE

Unaccompanied Children Will Be Sold As Elves.

Taylor Hunt grimaced at the ornate sign at the head of the stairs. "Cute." She squared her shoulders, took a deep breath to calm the butterflies in her stomach, opened the door to the right, and walked into a blinding pool of sunlight...and a six-foot wooden rabbit.

She grabbed at it as it toppled towards her. "Whoa, there, Peter."

From behind the carving a gravelly female voice said, "Actually, I call him Harvey. Sorry, but every time I slice into him he scoots out from under me."

Small hands encircled the rabbit's waist and hauled him back. A triangular face appeared between his ears. Definitely elfin, but no child. Taylor judged the woman to be in her fifties; there were lines at the corners of her bright blue eyes. "For the life of me, I can't get the roses right."

The woman stepped from behind the rabbit. She was perhaps five feet tall and probably weighed less than the wooden figure. She wore jeans and a dusty sweatshirt with Band Organs Do It with Pipes written across the chest. "Can I help you, dear?" she asked.

"Can you tell me where I can find Mr. Kendall?"

The woman gestured vaguely to her left. "Back there, getting Rico's stander on its feet."

"Uh-huh." Taylor had no idea what getting a stander on its feet entailed, nor, for that matter, what a "stander" was. She fought a moment of panic. She had had precious little time to do her homework. She'd just have to fake it. She had no intention of running back to Mel Borman with her investigative tail between her legs. She smiled at the blue-eyed rabbit lady, who began to dig at the rabbit's shoulder with a wicked steel gouge, three inches wide.

Oh Lord, Taylor thought, *I'd kill myself with that thing.*

Without looking up, the woman said, "Just plunge right on back. Never stand on ceremony at Rounders."

Taylor plunged.

Rounders Unlimited occupied the second floor of a building so old it probably belonged on the National Historic Register. The crumbling warehouse district down by the Mississippi riverfront in Memphis had begun to attract developers eager to turn the old warehouses into chic lofts, but the yuppification process hadn't reached this area. Maybe one look at *this* long-defunct machine shop and warehouse had sent the developers hunting for easier targets.

From the grimy wooden floorboards and crumbling brick walls, Taylor guessed that only minimum upkeep had been done since the original machinery had disappeared into scrap heaps and antique shops.

She threaded her way among sawhorse tables covered with the disembodied heads, trunks, legs and haunches of horses. Directly in front or her, a giraffe's head sat on its long neck, its black glass eyes level with her own. A pig and a frog shared another table, and in this *Alice in Wonderland* world, the frog was twice as big as the pig. The scent of fresh sawdust and wood shavings tickled Taylor's nose. Dust—like Mississippi river silt, too fine to see, impossible to dislodge—hung in the air. She could feel it sifting down into her hair, clothes, mouth and nose. She sneezed.

She edged past a room separated from the space by filthy glass panes nailed along the top of a four-foot wall. The loft stretched back past the reach of the skylights towards a pair of heavy steel doors. In the shadows stood more wooden animals, but no human beings.

"Mr. Kendall?" she called.

"Yeah?"

Nick Kendall had apparently been kneeling on the floor behind a large wooden horse painted to look like an Indian pony. He stood, wiped his hands down jeans even older than hers, and came towards her out of the gloom. He was well over six feet tall. A giant of a man with broad shoulders tapering to a narrow waist.

"Damn," Taylor whispered.

She'd assumed a man who taught amateurs to carve carousel animals would look like Santa Claus. This guy belonged on a dock somewhere unloading crates one-handed.

The minute he smiled, she knew that he was bad. Any female—from six to a hundred and six—would feel the impact of that grin right in the gut. She'd bet the lady carving the rabbit brought him brownies. The man was obviously a charmer. After the years she'd spent married to Paul—who'd showed the same easy charm as this guy Kendall, and had played it for all it was worth—she knew she should be immune. But a flare of heat in her belly warned her that she was still susceptible.

She shifted the strap of her leather satchel to a more comfortable position on her shoulder and extended her hand. She prayed her smile looked competent and professional. "Taylor Hunt, Mr. Kendall. I want to join your class."

He frowned, wiped his right hand down the front of his jeans again and shook hers quickly. His palm felt like badly tanned leather.

"Oh, yeah." He hesitated. "How about we talk in my office?" He gestured at a door to the window room. The office was small and held a scarred wooden student desk, a computer, a battered file cabinet and two mismatched kitchen chairs—one behind the desk, the other across from it.

Even seated—and with the desk between them—Nick Kendall's size was impressive and vaguely disquieting.

"Mel Borman didn't tell me you were a woman. I figured Taylor was a man," he said.

Kendall leaned back in his chair and looked her over. She felt like a mule being assessed for the number of rows she could plow in a day. She returned his gaze levelly and hoped her makeup was thick enough to hide the flush she felt creeping up her face.

"So, Ms. Hunt, how long you been a detective?"

The dreaded question. "I've been an associate of Mr. Borman's for just under two years." Technically correct. If Nick Kendall didn't know that you had to apprentice for a year before you could even sit for the Tennessee P.I. exam, she wasn't about to tell him. She also wasn't going to tell him that most of the time she answered telephones, ran papers to the courthouse, and occasionally tricked workmen's compensation cheats into showing that they could still mow the lawn and shoot pool.

"You used to be a cop?"

She took a deep breath. "No." Her stomach tied itself into a dozen granny knots, but she willed it to stay quiet.

"Isn't being a private investigator a dangerous job for a woman?"

"I was in more danger driving down here." Easier ground now. "Investigators spend most of their time sitting in front of computer screens or drinking cold coffee outside shabby motel rooms." Not strictly accurate, but close.

"How did you meet Borman?"

"My uncle Mark was a prosecuting attorney. He introduced me to Mel. Said he was honest and competent. After my husband's death, I needed a job. Mel needed an investigator. It was a good fit." No need to tell him of the weeks she'd spent bullying Mel until he agreed to take her on as an unpaid apprentice, or the sheer hell she'd endured from her family when he finally capitulated.

The darn chair hit her right on the tailbone, though the discomfort was probably more psychological than physical. She wasn't exactly deceiving Kendall—just omitting details. And she swore her inexperience would never make him regret hiring the Borman agency.

Kendall's grilling made her feel as though she were back in the fourth grade in the principal's office, with Mr. Davidson accusing her of hiding the garter snake in Mrs. Anderson's drawer. She'd never admitted that one either.

"Is this your first undercover assignment?" he asked.

"Of course not." Just the first one without Mel sitting two bar stools away in case one of the rowdies reached for her breast or tried to stick his hand up her dress.

"I've never hired a detective before."

She relaxed. Of course he was nervous—maybe even more so than she was. She gave him what she hoped was a reassuring smile. "Most people haven't unless they're trying to find a missing child or get the goods on a cheating spouse."

"I've never been married."

Alarm bells went off in her head. Most of the forty-year-old men she met were either married, damaged or gay. Her hormones indicated that he wasn't gay. That left damaged. Alcohol maybe, or drugs?

She sat up straighter. Why should she care? Mel's number-one rule was "Never get emotionally involved with The Client." Until this moment, she'd never felt the slightest twinge of interest in a client—but then, she'd never met one with the sort of grin that could con Little Red Riding Hood out of her basket of goodies.

"I'm not sure this is something a woman can handle."

Taylor's jaw set so hard that her teeth clicked. So *that*

was why he wasn't married. With effort, she kept the smile plastered to her face. "I can do anything Mr. Borman can do. We're talking carousel horses here, Mr. Kendall, not the drug cartels."

He raised an eyebrow. "I didn't mean you weren't competent." He leaned forward and rested his elbows on the desk in front of him. The sleeves of his sweatshirt rode up to reveal muscular forearms feathered with dark hair. "Ten of my signed pieces have been stolen, maybe more. I don't have a complete inventory of my stuff. As mine, they'd sell for ten to fifteen thousand dollars. With fake provenance claiming them to be real antiques, they could bring upwards of fifty thou. A few years back a genuine Illions went at auction for over a hundred and twenty-five thousand dollars. Multiply that by ten, and you'll have some idea of the scope. It may not be cocaine, but it ain't chicken feed. When that kind of money's involved, things can get rough."

Bigger than either she or Mel had thought.

"It should have been simple to trace the fake hippocampus Pete Marley bought," Kendall continued. "Unfortunately before I could talk to Helmut Eberhardt—the owner of the antique shop in Oxford that sold it—Eberhardt was killed."

For a moment Taylor thought she hadn't heard him properly. Then, as his words registered, she strained forward in her chair. The hair rose on the back of her neck as though the door behind her had blown open. One hint of murder and Mel Borman would yank her straight back to the office. He said P.I.'s didn't mess with murder unless the defense hired them to check evidence after the suspect was arrested and indicted. "Killed? Murdered?"

Kendall shook his head. "A fire. The Oxford cops called it an accident."

She relaxed. Mel Borman wouldn't mutate into Papa Bear over a simple accident. Maybe she wouldn't tell him. But that would never work. He invariably knew when she was lying or covering up. "Private detectives spend most of their time on routine tasks, Mr. Kendall, going over the same territory again and again, talking to people until something doesn't fit. Philip Marlowe and Sam Spade don't exist. If it were dangerous, I wouldn't be doing it and neither would Mel. That's what cops are for."

She changed the subject before Kendall could delve any more thoroughly into her experience or lack of it. "We have a more immediate problem."

"What might that be?"

"Mel said I was supposed to go undercover as one of your carvers. I can't hit a nail with a hammer. Fingernails grow back eventually—fingers don't. This place is crawling with power tools. I even saw a couple of chain saws. That woman with the rabbit had a chisel in her hand sharp enough to slice marble."

Kendall tipped his chair back on two legs and balanced it against the wall behind him. He chuckled.

Taylor felt that damn tingle again. Kendall's voice was deep and smooth. The wavy black hair just going gray at the temples, and the unusually large complement of even white teeth, added to his Big Bad Wolf impression. She concentrated on his nose—broken more than once from the looks of it. Dark, dangerous. The better to eat you with. This was the kind of man Mel usually tried to protect her *from.*

"Three-quarters of the people who sign up at Rounders have never touched a power tool or a chisel," he said. "Half of them are women over fifty. I've got a lady who flies in from Arizona one weekend a month to work on her jumper. She's seventy-seven and weighs maybe eighty pounds. Before she started her horse, her idea of a power tool was the emery board her manicurist used. If I could teach *her,* I can teach you. You look pretty tough."

"Not against a power saw."

"Maybe we can find some other cover for you."

"It's the perfect excuse to hang around and talk to everyone. Mel says no matter how bizarre the situation is, somebody always knows what's really going on. It's just a matter of asking the right person the right question. I'd just like to wind up the assignment with the same number of fingers I start with. I'd like to take it slow."

He frowned at her. "How are you at taking it fast?"

"I beg your pardon?"

"You have exactly ten days to find out who stole my animals."

She gaped at him. "What if it takes longer?"

Nick shrugged. "Then I have to cough up thirty-five thousand big ones to Pete Marley, the guy who bought the fake. I don't have it."

"But you didn't sell him a fake."

Nick leaned forward. "Listen, I live or die by my reputation. There are a lot of crooks in the carousel business; it's a tight little community. Right now everybody trusts me. I do what I say I'll do, when I say I'll do it. Period. If Marley doesn't get his money back within ten days, he's going public with the fraud. I can't afford that."

"But that's unfair. Mel says Marley'd never have known the horse was a fake if you hadn't pointed it out to him."

"Marley's mad as hell about being taken. He was ready to fly to Mississippi and kill Eberhardt himself, but by then the man was dead, and so was the only lead we had. Either I find out who stole the animal so that Marley can get the money from him, or I pay it myself. I was lucky to get a two-week grace period." He sounded grim.

No wonder. "Won't your liability insurance cover it?"

Nick shook his head. "The hippocampus and the other animals I carved were never part of the Rounders inventory. They're mine and not insured. The only way insurance would pay off is if I can prove that one of my partners is the thief. Rounders has partnership insurance against theft." He sighed and sat back. Taylor had to strain to hear his next words. "That's not possible."

"Why not?"

"My partners wouldn't steal from Rounders."

"Then who would?"

"That's the hell of it. It's got to be one of the carvers. Nobody else would know about the animals. I can't believe any of them would steal from me. They're my friends, my family."

"They're your students. They pay you to teach them to carve. Not the same thing."

"Why do I get the feeling you're not enthusiastic about what we do here?"

Taylor sighed. The man was a client. She didn't want to offend him. Still, he'd asked. "I admit I'm biased. Seems like an awful lot of money to spend on toys."

"Some people consider them art."

"Some people think collages made out of rotting lettuce leaves and bent safety pins are art."

Kendall rubbed the back of his neck and raised an eyebrow. He opened his desk drawer, pulled out a slick magazine and tossed it across the desk. "Hardly rotting lettuce and safety pins. Go ahead, take a look."

Taylor thumbed through the magazine, not really focusing on any of the brightly colored creatures that gamboled across its pages. She couldn't have said why one photo caught her eye. The big horse in the picture was covered with jeweled armor. Its short mane tossed in an invisible wind. It wore a jeweled leather bridle attached to a steel bit that pulled the corners of its mouth back to show its teeth. Lancelot must have ridden such a horse.

She could imagine herself flying free and invincible on such a great horse.

But this horse wouldn't ever fly free. It could only move in a stately circle, three of its four feet forever anchored to a wooden platform, while a calliope tinkled in the background. No martial music; no herald trumpets. An immense sadness and sense of loss welled up in her. She dropped the open magazine on the desk.

"You like him?" Kendall asked.

Taylor shrugged.

"Don't kid me. I saw your face when you looked at him. Pure lust. I've seen it before." He leaned across the table and whispered seductively, "You can build him."

Taylor reared back in her chair. He wasn't a wolf, he was more like an oversize demon tempting her to exchange fingers for art. "Come on. Even if I had the skill and could avoid doing myself serious injury, something like that would take years to carve."

"If you're willing to work, you can have him on his feet in two weeks."

"Now I know you're crazy." She stared at the shining horse—a warrior's horse—out of the corner of her eye. It drew her straight back into a childhood crammed with knights on horseback, Robin Hood, Odysseus, and Hannibal.

She'd always resented Rowena in *Ivanhoe* and all those other wimpy heroines who stood around wringing their hands and either getting abducted like Guinevere or rescued like Maid Marion. She wanted to be the warrior in the books she read. But her brother Bradley always said girls couldn't be warriors. Oh, yeah?

She looked straight into Nick Kendall's dark eyes. He raised one eyebrow and grinned at her. It was as though he could read her mind.

"You can do it," he said. "You picked a doozy of a horse, but if you work hard and let me help you, I promise you can do it."

For a moment she felt as though she could climb Everest

for this man. She gulped. "I don't have two weeks, remember. I have ten days. Not much time to spend on that." Taylor slapped the magazine shut. Of its own volition her hand lingered on the magazine; she realized her thumb was still marking her place. "What the hell," she said casually. "I've got to have something to work on if I'm going to stick around here. I can get started and then somebody else can finish."

His grin said that he knew she was hooked.

She felt that telltale flush spread up her throat and into her face. "So how do we work it?"

He sighed. Obviously he'd forgotten for the moment why she was here. "Normally you'd pay a fee for tuition and the raw wood we're going to use to build your horse. In your case, of course, we'll just let everyone assume you've paid. You will have to buy a set of chisels and one of those small handheld drills with the interchangeable grinders and cutters. You can charge them as expenses I'm paying Mel and leave them behind when the job is done."

Taylor nodded. She slid the satchel from her shoulder, dug around in it and came up with a miniature tape recorder. "I find it's easier to get the details on tape. Then I can transcribe my notes later. Okay with you?"

Kendall shook his head. "Not now. We've already been in here too long. Most people who come to Rounders are so pumped up to get started they can't wait to get their checkbooks out and choose their animals. You've already picked your animal, but if you're going to be a regular pupil, we'll have to get you started immediately."

"Can I have a moment alone with my fingers? I need to say good-bye."

"The sharpest tool you'll use today is a grease pencil. You're going to trace that horse, then we project the tracing onto a large piece of paper on the wall and you trace that.

Then you glue up the wood for the body and legs. You won't be carving anything for a couple of days.''

"With luck, maybe this will be wrapped up by then."

His face went dark. "Yeah. Sure."

He stood, and so did she. "Look," he said, "we're supposed to close at six, but Veda generally stays late."

"How come she's the only one out there?"

"It's Monday. You should have been here Saturday and Sunday."

"You're open seven days a week?"

"I have an apartment upstairs. I'm not always down here but I'm usually available."

Taylor sat on the edge of the desk and stuck her Nikes out in front of her. "Let me get this straight. You leave a bunch of perfect strangers down here for hours at a time?" She shook her head. He really didn't have the first clue about security. "I'm surprised you've got a single power tool left. No wonder they stole your animals."

He had the grace to flush. "I told you, they're family. Nobody even steals a cup of coffee. This is the first time in the five years we've been open that anything has been taken."

Taylor didn't believe that for a second, but she could see from the set look around his mouth that he did—and would fight her if she suggested otherwise.

"If you're free tonight we could go someplace for dinner, then we can come back here. I'll give you the whole story and the grand tour in private. That way you won't have to pretend to be gaga over carousel animals."

She shook her head. "No dinner, thanks. I can come back tonight, however."

He nodded and opened the door. "Come on. Bring the magazine."

Taylor realized her hand still lay on the cover. She picked up the magazine and followed Nick into the warehouse.

"WELL, OLLIE, HERE'S ANOTHER fine mess you've gotten me into," Taylor said into the telephone.

Mel Borman's rumble—his nearest approach to laughter—vibrated down the line.

"All your appendages intact?"

"So far. My neck hurts, I've got writer's cramp, and there's grease pencil embedded under my fingernails. I don't know a damn thing more than I did this morning except that tracing is not my long suit." She outlined the day and reported her conversations. "I came home to feed Elmo and take a shower, then I'm going back for a nice long chat with Kendall and a guided tour."

"What do you think of him?"

"I think he's a certifiable lunatic with a deadly combination of male hormones, charisma and a holy mission."

"What mission?"

"He wants the entire population of the United States to carve knockoffs of wooden animals originally intended to entertain children, and to treat them as though they were each the Mona Lisa."

"I like 'em."

"Fine. For grandchildren on Sunday afternoon. Not as the Holy Grail."

"They're fun, Taylor. People have fun carving them and looking at them. You remember that word *fun?*"

"From another lifetime." Taylor massaged the sore muscles at the back of her neck. "If what I did today is your idea of fun, I'd rather have a root canal."

"They're also big business and big money. Or at least Nick Kendall's are. In the world of carousel animals, his *are* the Mona Lisa."

"So I've been told. I'll let you know tonight after I've seen them whether or not I agree."

"Who cares if you agree? Collectors are paying upwards of fifty big ones for animals that they think are original.

Kendall's are probably every bit as good as the originals except that they were carved twenty years ago rather than a hundred. The man has an international reputation to protect, and whether you like them or not, he's paying us to protect it."

"Oh, boy, do I know that."

"You might have fun learning to do it yourself."

"There's that word again. *Fun.* You're paying me to do a job, not to have fun. Mel, there's something hinky about the setup."

"Hinky? You sound like a real cop."

Taylor propped the phone between her shoulder and cheek and rummaged in the kitchen junk drawer until she found an orange wood stick, then began to dig the grease pencil from under her nails. "Thanks, I think. He hired us to find out who stole his animals; I get the feeling he'd rather not know."

"Not surprising. He's got to realize it's an inside job."

"But the carvers are just students paying for the privilege of using the warehouse. Why would he want to protect them? If one of his partners is guilty, his insurance pays off. I'd think he'd want to find the rotten apple."

"Maybe he knows who did it."

"And doesn't want to be certain," Taylor said. Should she tell Borman about Helmut Eberhardt's death? She took a deep breath. "Mel…"

"What?" he asked.

"Nothing."

Elmo wound himself around her ankles. She picked up the cat and set him on the kitchen counter beside her. "The place is a sieve, Mel. Carvers drift in, carve a while, drift out, and may not be back for weeks or months. Nobody checks in. Nobody disturbs their stuff. Nobody keeps to a schedule, Kendall least of all. He's turned the top floor of the warehouse into a loft apartment so he's always available if a carver needs help. This comes from the only carver I've met, a semi-retired nurse practitioner named Veda Albright who's been working on this damn six-foot rabbit for six months and thinks Nick Kendall is a combination of the Dalai Lama and Michaelangelo. I suspect they all do. He's the rarest kind of con man—women fall in love with him, men respect him. You obviously do, and you're a tough sell."

"Yeah, I like the guy." Borman grumbled a moment. "You gonna fall in love with him?"

"Absolutely, positively not in this lifetime. No thanks. The next time around for me—if there is a next time—I want a tubby, balding CPA with glasses. Mel, the man worships carousels the way Druids worship oaks. He has built his career on objects that play loud music, flash lights, and are filled with wooden animals painted garish colors that go around in circles and never ever get anywhere. And most of them were built before nineteen-twenty."

"Don't lose track of the essential point, Taylor. Somebody went to a great deal of trouble to steal the things. Watch your back. And don't trust anybody—including Kendall. It's just possible he's behind this himself."

"Why would he hire us?"

"Double bluff. Trying to protect his reputation. Insurance? Who knows? Just don't trust him too far."

"Mel, dear, you've taught me well. I don't even trust you too far."

"Thank you very much, Ms. Hunt. Call me the minute you get home after this meeting, no matter how late."

"Yes, mother."

As Taylor hung up, Elmo rowled at her in his deep Siamese voice. Absently, Taylor ran her hand along his sleek golden side and scratched behind his dark ears. He continued to berate her for his empty food dish.

"You're an unforgiving so-and-so," she told him, leaning

down so that he could butt his triangular head against her cheek. She scooped him up, draped him around her neck like a feather boa, then dropped him on the couch. She poured dry cat food into one side of his dish and dumped a can of his favorite canned liver into the other. Elmo dug in.

Then she fixed herself a tuna sandwich.

Elmo protested. Filled cat dish or no, any available tuna was supposed to go down his gullet, not hers. She ignored him, cleaned up the kitchen and padded barefoot across the brick floor into the bathroom under her sleeping loft. In the large closet attached to the bathroom, she peeled off her clothes and dropped them into the hamper in a pouf of dust. Elmo sneezed daintily and regarded her with malevolent blue eyes.

She stood under a hot shower, scrubbing her body, her short nails and hair until she felt dust-free. She toweled her hair and ran a comb through it, then moisturized her face. She pulled on cotton underpants and a sports bra, a bulky black fisherman's sweater, tight black jeans and, finally, black running shoes.

Eight-and-a-half minutes total.

No more hours spent on long streaked hair, body waves, acrylic fingernails, weekly manicures and pedicures, Swedish massages, bikini waxes and body wraps when she was swollen from P.M.S., or when Paul wanted her to make an especially good impression on one of his prize clients.

No more high heels, panty hose, tiered jewelry case. No more endless hours spent creating herself.

She'd been just like one of Kendall's horses—her honest wood covered by layers of garish paint.

She reached for her satchel as the telephone rang. She was tempted to let the answering machine pick it up, then relented. "Hello," she said.

"Taysie, darling, it's mother."

Taylor sighed. "Hi, Mom."

"Darling, I haven't heard from you in days. I drove by to check on you but you've changed the entry code on your gate again. You really should give me a key and the code. What if something happens to you out there all alone?"

"Mel has both the code and a key to the cabin, Mother."

"He's not family. He's only your boss, and only so long as you refuse to give up this detective business."

Taylor heard the edge of exasperation in her mother's voice. "It pays well and I enjoy it."

"You could do so much better. CeCe Washburn tells me she's opening a branch of her antique store in Germantown. I know she'd love to have you help out."

"At minimum wage plus commission, no doubt."

"Darling, if money's the problem you know—"

"Money is not the problem."

"Oh, Taysie, your brother and I only want you to be happy and settled again. And to see you occasionally. Tell you what, meet me for lunch at the club tomorrow. I promise I won't mention Mel Borman or your job."

"Sorry, Mother, I'm working tomorrow."

"You have to eat, dear."

Guilt flooded her. Her mother did want her to be happy. Their definitions of happiness had simply ceased to coincide. "All right, Mother."

"Wonderful!"

Taylor heard the elation.

"Latish? One o'clock? I have a hair appointment in the morning. Oh, and Taysie, could you—you know—fix yourself up a little, dear? I mean, it is the club, after all."

Taylor dropped her head into the hand not holding the telephone. "I'm sorry. I told you I'm working. If you want me to dress up, I'll have to decline."

She heard the quick intake of breath, then the resignation. "No, please come. Do the best you can. You never know who'll be there. Mr. Right might walk in the door."

"Mother, if he's Mr. Right, he's going to like me in jeans and a sweatshirt."

"Of course he would...if he got to know you."

The implication was obvious. No man at her mother's country club would bother to get to know a woman who wore jeans and a sweatshirt to lunch. Probably true.

Taylor braced for the inevitable lecture.

"You are much too lovely a woman, dear, to spend the rest of your life without a husband. And life is so much easier if the whole economic burden isn't on your shoulders. But sometimes the image you project is a little...well, tough. Men like a woman to be a little soft, darling. Smile more, relax a little. You have such a lovely smile. Grief has to come to an end sometime—"

Taylor cut her off before she could set off down that stretch. "Sorry, Mother, I have to go."

"Where?" her mother asked quickly. "You have a date?"

Taylor flashed on Kendall's dark eyes and crinkly smile. For a moment she wondered what it would be like to date a Big Tin God. The warmth that flooded her was annoying. She cut her mother off more sharply than she intended. That was Kendall's fault. "No, Mother, not a date. A business meeting."

"At this hour? Taysie, you know I hate having you drive those back roads at night."

"Mother, it's seven o'clock. I drive a pickup truck with four-wheel drive and a telephone. And I carry a gun."

"Oh, Taysie!"

"Bye."

Taylor hung up the telephone and wiped the thin film of sweat off her upper lip. How could she ever tell Irene Marshall, her exquisite widowed mother, that what she perceived as grief over Paul Hunt's death was Taylor's revolt against his lifestyle and Irene's? That Taylor had never grieved for Paul, only for the manner of his dying? That his death had released her into a world in which people were not judged by bank balances, degrees, professions or their latest plastic surgeries?

How could she ever tell her mother that life with Paul had been hell, and that for all his looks and charm he had been an unfaithful, wife-beating louse?

CHAPTER TWO

LIGHTS BLAZED FROM THE CHIC LOFTS in the redone warehouses on the way to Rounders, but once Taylor turned left into the alleyway leading to the square on which Kendall's building sat, she felt as though she were plunging into the mouth of a cave.

Suddenly headlights ahead blinded her. She threw up one hand and stomped on the brakes.

Horn trumpeting like an angry elephant, a car shot by and barely missed her left front fender. "Damn fool!" she snarled. In her rearview mirror she saw the car spin around the corner onto Front Street. Her heart pounded in her throat as she inched forward.

By the time the parking area in front of Rounders opened before her, her adrenaline rush had subsided, but not her fury. Her tires crunched and bumped across a disused railway spur, and she pulled to a stop in the glow cast by the light over the door.

She turned off the key, but sat in her car with the windows up and locked while her heart rate returned to normal. The buildings on either side loomed black and faceless like punch-drunk boxers who refused to go down for the count. Apparently, no one lived in this particular square but Kendall.

NICK READ THE SAME PARAGRAPH for the fourth time, realized he still didn't have the foggiest notion what it said, and dropped the carousel magazine onto the table beside him.

What had possessed him to hire detectives?

He leaned back and let the intricate rationality of Bach's "Goldberg Variations" wash over him. Max had introduced him to Bach and Mozart. Max Beaumont—partner, expert carver, the closest thing in Nick's life to a father figure. Could such a man betray him? Steal from him?

Surely not Max.

Josh Chessman then? Cheerful, fumble-footed Josh with his myopic eyes and his childlike delight in discovering that he too, could handle a power saw? Josh, his other partner, who had braved unshirted hell from his wife—at least until she realized that such an interesting hobby would look good on his resume—to invest in Rounders?

Not Josh.

So if Nick ruled out both of his partners, the culprit had to be one of the regular carvers.

Veda? Veda loved them all as much as he did. Maybe loved Max considerably more.

And why would Marcus Cato have to steal? He didn't gamble or do drugs. If he needed money, all he had to do was cut out another brain tumor. Nick didn't know much about surgeons, but he supposed even a neuro could remove an appendix or a gall bladder to make emergency payments on his Mercedes.

There were rumors Charlene had threatened to kick Marcus out if he started another affair. If she caught him messing around again, she might carry through with her threat. Cato might be accumulating a safe nest egg that Charlene's lawyers wouldn't be able to get their hands on.

Then there was Rico Cabrizzo. He said the animals reminded him of the year he spent as a carny shill before his uncle dragged him home and got him into law school. He made big bucks, but he spent them just as fast and liked "living large," as he called it. Nick liked him, but he had to admit Rico seemed the best bet for the thief.

Unless Nick had calculated wrongly, the thief had to be among those few people. The other twenty or so carvers were novices and most likely unaware of how much money Nick's animals were worth. Unfortunately, the most likely suspects were the people closest to Nick.

So why the hell had he hired Borman?

Not for the first time, he wondered if he should write Taylor Hunt a check for the day's work and send her packing. He'd hired Borman himself, not this woman who didn't understand the first thing about Rounders. Talk about attitude.

Still, if Borman trusted her, she must be competent.

She was sure better looking than Borman. And she had those long, muscular legs...

Where the hell had that come from? He felt himself harden. Too long since any woman had shared his bed, much less even the smallest portion of his life. And this one...tall, muscular, brainy. Not the usual downy dumpling he preferred. But she stirred him all the same. He liked the way her hair swung around her face. He liked the way she looked him straight in the eye, even when she was disagreeing with him.

Bad timing. He had a problem to solve and didn't need to complicate his life further by lusting after any woman. Certainly not the detective he'd hired to save his ass.

Not just his ass. His whole way of life. He couldn't go around suspecting all his closest friends. He had to know who had betrayed his trust so he could exonerate everybody else.

Suddenly he grinned as he visualized Rico Cabrizzo's first encounter with Taylor. Little Rico invariably hit on tall women five minutes after he met them, but Taylor seemed quite capable of decking Rico if he annoyed her. Nick laughed out loud at the picture.

A horn honked. He went to the window and saw Taylor's truck outside the front door. His stomach churned at the prospect of telling her about his friends. He buzzed the door open and watched her climb out. She glanced around her as though the dark square frightened her.

TAYLOR WAITED UNTIL SHE SAW NICK silhouetted in the upper window and heard the front door buzz. Then she slid out, locked her truck and hefted her satchel.

Something skittered away into the darkness. A rat? Sounded as big as a railcar. She shuddered.

She stepped into the dimly lit hall. The door eased shut behind her. "Up here." Kendall's voice came to her from the staircase.

She climbed the stairs past the closed door to the workshop. Light spilled down from the third floor where Kendall stood in the doorway of his apartment.

Suddenly her heart began to beat faster. What did she know about Kendall anyway? She strolled past him with studied casualness and plunked her satchel on the floor inside the door. Her gun, a nine-millimeter Glock, thunked against the wood.

The loft was brightly lit by track lighting fixed to overhead trusses. The brick walls had been painted white. The room held a few pieces of simple furniture beautifully crafted of pale wood. Gleaming. No dust here, but a faint aroma of furniture polish.

A white Euro-style galley kitchen opened to the right. To the left, eight-foot partition walls carved out what must be bedroom and bath. At the back of the room, a solid wooden grid covered what looked like a freight elevator. Floor to ceiling bookcases holding mostly art books and a few paperbacks fitted into the short wall beside the door.

As Kendall shut off the stereo, Taylor decided he no doubt needed this oat-colored oasis at the end of ten-hour days spent with rioting colors and blaring music.

"Right on time," he said.

"I try. This is nice." She waved a hand at the room.

"Thanks. Want a drink?"

"No, thank you." Taylor inched her tape recorder from the pocket of her jeans. "Let's get to it, shall we?"

Kendall shrugged, pointed to a burled walnut table in the dining alcove. Taylor set the tape recorder upright in the center of the table beside a mahogany bowl piled with polished wooden fruit, pulled out one of the comb-back Windsor chairs and sat down. Kendall sat opposite.

"Beautiful table," she said, and switched on the recorder.

"Thanks again. I built it. I built all this." Kendall waved a hand at the apartment. "My grandfather was a cabinet-maker. Specialized in restoration and fancy stuff. Taught me to love beautiful wood."

"Did he teach you to carve carousel horses?"

Kendall flushed and looked down at his hands. Taylor frowned. It had been a casual remark, an ice breaker.

"Something like that."

"So, how'd you find out your animals had been stolen?"

"What? Oh." He seemed to pull himself back from a great distance. "I don't just carve new carousel horses, I also restore old ones. Pete Marley called me from Seattle and said he'd just bought a hippocampus from Helmut Eberhardt's antique shop in Oxford while Marley and his wife were down at Ole Miss for some sort of training seminar. Marley wanted me to come out to Seattle, all expenses paid, to restore the thing. It sounded like a hell of a vacation, so I gave him a cousin's price and went. I didn't recognize the hippocampus right off. I don't guess I'd looked at the thing closely since I carved it twenty years ago."

"But surely it wouldn't have needed restoration after only twenty years."

"That's just it. It shouldn't have, but it did. The paint was flaking and peeling. In places the glue had separated. There were spongy areas under the belly that felt rotten. It was supposed to have been in somebody's attic for forty years. I could believe it."

"So Eberhardt—or whoever did the faking—was expert?"

"Had to be Eberhardt. I won't go into all the techniques crooked antique dealers use to make things seem old, but Eberhardt obviously knew them all and used most of them on the hippocampus."

"So what tipped you that it was yours?"

"Once I got suspicious I went to the shop in Seattle at three in the morning so I could check it out. The last thing I wanted was to tell Marley he'd been had if I wasn't certain. Next morning I went to see him and rechecked the provenance." He raised his eyebrows in question.

She nodded. "I know about provenance. The history of the thing, who's owned it, where it came from—the documentation that assures it's authentic."

"Yeah. In the thirties, a hurricane knocked down a great old carousel on a beach in New Jersey. Nobody valued carousels much then—it was the middle of the Depression—so they bulldozed it and the Ferris wheel beside it, covered the whole shebang with beach sand and left it."

Taylor shivered. "I may not care much about carousels, but that seems like a terrible tragedy for the children, if for no other reason."

"It was. There was a guy named Joe Kolzcek who had helped run it. One night, a couple of weeks after it was bulldozed, he and some friends got drunk, dug out some of the animals and carted them off. Kolzcek was living in a furnished room. His wife Nell was staying in Mississippi

with her folks, expecting their first child. He probably figured that at least she'd get enough to eat down there. Anyway, Kolzcek wrote her all about the animals he'd rescued.''

"Seems pretty cut and dried. Marley had the letters from
Kolzcek to his wife?''

"Photocopies. That should have tipped him off, but he's
new at this. Anyway, after Nell's baby was born, Kolzcek
moved back to Mississippi and farmed with Nell's father.
Apparently Kolzcek brought three animals back with him.
He died on Iwo Jima. Eberhardt supposedly found the carousel animals in Nell Kolzcek's attic when he bought her
estate last year after she died.''

"Sounds like perfect provenance to me. The hippocampus
is documented every step of the way.''

"Right. Except for two things. First, Joe Kolzcek never
called any of the animals by name. His letter just mentions
'three animals.' ''

"He might not know a hippocampus from an American
eagle. I certainly don't.''

"Sorry. The front half is a horse, the back half is a fish.''

"Thanks,'' she said, then added, "Weird.''

"Anyway, there was no hippocampus on the carousel.
Only horses.''

Taylor let out a long breath. "Oh, boy.''

"How much do you know about faking antiques?''

"Not a lot.''

Kendall looked at her, a wry smile on his face. "I know
a lot. You can fake provenance as easily as you can fake
the piece itself if you're willing to take the time. But Eberhardt was smarter than that. The provenance is probably
genuine. It simply doesn't go with the animal he sold.''

"What makes you think Eberhardt sold the others?''

"Why stop at one? There may be ten happy collectors
gloating over their prizes all over this country, all certain
they've got the bargain of the century.''

"Forgive me for saying this, but if they're happy, why do you want to burst their bubbles? Why not just let sleeping dogs lie?"

"For one thing, I can't afford to simply write off a hundred-fifty thousand dollars of inventory. But, more important, even if we head Marley off, sooner or later someone knowledgeable may figure out he's got a Nick Kendall original and not a Muller or an Illions. I can't take that chance. My reputation is all I have."

"Wouldn't Eberhardt be afraid you'd see one of the stolen animals somewhere and recognize it?"

Kendall shook his head. "Assuming all the animals were sold in the same condition, probably not. Once someone else restored them, even I might not recognize them. Besides, Eberhardt was smart. He didn't sell to the trade, didn't advertise in the carousel magazines, or put any of the animals into a carousel auction. He apparently set out only one animal in his shop at a time, and made certain that it went to someone who knew nothing about carousels. Marley took his wife shopping for antiques in Oxford one afternoon when they didn't have classes at the university. He fell in love with the hippocampus but obviously didn't know anything about carousel animals. Eberhardt found out he was from Seattle. There are plenty of carousel restorers in California. The chances that he'd get *me* to come all the way from Tennessee to restore it were slim to none."

"If this Pete Marley had been a knowledgeable collector from this part of the world, do you think Eberhardt would have refused to sell him the hippocampus?"

"Maybe. Maybe not. When I started carving horses, I imitated the originals even to the point of using the old carving tools and glue. The hippocampus was a beautiful fake, especially after Eberhardt got through soaking it and baking it and going over it with a heat gun."

"I thought restoration lowered the value of an antique."

"Even fine animals can be layered with fifty years' worth of park paint. A perfectly restored antique is worth considerably more than a grungy mess. There is almost no such thing as an antique carousel animal in mint unrestored condition."

"I see," Taylor said, "but that doesn't explain who made arrangements with Eberhardt to steal them."

Kendall pushed his chair back and stood. "That's what you're here to find out. I need a drink. Sure you don't want one?"

Taylor shook her head. He went to the large white Sub-Zero built into the kitchen and came back with a long-neck Coors. She was certain he was stalling.

He prowled, moving with the loose-limbed assurance of a big cat. Taylor watched the muscles under his shirt and wondered if he worked bare-chested in the summer. She blinked away the vision just as he tilted the bottle and let the beer drain down his throat in a solid stream.

"Assume we find the thief before the ten days are up. Even assume we locate all the buyers. What happens then?" she asked and hoped her voice didn't betray the sudden rise in her blood pressure.

"I try to buy them back at a price I can afford."

"You can't even afford to pay Marley. How are you going to buy them all?"

"I'll sue Eberhardt's estate."

"You have to prove he bought the animals knowing what they were and did the faking himself. Besides, a suit could take years to settle."

"You got any better ideas?"

Taylor sighed. "Not at the moment."

"Then find out who did it and when."

"Then what?" Taylor asked. "Have you reported the thefts to the police?"

Nick shook his head.

"But if you did, maybe your homeowner's insurance would pay at least a part of the cost."

"I checked. Not without a special rider."

"Damn." Taylor bit at the cuticle on her thumbnail, then dropped it quickly into her lap. In the days when she wore long acrylic talons, biting her nails had been impossible. Now she found that she reverted when she was nervous.

"I'll take care of the problem myself." Nick sounded grim.

Taylor watched as he flexed his large hands, then let the fingers curl against his palms. "Whoa! If you're planning to beat somebody to a pulp I don't want any part of it."

"I don't beat people."

"Then you plan to turn the thief over to the police?"

"None of your business."

She hoped for his sake that one of his partners was the thief. Otherwise Nick Kendall might wind up bankrupt. Taylor made a mental note to warn Mel to get a cashier's check for their first week's work. "One thing. If Eberhardt's shop burned up, how do you know the rest of the animals weren't turned into cinders?"

"Since there was only one animal there for Marley to buy, I'd guess Eberhardt was parceling them out one at a time. Maybe there was one in his workroom when it burned, but probably no more than that." Nick set the empty bottle on the kitchen counter and returned to the table. He reached into the wooden bowl for a bunch of teak grapes and began to roll each grape gently between his index finger and his thumb. Taylor couldn't take her eyes off his hands. They caressed the fruit as if it were skin.

She gulped and fought back a sudden fantasy of those hands on her body. The resultant heat from her belly disconcerted the hell out of her. She dragged her attention back to his face. She'd been alone too damn long.

As though sensing her gaze, he glanced up at her. "I've got to know who's behind the theft. And then I've got to fix things."

CHAPTER THREE

"YOU SUSPECT SOMEBODY SPECIFIC, don't you?" Taylor asked quietly.

Kendall's hands went still. After a moment he dropped the grapes and picked up a pear. He began to roll it between his palms.

Taylor watched him move the pear back and forth. He seemed to be treating the wooden fruit like oversize worry beads to keep himself calm. Unfortunately, watching his hands had the opposite effect on Taylor. She cleared her throat. She wanted to learn about this man as a client, not as a male.

After a minute—without taking his eyes off his hands—he began to speak. "No. I don't know who—not exactly. But you'll see when I show you the storeroom that it had to be someone very familiar with Rounders."

"I'm sure all this hurts you," she said gently. "I've seen it before."

He glanced up in surprise.

"The first year I was with Mel we busted a very nice lady, well respected in her community, president of the Missionary Society." Taylor shrugged. "Over five years she'd embezzled half a million dollars from her boss. When we showed him the proof, he cried. I've never forgotten that."

Nick dropped the pear, stood and began to pace again. "These people are all the family I've got left." He struck the edge of the nearest bookshelf with the flat of his hand. The force of the blow rattled the walls.

Taylor jumped. She watched him force himself back under control. His hands drew into fists. The muscles of his broad back worked under his sweatshirt. A moment later he turned, seemingly calm again.

"When I was sure the hippocampus was mine, I called Rounders from Seattle," he continued as though his outburst had not occurred. "My partners, Max Beaumont and Josh Chessman, were handling my carving classes. They rallied the carvers who were here that day and took inventory."

"Did you tell them about Eberhardt?"

He nodded. "Yeah. I told them I was catching the next plane home and planned to drive to Oxford to talk to Eberhardt. But I got there too late."

"But if you had even the faintest suspicion one of them might be guilty, why alert them?"

He shook his head. "I didn't suspect them. Not then. I don't want to suspect them now. Until Eberhardt died, I just figured somebody had broken in—you know, a regular burglary. Anytime. Anybody."

"You could be right. The thief doesn't *have* to be somebody you know."

He snorted. "A random thief who didn't bother to steal power tools? Who selected ten of my animals—nobody else's?" He shook his head. "No, the people who were here the day I called are the only ones who knew I'd found out about the theft and planned to talk to Eberhardt." He leaned back against the bookshelf and closed his eyes as though his moment of anger had drained him completely.

"But if the fire was a coincidence…"

"Perfect timing. Somebody who was here that day could have called Eberhardt and told him I'd found out about the theft."

The hair stood up on the nape of Taylor's neck. "You think Eberhardt's death was…more than an accident."

"My guess is that Eberhardt started the fire to get rid of

whatever animal he was working on at the time, but it got out of hand and trapped him.''

"Maybe he burned all the animals he hadn't sold yet?" Taylor suggested.

"I can't count on that. And I won't." He opened the refrigerator, reached inside as though for another beer, then dropped his hand and turned back. "I've had more than enough." He grinned at her sheepishly. "Two beers is my limit. Shows I'm upset. Sure you won't have something? Diet soda maybe?"

Taylor shook her head. "I'm fine." She reached across the table as though to reassure him, then drew her hand back and sat up straight. *Stick to business.* "Tell me about the people who were here the day you called," Taylor said gently.

He sighed and came back to the table. "Okay. Both my partners were here. Max Beaumont is a retired army colonel with an adequate pension. Josh Chessman is chairman of the marketing department at the university. He makes good money, plus he does a lot of consulting. Besides, his wife has money. The carvers here that day were Marcus Cato— he's a neurosurgeon who's richer than Trump—Rico Cabrizzo—he's a criminal lawyer—and Veda Albright."

"The rabbit lady?"

"She couldn't move Jell-O."

"She could hire help."

"I can't believe it was Veda. Hell, I can't believe it was anybody."

"What about Cabrizzo? He's your lawyer, right?"

Kendall nodded. "I like Rico, but he's a tough little Boston hood who implies he has mob connections. He says it 'enhances his aura with women.'" He hesitated. "Cato? He has a roving eye and a wife with expensive tastes."

Taylor appraised him. "So he might actually need money?"

Nick shrugged.

"Any of those people out of town the night Eberhardt died?"

"Nobody's asked them."

"Okay. Tomorrow I find out. Can I have that grand tour now?" Taylor walked towards the back of the apartment.

"Where you going?"

"Isn't that a freight elevator?" Taylor pointed to the far end of the room. "I assumed that's how the animals were stolen. I need to see how big it is, how many trips it would take."

Kendall looked apologetic. "Look, do you mind if we walk down? I hate that damned thing."

"Sure," she said, glancing at him curiously. "Doesn't it work?"

"Yeah. It works all right." He drew a hand down his face and smiled sheepishly. "I'm claustrophobic as hell. While we were moving in, the damn thing got stuck between floors. Max got me out in five minutes, but it felt like an hour. I never use it except to bring up wood I can't get up the stairs."

Taylor smiled at him. "I'm not too thrilled with heights. I understand." She picked up her satchel and slung it across her shoulder. "You leave your apartment door unlocked?"

"Sure. Door at the bottom of the stairs is locked. So's the back staircase beside the elevator. We only use the second floor. There's a metal door on the freight elevator. It stays padlocked on the outside."

In the second-floor workshop, moonlight spilled through the high front windows and animated Harvey the rabbit's glass eyes. The bits and pieces of carving on the tables loomed as eerily real as body parts of newly butchered animals. Taylor shivered and edged closer to Nick. Her shoulder brushed his arm and she felt an instant resonance as though someone had thrummed a tuning fork against her.

But she stayed close; his bulk made her feel safe from everything except her own emotions.

The moment he flicked the light switch, the room became commonplace and familiar, and she moved a pace away, then followed him to the heavy metal doors that closed off the back third of the warehouse from the workshop.

"Welcome to Oz," he said and held the door open for her.

"Not locked?" Taylor asked.

"Why? The whole place is locked at night." He turned on the lights.

It was as though some long-dead emperor's menagerie had been frozen in time. The room was crammed with carousel animals—child-size to giant—glowing with brilliant paint, festooned with jewels, hung with fat pink and yellow roses, caparisoned with silver armor. Horses danced, pranced and leapt into the air with tossing manes.

There was a running stag complete with antlers, a frog sporting a red vest and pantaloons, a tiger slipping along in the shadows like a wraith. The animals posed in uneven rows back to the wooden grating that barred the freight elevator.

Taylor had the unnerving feeling that the moment she left they'd caper into life and frolic the night away, only to freeze once more come daylight.

Since the lights illuminated only the front of the room, she noticed, someone might be able to remove animals from the back without anyone's noticing. Taylor clutched her satchel in front of her to avoid knocking into animals as she threaded her way among them.

"Are all of these yours?" she whispered as if afraid to wake them.

Kendall laughed. "Hardly. They belong to students who haven't taken them home or who want to leave them here. We're hoping to set up a museum someday."

"Students did these?"

"Yeah. Veda did the frog."

"Clever."

As she reached the shadowy back of the room, Taylor could now see that there were gaps. "How many of yours are left?" she asked over her shoulder.

"Ten or so. I carved a lot of animals when I got started. They're my savings account."

"I beg your pardon?"

"I sold a couple to finance Rounders. If I have to pay off Marley and the others, I'll try to sell these for as much as I can get. Takes time."

She'd been thinking of the loss of the animals as tragic for Nick, but it wasn't as though he couldn't carve others. Now she saw them as he must—all his ready capital gone in a heartbeat. Whoever took them knew that, and didn't give a damn.

To lighten his mood, she said, "The horses all look so different."

"The ones with the sweet faces and the big eyes are Denzels. The armored horse you picked to carve is a Muller. I'll find you a couple of books so you can read up and sound as though you know what you're talking about. Some of our carvers are experts."

At the far back sat a matched pair of single-bench gilt carriages adorned with simpering cherubs and pictures of nubile Victorian ladies. A heavy purple velvet throw had been tossed over the seat on the left. "Does anybody ever actually ride in these things?" Taylor asked. "When I was a kid, we thought the carriages were for wimps."

"The occasional mother or someone with a baby too young to hold on," Nick said. He leaned against the wall and thrust his hands in his pockets. "If you want your carousel to be authentic, you've got to have at least a couple."

Taylor ran her hand along the top of the carriage and

turned to walk back towards Nick. Suddenly both feet slid as though she'd hit a patch of glare ice. She caught herself on the arm of the chariot. "Whoa!" She looked down. "There's something sticky down here. Somebody spill some glue?" Then she noticed her palm—something dark and sticky there too. At that moment she noticed the smell—metallic and salty. Her stomach churned.

"Nick," she said quietly, then more urgently, "Nick. Get back here."

"What is it?"

Taylor held up her hand, then pointed at the carriage. How could she not have realized that the fabric was lumped up that way? She watched Nick pull back the velvet throw.

For a moment Taylor feared the woman on the bench was Veda. Like Veda, she'd been small with gray hair. But this woman's hair was perfectly set. Even violent death had not disturbed it.

She'd been folded up like a child asleep on the backseat of a car and covered by the purple throw.

Her blood had puddled—cordovan-colored and viscous—on her body, the seat and the floor. The throw on the back of the chariot must have taken the initial spray. The thick pile had already begun to stiffen as the blood dried. The wood chisel sticking out of the side of her throat must have severed the carotid artery. She hadn't died instantly. Her heart had continued to pump until no blood remained. Taylor prayed the woman had been unconscious, had not lain there unable to speak and aware of what was happening to her.

Taylor was surprised she felt no revulsion, only an overwhelming pity. The woman was so small. Except for the blood, she seemed to have curled up for a nap. In the fluorescent light her skin shone like gray wax. Her eyes, already beginning to film, stared at the leaping stag. Death had wiped even wonder from her face.

"Damn," Kendall whispered. He touched the woman's wrist. "No pulse."

"How could there be? Don't step in the blood," Taylor said and turned away. Her mind functioned with appalling clarity. Perhaps when the shock wore off she'd have hysterics, but at the moment she merely felt numb.

Kendall glanced up at her, then stared. "You okay? You're a little white around the gills."

"Fine. I'm fine." She drew her arms across her body. "Just cold." She clamped down on her teeth before they began to chatter.

Nick slid his arm around her waist and began to walk her away from the corpse. "Come on out of here. We've got to call the police."

She leaned into him and absorbed the warmth from his frame into her bones. "Who is she?"

"Damned if I know. Never saw her before in my life."

"WHAT THE HELL ARE YOU DOING HERE?"

Taylor opened her eyes and sighed. "Danny! I thought you were too high and mighty to get called out at night." She stared directly into the eyes of Detective Danny Vollmer, Homicide. They were exactly the same height.

"Not when you're involved."

"I see." She jerked a thumb at the forensics team scurrying about in the storeroom. "Who ratted on me?"

Vollmer's smile twitched the ends of his thick graying mustache like a cat's whiskers. "You'll never know. Answer the question."

"I'm working. Kendall's my client."

"The heavyweight? He do it?"

"I seriously doubt it. He'd hardly have let me wander all over the room if he knew there was a dead body there."

"Unless he wanted you to find it for him."

"Cute. You know I hate cute."

"God, Taylor, how long are you going to keep this detective joke up? This is murder."

"It wasn't until now." Taylor shuddered.

"What was it? Cheating wife?"

"He's not married."

Vollmer stiffened. "So what were you doing here?"

"I told you, I was talking to my client. If and when I decide that what I'm working on is important to this murder, I'll tell you about it."

"Dammit, Taylor, you don't make that kind of judgment. I do."

"Danny, back off, okay? I don't have to talk to you at all. Not without a lawyer." She heard her voice from far away.

"Hey, this isn't an interrogation, sweet cheeks, it's merely an interview." He cocked his head to stare at her. "You okay?"

She nodded. "Why does everybody keep asking me that? I'm fine. Just fine."

"Right. If you say so." He glanced at Nick, who slouched against the wall by the office. "So how well do you know this man?"

"Met him today." Taylor glanced at her watch. One-thirty in the morning. "Yesterday."

"You sure he didn't kill her?"

She pressed the heels of her hands against her eyes and took a deep breath. She felt as though she'd been running for hours. "Look, Danny, from what I've seen today, this place is Swiss cheese. I'll bet you found the loading dock doors and the back stairway unlocked. Am I right?"

"Yes." Vollmer perched on one of the other tables, then grimaced when his hand touched the thin film of sawdust that covered it. Taylor laughed. Danny spent most of his salary on Gucci loafers and the occasional Armani suit. She watched him stand and, fastidiously as a cat, brush off his immaculate slacks and Benetton sweater.

He had the grace to smile and shrug. "Place is a firetrap."

"No, it's not." Taylor pointed overhead. "Sprinklers. Extinguishers every ten feet around the wall. No Smoking signs everywhere. Electrical panel box back by the rear exit. All very safe." She dug her fingers into the knotted muscles at the back of her neck. She wanted to go home, to bed, to sleep for a week. "She was killed here?"

"With all that blood? What do you think? Assuming Kendall was upstairs, would he have heard someone come in?"

"I have no idea. He's got the freight elevator closed off in his apartment. The walls are old and thick. Who was she?"

Danny shook his head. "No purse, no ID. Why would anyone be back there?"

"I don't know."

"Okay. Sit. Wait. Don't interfere. I'm going to go talk to this Kendall. Hell, he didn't need to stab the woman. He could just break her in half and throw away the pieces."

Taylor worked her bottom farther back on the table so that her feet came off the ground. She'd have to stay alert while Danny questioned Nick. He had no idea what a tenacious little devil Danny could be when aroused. And Nick would irritate him by his sheer size. Taylor knew how deeply Danny resented big people. He'd told her that one afternoon as they lazed in bed over the Sunday *Times*. He'd admitted she was the tallest woman he'd ever made love to.

He said he'd come down here because of her. After eight months apart, she prayed that didn't mean he still cared about her.

Kendall leaned against the wall with his hands in his pockets. He looked as tired as she felt. The strong bones surrounding his eyes seemed more prominent; there was a tinge of blue in the hollows of his temples. His broken nose cast an irregular shadow on his cheek, and he had the beginnings of black stubble along his jawline. For all his size, Taylor thought he looked terribly vulnerable. She wanted to go to him, to reassure him that everything would be all right.

No. She wanted to slip into the curve of those brawny arms of his and let *him* do the reassuring. Her head would fit comfortably in the hollow of his shoulder... Not at all a professional reaction for an up-and-coming private investigator.

She sat up and blinked. What she felt was exhaustion, delayed shock—whatever. Maybe even a flashback.

Murder tilted the world on its axis, screwed up the geometry. She'd found that out when Danny told her Paul had been killed. Nick didn't understand that yet, but he would. God help him.

NICK KENDALL TRIED TO CONCENTRATE on Vollmer's questions. He should be feeling sympathy or grief or horror. Instead he felt bewildered. The body hadn't looked as though it could ever have been human. It seemed to belong among the wooden animals. Even the blood seemed fake.

He'd seen death in the army. But Rounders was a sanctuary. Violence shouldn't be able to intrude here.

In the hours since he'd discovered the body, his mind had written and rewritten a scenario in which the dead woman was a vagrant—a stray killed by a stranger who picked Rounders by chance and convenience.

It wouldn't wash. When he'd touched her wrist, he felt cashmere. And when he'd stooped to pick up one black leather pump that had fallen onto the floor, Taylor had stopped him before he touched it and left fingerprints, but he could tell it was well cared for and expensive.

The woman had come here or been brought here for a purpose. Someone with a key had let her in, taken her to the one place her body would be likely to stay hidden for a while, killed her, and gone away again. Easy enough to come back later and remove the body before it began to smell.

The killer knew Rounders. Knew the storeroom was seldom visited.

He looked at Taylor. She smiled at him as though the two of them were the only people in the room. In a sense, they were. They were bound by their discovery.

He felt himself draw strength from her presence. She couldn't have discovered many dead bodies, but she hadn't screamed or thrown up. There was a moment when he thought she was going to faint, but she'd wrenched away, dialed 9-1-1, and stared out the window until the first squad car arrived.

"Excuse me?" He pulled his attention back to the detective, shaking his head as the question was repeated. "I have no idea who she is or why she was here. I didn't hear anyone come in this evening, but then I probably wouldn't."

"Not even if they used the elevator?"

"Probably not even then. It's behind a wall in my apartment. Doesn't make much noise. And I had a CD on."

"When did you lock up?"

"The last carver left about six-thirty. Veda wanted to finish carving her rose, so I stayed with her and gave her a hand."

"Did you lock the loading dock?"

"Never opened it. Haven't been down there for three or four days. To the best of my knowledge it was locked, but I can't swear to it."

"Who has keys?"

This was the question he'd been dreading. He realized he was the obvious suspect. It was to his advantage to implicate as many others as possible. Still, he felt his words were a betrayal. "My partners, Max Beaumont and Josh Chessman."

"And you, of course."

"Of course. But there's a complete set on a key hook in the office in case any of the carvers need them."

Vollmer stared at him. "Anybody? My God, Taylor wasn't exaggerating when she said this place was Swiss cheese."

Taylor. Not "Ms. Hunt." Nick glanced over at the table where Taylor sat with her elbows on her knees. Her unwavering eyes stared back into his. How well did these two know one another? He looked at Vollmer more closely and felt the man's antipathy. He was surprised to realize he returned it.

Nick hunched his shoulders, felt his stomach muscles tighten. "We're all friends at Rounders. The place is locked up at night."

"Ready to be unlocked with a key anyone could have copied during the day." Vollmer ran his hands through his thick hair, then moved aside to study his reflection in the window of the office behind him. After a moment he swiveled to peer at the rest of the room. "Hell, you got power tools? Stuff that would be easy to fence?"

"Nothing missing so far as I can tell."

"Right." Vollmer sighed. "These partners—give me addresses and telephone numbers. And any carvers who were here today."

"Is there a car out back?"

"Why?"

Nick leaned his head back against the windows and closed his eyes. His eyes burned from the dust that he ignored during the day. He couldn't get the smell of wood glue and old blood out of his nostrils. God, he was tired. "No woman's going to walk these streets after dark alone. Either she drove herself or somebody drove her."

"Only Taylor's truck's out front," Vollmer said. Both men turned to look at her.

She raised her hands. "I didn't walk, Danny. Three steps from the truck to the door, period. And I made sure Nick was watching me from upstairs when I did it."

"Okay," Vollmer said, and turned back to Nick. "There's a big blue truck by the loading dock that says Rounders Unlimited on the side. That yours?"

Nick nodded. "No other car?"

Vollmer shook his head. "So, you mind if we check out your truck?"

"You don't have to let him," Taylor interjected. "Not without a warrant. It's technically outside the crime scene."

Vollmer looked daggers at her. "Get your J. D. when you got your P.I. license, did you?" He turned back to Kendall. "Unless you got something to hide…"

"Go ahead," Nick said. He'd noted that Vollmer recognized Taylor's truck instantly. He glanced at her. She had moved the pig's head to a corner of its table and now leaned back on her hands. God, what a body the woman had. He felt his groin tighten. Amazing how lust could override even fear and exhaustion. He glanced at Vollmer, who played once more to his reflection in the office window. Vain little bastard, he thought, and glanced over at Taylor.

The track lighting had turned Taylor's cropped hair into a shining bronze helmet. Her gray eyes beneath their dark brows were in shadows. Suddenly he wanted to see into those eyes, see what she was thinking, know whether she was watching him or watching Vollmer.

Vollmer said abruptly, "That's it for you for tonight. I'll want to talk to Mr. Kendall some more after we finish working the crime scene." He turned towards Taylor. "You'll be going straight home, am I right?"

Taylor slid off the table. "I want to speak to my client, then you can have one of your guys see me to my car. Suddenly, this doesn't seem like the safest neighborhood."

"Talk to your client tomorrow. And I'll see you to your car."

Taylor caught Nick's eyes.

"The lady is my guest, detective. I'll see her to her car." He heard Vollmer's exasperated snort.

Nick followed Taylor down the stairs and out into the damp autumn air. Patchy fog grasped at them. The asphalt shone like molten tar in the light that spilled from the open door. Taylor gulped the chill air gratefully.

"I'm sorry about all this," said Nick.

"Why? You didn't kill the woman, did you?"

"Sure. I try to kill a woman a week. Keeps my creative juices flowing."

She touched his arm. "Sorry, that was a stupid remark. I guess I'm more uptight than I thought I was."

"This the first time you've seen a dead body?" Nick asked.

"Of course not," she lied, trying to echo his tone. "I try to see a dead body a week. I've got creative juices too, you know." She added briskly, "I'll call Mel from the car. You realize you'll probably have reporters calling?"

"Yeah. This changes everything."

"How?" She could guess what he planned to say and did not want to hear it.

He waited while Taylor unlocked her door, climbed in and fastened her seat belt. Then he said, "I can't have you mixed up in murder."

"I'm already about as mixed as I can get. Even if you fire me, I'm still involved. And I hope you don't fire me because I need the job."

"Vollmer's not going to like that."

"The hell with Vollmer."

"Will you be all right? How far away do you live?"

"The other side of Collierville." She shook her head. "I drive it every day. I could drive it in my sleep."

"Don't try that tonight."

She smiled and turned the key. "See you tomorrow morning."

Nick watched her taillights until they disappeared beyond the railroad trestle and out of sight. She was a new experience for him. He liked women in his bed, but they weren't central to his existence. He certainly never relied on them for anything important. But he suspected Taylor Hunt would honor her commitments, no matter where they led.

That might not be good for either of them.

TAYLOR BEGAN TO SHAKE as she hit the city limits. She fought nausea until she found a well-lighted all-night gas station, pulled in and cut her engine. The car felt stifling and her sweaty palms slid on the steering wheel. She knew she shouldn't open her window even in this relatively safe location, but she knew if she didn't get some fresh air, she was going to throw up.

She realized suddenly that the sour odor of dried blood clung to the inside of her truck. She looked at her hands. She'd washed them but, like Lady MacBeth, she could still feel the spots of blood burning on her palms. She sniffed. They smelled like Ivory soap.

Her shoes. She'd slid in the blood. The crosshatching on the soles of her Nikes must still carry traces. Frantically, she bent to pull them off. She'd throw them in the open back of the truck and drive home in her bare feet. Anything to get away from that smell.

A yellow slip of pasteboard was stuck to her right sole, glued there by traces of dark blood. It must have been on the floor near the body. It could only have adhered to the sole of her sneaker after she stepped in the woman's blood, but before it dried.

She pulled off the pasteboard, turned on the overhead

light and saw that it was a valet parking slip from The Peabody hotel, stamped at 6:45 tonight.

She caught her breath. According to Nick, no one from Rounders would have been in the storeroom at that time, so the slip probably belonged either to the dead woman or to her killer. The dead woman did not look like the sort of person who would drive casually into the Rounders neighborhood if she could get someone else to drive her. In this case she picked the wrong chauffeur—her killer. The chances were good that the car that belonged to the ticket also belonged to the corpse.

The Peabody was notoriously strict about letting cars go without parking tickets, particularly for valet parking. If the car had left the valet parking lot, the attendant would have kept the parking slip. That car still had to be there unless someone—probably the killer—had raised an almighty stink to get it out. And no killer in his right mind would do that, would he—or she? And risk identification?

For a moment Taylor considered driving straight back to Rounders to give the slip to Danny.

But only for a moment. She told herself she might have picked that slip up anywhere—anywhere, that is, after she stepped in blood. All right, and *before* the blood dried. So maybe she was fudging. Her first loyalty was to her case and to her client.

Taylor threw her shoes through the back hatch of her truck into the bed, and drove off. She felt considerably better and only slightly guilty.

She called Mel Borman from her car phone and offered no apology for waking him up. After he heard about the murder, he didn't ask for one. Taylor concentrated on her driving, speaking into the car mike that hung from the sun visor. She knew Borman hated the tinny sound, but she needed both hands on the wheel. She clicked off her brights to accommodate an oncoming truck.

"One more thing."

"Here it comes. I knew there was something you weren't telling me."

"You know me too well." Taylor clicked her brights on and negotiated a sweeping curve down the narrow sunken road. "I just found something."

"One of these days, Taylor, I'm going to be visiting you in jail or identifying your body. I don't look forward to either eventuality."

"Never happen. Listen, you old bear." She concentrated on avoiding the pin oaks and scrub locusts encroaching on the shoulder. The road was treacherous in the daytime; at night it was an obstacle course. She told Mel about the ticket. "Should I take it back to Vollmer right now?"

Silence. Then Mel said, "Check it out first, then make sure *he* discovers it. Could be nothing. You have no way of knowing where you picked it up. Your shoes stayed wet for some time."

She let out a contented sigh. "Danny will be wild."

"Yeah. But he can't do much about it."

"Okay," Taylor said, "first thing tomorrow I'm going to find out if that car is still there. If it is, I'll get it out, take it down to Mud Island, and go over it with a fine-tooth comb. Can you meet me?"

"I've got a meeting at eight."

"Then I'll ask Kendall. He might recognize something I don't."

"Taylor, he's the obvious suspect in this thing. Remember Occam's razor."

Taylor laughed. "Yeah, yeah, yeah. Your favorite theorem. 'Keep it simple, stupid.' The obvious solution is usually the correct one. I remember. But somehow, I don't think the obvious suspect is the correct one in this case. Nick seemed genuinely stunned."

"Still, watch your back."

"That's what I've got you for." She turned the wheel. "Damn. Mel, I've just remembered something else. A car nearly ran into me as I turned into the Rounders parking lot. Going fast."

"How long before you discovered the body?"

"Maybe half an hour. The timing works out. The blood was congealing but still wet when we found the body."

"What about the car? Get a license number?"

Taylor snorted. "I wish. No license number, no model, no color. Just know it's a car and not a truck or van."

"You tell Vollmer?"

"I told you I just remembered," Taylor said. She sighed wearily and turned into her driveway. "I'm home and I'm whipped. I'm not going to get more than four hours' sleep. I'll let you know what we find. Good night, you old grizzly."

"Taylor, this is murder. I ought to yank your butt out of there."

"My butt stays where it is until I find out who stole those horses."

Before Mel could answer, Taylor hit the "end" button on her car phone.

She punched in the code that opened the heavy iron gate at the top of her lane. The gates swung open silently. She drove through, hit the button on the clicker and waited while they closed behind her. Behind these gates she was even safe from her mother and her brother—at least until they wormed the gate code out of her again. She shrugged. She'd change it the minute that happened.

The one-lane gravel drive wound down the hill and up again towards the little cabin. It was every bit as dark as the parking lot at Rounders, but she felt welcomed, not threatened.

Except by Elmo. She heard his yowl before she closed the door of her truck.

She picked her Nikes up from the back and walked to the door in her bare feet. Elmo launched himself into her arms the minute the door was open. He flopped over onto his back and began to purr.

She felt as though she'd been dragged backward through a knothole today, but as always, this place soothed her soul. She carried Elmo out to the swing in the yard and settled down. Now, as the swing moved gently to and fro, she let the cold air revitalize her.

How her mother hated this place. She still told her bridge club that Mark had died of lung cancer, as if everyone in town didn't know he'd died of AIDS. It was as though Mark's legacy to his niece had been his final slap in the face to her mother's respectability.

Taylor remembered the funeral. Her mother had tightened her jaw and ignored Steven, Mark's partner. Taylor had made a place for him in the front row of mourners and had clung to him during the ceremony. She and Steven were the only members of the family—and Steven *was* Mark's family, whatever her mother thought—who wept openly.

Steven had been so sweet when Mark's will left everything to Taylor. "I've got plenty of money, Taylor," he said, his eyes misting over. "Mark said you were the only member of his family worth knowing. He used to tell me that one day you'd grow up and walk out on them all."

So she had. It had taken two more years and another series of disasters, but when the metamorphosis was forced on her, she'd known where to run. Thanks to Mark, she had sanctuary.

The telephone rang. She cradled Elmo and raced into the house to answer it before the machine kicked on.

"Hey. Wanted to make sure you got home."

"Nick." Taylor dropped into the battered leather wing chair beside the telephone. She winced as Elmo landed on her shoulder with claws extended. "I'm glad you called."

His deep voice sent a warm glow coursing along her veins. It had been a long time since any man—besides Mel—had shown a real concern for her.

"Vollmer and his team just left."

"Did they search the place?"

He chuckled. "They gave up in disgust. Vollmer said he'd be back tomorrow morning when they could see. I'm not opening Rounders, but Max and Josh are coming down around ten."

"Good, that gives us plenty of time." Taylor outlined her plan. She expected Nick to protest, but he didn't.

"Nick, do your partners know about me?" she asked.

"They do now. I had to tell them why you were here."

"Damn. Oh, well, I suppose I'll never get that horse carved now. I might as well work openly. Maybe whoever killed that woman will get upset enough to go for me."

She heard Nick's quick intake of breath. "Are you crazy? I won't let that happen."

"I was kidding. I can take care of myself. Nobody's going to think I'm a threat."

She hung up. And that's when the day crashed in on her. She had barely enough strength to lock the front door, brush her teeth, wash her face and crawl up the ladder to bed.

She snuggled down and settled Elmo in his customary place in the hollow of her stomach. She wanted desperately to rest, but instead the still face of the dead woman rose in her mind. Finally just before sleep came, another face took its place—Nick Kendall, laugh lines around the eyes, crooked smile, broken nose and all. That was worse. The dead couldn't do her any harm.

She had a feeling that if he put his mind to it, Nick Kendall could twist her life around like a corkscrew.

CHAPTER FOUR

TAYLOR PULLED INTO THE PARK at the north end of Mud Island just before eight in the morning. Nick leaned against the side of a shining blue Lexus with his arms folded across his chest. He looked as big as a tree.

Taylor opened her door and slid across to the passenger side. "You drive."

He shrugged and folded himself behind the wheel of Taylor's little truck.

"Sorry," she said, "seat adjustment's beside you, but this baby truck wasn't meant for giants."

Nick slid the seat back as far as possible. His head still grazed the roof.

"Where's the Rounders truck?" she asked.

"I drove to Max's at dawn and swapped off for his Lexus. Truck's locked in his garage."

"Good thinking. Any trouble getting away from Rounders?"

He shook his head. "Apparently reporters don't get up this early."

"I checked the morning paper. There was just this squib in the Metro section."

"Maybe we'll luck out. It's not the sort of publicity Rounders needs right now."

Taylor said dryly, "We got bumped by a major shoot-out at the Three-Three Club after midnight. One gray-haired lady doesn't rate much space when you've got a dozen drug dealers wielding semiautomatics."

"I guess we ought to be grateful for small favors." He drove past the courthouse and slowed by the park. "With luck, we'll be back at Rounders before the cops show up." He glanced at her. "You look different."

"From your mouth to God's ear." She settled her black fedora at an even more rakish angle and shoved her oversize sunglasses up on her nose. "The hat's a cliché, but it's the only one I own. Better than nothing. I would prefer the doorman at The Peabody not be able to identify me to Danny. If Danny finds out, he's going to go ballistic."

"Could you lose your license?"

"Not at all. He can't bring charges. He'll just rant and rave a little. He has a terrible temper, but he gets over it quickly. We're not really interfering with the investigation. Who says that ticket has anything to do with the corpse? We'll know after we check it out. Then we make sure Danny gets it."

He glanced over at her. She wore a black cashmere blazer over a black turtleneck sweater, dark gray wool trousers and high-heeled suede boots. She also wore makeup, black kid gloves and broad gold hoop earrings.

"My usual ratty jeans and running shoes are in my gym bag in the back, but they'd stand out where we're going, particularly if the car we're picking up is a Caddy or a BMW. This way I look like all the other businesswomen leaving for a day of pharmaceutical sales or marketing meetings. Hopefully they won't remember me when I bring the car back."

"I'd remember you. Unless those guys are blind and deaf, they'll remember you too."

She gazed at him curiously. "Is that a compliment?"

"You might say that. You'd do better with padding, buck teeth and a wig. Even then you'd probably stand out."

"That's because I'm tall."

He chuckled. "That too."

He waltzed the little truck through traffic with practiced ease. In the morning light Taylor could see that the hands that had so sensitively rolled that wooden pear last evening were not merely large, they were rough—with broad fingers and tufts of fine dark hair on the knuckles. An artisan's hands.

She took a deep breath and stared straight ahead. "Exchanging cars with your partner was smart. I wouldn't have thought of it."

Nick grinned and avoided a Toyota that recklessly cut in front of him. "The Rounders truck was painted to be showy. Besides, it's the biggest pickup made. Maybe I have a flare for this cloak-and-dagger stuff."

Taylor looked at his profile. *Maybe you do,* she thought. *I hope you're not cloak-and-daggering me.*

"Let's hope nobody strips Max's Lexus before we get back. He loves that car just slightly less than he does his son and grandson."

"Pull over right there," Taylor said. "I'll walk through the lobby and out the back."

Twenty minutes later, she slid a silver-gray Mercury sedan into a space between her truck and Max's Lexus.

Nick came toward her from the bank of the Mississippi. The early morning sun turned his hair into a sable pelt. Strip him down—now that was an interesting image—put buckskin britches on him and he'd turn into one of the old-time mountain men right before her eyes. She squinted and tried to imagine him in buckskins. Disquieting. Have to be made from a *very* large buck.

She squirmed on the seat uncomfortably, blinked to bring herself back to the present, and climbed out of the sedan.

"Here, put these on." She handed him a pair of surgical gloves. "And don't lean on anything. She pushed the button for the trunk lid, then popped the glove compartment, reached in and pulled out a handful of papers. "Damn." She handed the documents to Nick.

The registration was in the name of Clara Fields Eberhardt of Oxford, Mississippi, and signed by Helmut Eberhardt, spouse.

The sun dipped behind a cloud. Nick covered the fluttering paper with his hand and held it against the hood of the car. Taylor grabbed at her fedora as it lifted from her head.

The bright autumn morning turned chill and threatening in an instant, as though a giant hand had grabbed the sun and shaken it by the scruff of the neck.

Taylor stuffed the fedora in the pocket of her blazer, and shivered.

She took the registration Nick handed her and slid it back into the glove compartment. Then she pulled a penlight from her handbag and searched under the car seats. "Clean as a whistle." Next she shone the light into pockets on the sides of the car. Nothing.

"Woman was a neat freak." Taylor sat back on her heels. "We, the organizationally challenged, salute you." She went to the back of the car and opened the trunk.

"Bingo," Nick said softly. A soft-sided Louis Vuitton overnight bag lay in the trunk. "If she planned to stay at The Peabody last night, why isn't this in her room?"

Taylor shook her head. "Maybe she never checked in. Just dropped the car and met somebody. Maybe she planned to drive back to Oxford last night."

"Then why pack at all?"

"Good point." Taylor smiled up at him. "If her reservation was guaranteed for late arrival, she could drive in, drop the car, meet whoever she was meeting, do her business, come back to the hotel and bring her bag in then."

"Only she never got back."

The wind had turned ugly, whipping Taylor's short hair across her face, stinging her eyes. Instantly, Nick stepped up to her, blocking the wind, shielding her as effectively as a wall. "Better?" he asked.

"Thanks." Most men would not have noticed. His eyes were warm. She looked away quickly. "Here goes." She opened the bag.

Taylor saw that Clara Eberhardt had carefully wrapped her clothing in pink tissue. Taylor hated the idea of violating this woman's privacy, but she steeled herself and unwrapped each neat package gently, grasping the paper that threatened to become airborne.

Inside were a complete set of skimpy peach silk-and-lace underthings and a pair of thigh-high white lace stockings. Did these things actually belong to Clara Eberhardt—with her cashmere sweater and her neat black pumps? Maybe Clara indulged her fantasy life where it didn't show.

Another sweater: cashmere, powder blue. A pair of gray flannel slacks. Black suede flats. Very expensive. Knee-high panty hose. Dior.

A quilted satin jewel case, containing a heavy antique gold chain and earrings—a matching makeup case. Only the best. No spilled powder, no messy lipstick. Deodorant. A small medicine bottle labeled Dilantin. Heart problems? No shampoo or conditioner, but then The Peabody furnished those. Either Clara didn't wash her silver hair every morning or she knew that she'd find what she needed already in place.

No robe, no nightgown, no pajamas. Clara slept naked? Alone? Did she plan to come back to The Peabody for a tumble with the person she met? Maybe someone waited for her all night, frantic when she didn't show up. A wave of pity washed over Taylor. This woman did not deserve to die alone, mute, drowned in her own blood. At this point Clara deserved justice. Taylor prayed she'd have a hand in obtaining it for her.

Taylor found a slightly raised area along the bottom of

the case—rectangular, perhaps five inches by seven. Carefully, she drew out a cordovan leather notebook. Slim, detailed with cutwork. Very beautiful, probably very old.

"Look what I found." She held it up to Nick, who took it carefully between his index finger and thumb. "Why don't you take it over to my truck? I'll put everything back. Be there in a minute." Taylor replaced everything precisely as they had found it, closed but did not zip the lid of the bag, and closed but did not latch the trunk.

"It's an appointment book," Nick said, when she climbed into the truck. "Mostly initials. Here, look at yesterday."

"*Meet pb 7:30.*" Taylor looked up. "Pb must stand for Peabody. Unless you know someone connected with Rounders whose initials are P.B."

"Not offhand."

Taylor thumbed carefully through the book. Unlike the date books that Mel demanded she keep, this one held only unprinted pages. Clara had written down dates, times, appointments as she needed them. Only about a dozen pages had been used.

"We got time to take this to a copier?" Nick asked.

"No need," Taylor said. She brought up a small camera from behind her seat. "Just point and shoot."

"We got enough light?"

"Absolutely. At least, I think so."

Nick Kendall laid the book on the seat between them, then held her flashlight so that she could take pictures of the pages. She took several of each sheet.

Nick looked at his watch. "Let's get this thing back. It's getting late."

"Right." Taylor replaced everything in Clara's car and climbed in. "See you back at Union and Second."

She returned the car to valet parking. Nick picked her up in her truck, then they drove back to Mud Island so that he could collect Max's Lexus.

"Okay," Taylor said as she moved into the driver's seat. "Musical cars is over for now. I'll drop this film off and meet you at Rounders."

BOTH PULLED UP IN FRONT of Rounders at nine. Only then did Taylor realize she'd had no breakfast and was ravenously hungry.

"At least we beat the police," Nick said as he opened the front door.

"And the reporters. Whoever was on the crime desk last night dropped the ball, for which you can be eternally grateful. Reporters can be insensitive monsters."

She sounded bitter. Nick wondered when she'd run afoul of reporters, and made a mental note to ask Mel Borman the next time he spoke to the man. Vollmer would know, but Nick wouldn't lower himself to ask Vollmer what century they were in.

"Is there an area they might have missed last night? In the storeroom, I mean?" Taylor asked.

"Why?"

"I need to get this valet parking stub back."

"There's yellow police tape across the storeroom doors and the loading dock."

"Damn! I should have thought of that." Taylor sighed and turned to him. "Any bright ideas? I can't withhold the darn thing, and I certainly don't want to hand it over to Vollmer and tell him where I found it—if I can avoid it."

"Come on." Kendall walked down the alleyway beside Rounders. The sick-sweet scent of rotting vegetation from the vacant lots mingled with the acid smell of rat droppings, and raised Taylor's gorge. She avoided the puddles, wishing she'd stopped to change her good boots for her running shoes. Kendall forged ahead with casual familiarity.

Around the corner of the building, Taylor got her first look at the loading dock. Concrete, set at the height of an open truck bed. The freight elevator was closed by a steel door with a handle at its base. A heavy steel padlock latched handle to haft. Beside it, another smaller steel door probably led to the back stairs.

Taylor shivered and hugged herself. She visualized Clara Eberhardt walking up those stairs or climbing into that elevator, unaware that she had only a few moments to live.

Here, too, the police had strung yellow tape, effectively blocking both entrances.

"Damn," Taylor said. "If we just drop it out here, the wind could blow it away before they find it."

"Nope. I can slide it under the door. See? Doesn't quite meet at the bottom. Helps to have long arms."

"Don't leave fingerprints," Taylor cautioned. "I wiped mine off last night."

Nick stared at it. "How'd you manage to keep the original stub?"

"Told the man I needed it for my expense account. He gave it to me."

"He'll remember you. Maybe we should have gotten someone else to pick up the car."

"Let's hope he's off duty when the cops show up." She shrugged. "If I have to tell Danny, I will. I'll keep you out of it. He's already suspicious of you as it is."

Nick slid the stub under the door. "That'll have to do."

"Right. Let's get around to the front and inside before they catch us," Taylor said. "Lord, it's cold back here."

Nick reached an arm around her and pulled her against his side. He released her instantly, but Taylor wouldn't have been more surprised if he'd thrown her down and sat on her.

That one second was long enough for Taylor to realize how good it felt to have a man's arm around her again, and how long it had been since she'd felt that simple pleasure. As he walked ahead of her down the alley, she looked critically at the set of his broad shoulders. Maybe it was time to stop being such a damn recluse.

FOUR PEOPLE WAITED IN THE WORKROOM. Taylor recognized Veda. The other woman was as tall as Taylor and bone thin. Despite the No Smoking signs, she smoked languidly and dropped her ashes into an empty paper cup in her hand. She wore a sour expression that said she didn't want to be here.

"God, Nick, this is awful!" The man with her stood perhaps five-seven and weighed well over two hundred flabby pounds. As he ran a hand over the thin fringe of graying hair that encircled his head, he rocked back and forth on his toes in a steady rhythm that made Taylor queasy. His slightly pop eyes and wide mouth reminded Taylor of Veda's frog in the storeroom.

"Taylor Hunt," Nick said, "this is Josh Chessman and his wife Margery. Veda, you know."

Veda nodded and bobbed.

"Veda," he said, "we're closed today. Didn't you read the sign?"

"Of course I did, Nick dear. I ignored it. I came to help."

"Thanks, but I'm not sure what you can do."

"Offer moral support, make coffee, answer the telephone, chase off reporters for a start."

Nick smiled at her. "'Course you can. Thanks."

"I stopped for doughnuts and the coffee's perked."

Taylor's stomach rumbled. "Bless you, Veda, I'm starved."

Veda scurried off to Nick's office.

"Max Beaumont, Ms. Hunt," the second man said, and advanced to shake her hand. He was nearly as tall as Nick, but with a fine-boned thoroughbred elegance that seemed to belong in a hunting jacket or a tuxedo. He wore jeans and a sweatshirt—the standard Rounders uniform—but the jeans were designer and pressed with a knife-edge crease. His gray hair was cropped close to his head like Julius Caesar's. His pale gray eyes were glacial. "I won't ask where you were or what you were doing, Nick. This is a bad business."

"Worse than you can imagine," Nick answered.

Taylor shook her head at him. He took the hint.

"In what way, Mr. Kendall?" Danny Vollmer spoke from the doorway. None of them had heard him come up the stairs. He and his partner entered the room.

"Can't get much worse than murder, can it, Detective Vollmer?" Taylor asked. She stepped in front of Kendall.

Vollmer narrowed his eyes and glanced quickly from her to Kendall.

"Any idea who the woman was?" Max Beaumont asked.

Vollmer shook his head. "Whoever killed her took her purse. We're searching the Dumpsters in the neighborhood." He spared a final glance for Taylor—a glance without any warmth—and turned to the others. "Any of you know a fiftyish woman, five-two, a hundred and ten pounds, gray hair, hazel eyes? Well-dressed, probably rich?"

Margery Chessman dropped her cigarette into the cup. It sizzled like a firefly hitting a candle flame. "I know fifty women of that description, Mr...?"

"Sergeant Vollmer, ma'am."

"I, myself, almost fit that description. We are clones, sergeant. We sit on hospital and museum boards, we run corporate offices. We are—although the men seem unaware of it—the movers and shakers of this city."

"Yes, ma'am." He turned to the others and raised his eyebrows. They shook their heads.

"Any identifying marks, Detective?" Max Beaumont asked.

"Except for a three-inch hole in her neck, none that I could spot." Vollmer reached behind him. His partner handed him a manila folder. "We brought pictures." He pulled out a set of glossy eight-by-tens and passed them to Beaumont with a flourish. He winked at Taylor.

She rolled her eyes.

Beaumont took the pictures, glanced at them dispassionately and passed them to Josh. Josh caught his breath and averted his eyes. Taylor thought that made him look even more like a frog. He even seemed to be turning green. "I'm sorry," he said apologetically. "I've never had a strong stomach. Poor woman."

Margery took them from her husband, stared at them a moment, and handed them back to Vollmer.

"Thank God, she's not one of my committee women," Margery said.

"Do any of you recognize her?" Vollmer asked.

"Oh, my, no. At least I don't think so," Chessman said. His thick white eyebrows met. He frowned and clicked his tongue against his teeth. He pulled a handkerchief from his pocket and wiped it across his sweating pate, then rubbed it between his palms.

Vollmer turned back to Margery Chessman. "Mind telling me where you were last night?"

"Good grief, am I a suspect? Surely no woman could do what was done to that poor soul."

"Didn't take much strength. That chisel was as sharp as a razor."

Taylor heard the edge of impatience in Vollmer's voice. He spoke to Margery, but his angry eyes were on her. Did Danny know what she'd been up to with Nick and Clara's car? No way. Still, his patience was wearing thin. Taylor was certain she was to blame. She simply didn't know why. She smiled at him blandly.

"So, if you could just tell me where you were?" Vollmer repeated.

Margery raised her shoulders and clasped her hands across her bosom. "Very well. I was at home cooking dinner for Josh.'' She turned to her husband. "He got home around—what—eight or so?''

Chessman nodded. "That's right.''

"And Mr. Chessman?''

"Dr. Chessman, Sergeant,'' Josh corrected. "I was in my office finishing a paper that I had to send to my journal referee this morning.''

"Anyone with you?''

Chessman gulped, and his Adam's apple moved convulsively.

Taylor half expected to see a four-foot-long tongue dart out to capture a passing fly.

He continued, "The place cleared out around six. My lights were on, of course, but I shut my door. Nobody stopped to chat.'' Then his face brightened. "Margery called me, though, didn't you, darling? About seven-thirty?''

"That's right, Sergeant. I wanted to ask him how soon I should start the grill for the lamb chops. He was definitely there. He answered the telephone on the second or third ring.''

Taylor watched their smooth interplay. Obviously they were used to working in tandem. She'd seen her mother and father do it. They might not have an ideal marriage, but they certainly ran a well-oiled partnership.

Vollmer turned to Max Beaumont.

"Working at home alone. Nobody called, nobody came. No alibi.''

"What were you working on, Mr. Beaumont?''

"I am restoring my family's old home. I inherited it several years ago—just after I retired from the military. I needed a project. At the rate I am progressing, it should be finished the day before I die. My family is remarkably long-lived.'' He tried to chuckle, but it fell flat. "Last night I was trying to get a dozen layers of enamel off the fireplace tiles in the living room.''

"Could anyone have seen you from outside?"

Beaumont shook his head. "I have plantation shutters across the front windows."

"I see."

At that moment Veda slipped out of Nick's office and handed Taylor a steaming mug of coffee and a glazed doughnut in a paper towel. "Here, dear," she whispered.

Taylor smiled her thanks.

"Ma'am? You'd be…?" Vollmer asked.

"Veda Albright, Sergeant. And no, I do not have an alibi. I left here sometime before seven and drove straight home. I didn't leave until I saw the story in the papers this morning. My only companions are my cat and my bird. Neither would do very well in the witness box, I'm afraid." She smiled gently.

"Right." He turned to Taylor, who had a mouthful of doughnut. He seemed to reach a decision. "Can I see you a minute outside, Ms. Hunt?"

Taylor took a gulp of blessedly hot coffee. "Can't it wait, Detective? This is the first food I've had all morning."

"Now, please," he said with suspicious calm.

Taylor sighed, set cup and doughnut on the nearest table beside a pair of cloven hooves, and followed him out the door and down the stairs.

He held the front door for her. She stepped out onto the sidewalk.

"Danny, it's cold out here, dammit," she said. The wind whipped bits of garbage and paper around the square like lost souls.

He whirled, took her upper arms and pulled her so close that their noses almost collided. "What the hell do you think you're playing at? You think I like having you messing around with a damned murderer?"

She yanked one arm free and used her freed hand to slap

his other hand down. "Stop that. Don't you pull that Prussian temper on me."

"You get your cute little rear end right back to Borman."

Taylor flushed. "I'm trying very hard to be nice, Detective, but you are not making it easy. Understand me, please. My rear end is no longer your concern."

"It is when it's mixed up in my murder investigation and you're working for the principal suspect."

"Oh, get a grip! You have no evidence that Nick Kendall is any more involved in this than..." She flipped a hand towards a tall man leaning against an overflowing grocery cart across the square.

Vollmer snorted. "Right. And I'm Grandma Moses. Kendall was there alone." He ran his hand over his hair, smoothing it against the wind. "He had access to dozens of those damn chisels. They're everywhere you look." Vollmer leaned casually against the dirty brick wall, realized what he'd done, and stood away, brushing himself down carefully.

Despite herself, Taylor smiled. He hadn't changed. "Okay, but do you know which set it came from?"

"Set? What do you mean 'set'?"

"If you'd bothered to ask, you'd have found that every carver has at least one set of chisels of different sizes and shapes. The school has half a dozen more sets. Somebody's missing a chisel."

"Damn." He reached past her to open the door, then shoved her through, shutting it behind them. They stood close to one another in the dark foyer at the foot of the stairs. "So what are you working on for Kendall?"

"Nope."

"Fine. Just fine. I'll ask Borman." Taylor started up the steps. "Wait."

She hesitated.

"I've missed you, Taylor." He took her hand and reeled

her back to his level. "When I saw you last night, all I could think about was you sitting there swinging those damn long legs." He ran his fingers up under the hair at the base of her skull. "Taylor. We were good together. We could be again."

The man had the sexiest voice. And those hands. She felt remembered heat flooding up from her center and his hot breath against her face. He drew her to him. His breath wasn't all she felt against her. It would be so easy to forget all their problems. Hadn't she just said it was time to stop being a recluse?

She pulled herself up short. Danny still knew the buttons to push. She wasn't about to fall into the trap all over again.

"You're on duty, Detective."

"I get off at four."

She stepped away from him. "I'm sorry, Danny, truly I am." She sighed. "We won't work. I'm a different person now." She saw his jaw tighten, the light die out of his eyes. Women didn't often say "no" to Danny Vollmer. Not women he'd bedded.

She heard the sudden anger in his voice. "Changed? That mean you've stopped being a ball-breaking bitch or what?"

She gripped the banister, then realized he couldn't even make her angry any longer. She felt a wave of loss and said sadly, "No, Danny, I'll probably always be a ball-breaking bitch, but I've sure gotten better at identifying control-freak bastards." She ran up the stairs.

Behind her, he called, "Taylor! God, Taylor, I didn't mean that. Taylor!"

She kept going.

VOLLMER LET THEM ALL GO with promises that they'd be interviewed again once the dead woman's body was identified. Veda stayed to man the telephone, and the others decided to meet at Max's house at five to decide on a course of action.

"Come on, Nick," Taylor said. "I'm starved. Buy me some breakfast." They passed Vollmer's partner on the stairs. Taylor knew him slightly and nodded. "Detective Harrison."

He didn't return her greeting, but stood halfway up the stairs and watched them until the front door closed behind them.

The tall man she'd seen earlier abandoned his grocery cart and started towards them. "Sir?" The man addressed Nick. "Can I speak to you?" He was pulling a small tape recorder out of his jeans as he walked.

"Come on," Taylor said urgently. "I think the crime desk finally woke up."

"The guy probably wants a handout."

"He wants a story. That's a reporter, not a vagrant. Take my truck." She tossed him the keys.

Without another word, Nick climbed into the driver's side of the truck, turned the key and waited for Taylor to get in.

The reporter tapped on the window. "Sir, if I could ask you a few questions?"

Nick ignored him, reversed and drove away.

"Whew!" Taylor turned to watch the man, who stared after them forlornly. "Close one."

"I'm going to have to talk to them sooner or later."

"Why? Let them get their info from Danny. He's used to it." She fastened her seat belt and leaned back. "By tonight they'll have her identity—and other fish to fry." She clicked her tongue. "I hope."

"Yeah. So where we going for breakfast?"

"How fast do you think we can get to Oxford?"

"I can make it in an hour if your radar detector works," Nick said, then swiveled to look at her. "Remind me not to ask you to lunch. You might want to go to Paris."

Taylor laughed. "Actually, I wanted to break into the Eberhardt's house before Danny finds out who she is."

"That's illegal."

"So's speeding. Besides, it's only illegal if we get caught. I'll break and enter. You can sit in the car and bail me out if the cops show up."

"I'm going to be right beside you if you waltz into the Eberhardt house. Count on it."

He sounded just as bossy as Danny, but she felt a wave of warmth. Danny wanted to control her. Apparently Nick wanted to help if she needed him. A small difference, but an important one.

After they passed the Mississippi line, he said, "Vollmer thinks I did it, doesn't he?"

"Yes."

"I didn't."

"I know that." *At least I think I do.* "But you had means and opportunity. Once they identify the body, they'll say you had motive as well."

"Clara was blackmailing me about the horses?"

"Or her husband's death or something. The point is, Danny wants you to be guilty."

He glanced at her. "He's in love with you."

Taylor flushed. "Not love. We had a thing for a while. It's been over for months."

"Not for him."

"It has for me." She watched the pines and kudzu flash by. How much should she tell Nick? If Danny planned to arrest him, he had a right to go armed with as much knowledge as possible. She took a deep breath. "My husband, Paul, was killed in a drive-by shooting at an ATM. Danny and his partner caught the case and then caught the three men who did it. I was vulnerable, he was attractive. My hero."

"What went wrong?"

"He wanted to own me. Nobody does that, not anymore."

She felt, rather than saw, Nick take his eyes off the road long enough to stare at the set of her profile. "Maybe he's just worried about you."

"I don't report to anybody but Mel, and then only during business hours." She sounded determined.

"What are we looking for in Oxford?"

"We've got to find the records on those remaining animals."

"You think whoever stole the animals killed Clara?"

"Don't you? It's possible the same person killed Eberhardt and burned his store down, too." She looked at him.

The knuckles on his hands were white around the wheel. "Yeah. I may have been wrong about Eberhardt torching his own place." He glanced over at her and looked back to the road quickly. "What gets me is that one of those people back there could betray everything Rounders stands for—just for money."

He frowned and stamped down on the accelerator to pass a truck. When they were safely back in the right lane, he continued. "All I've got going for me are these." He lifted his hands from the wheel for a moment. "I'm not an artist, I'm a glorified carpenter who likes to teach. Rounders—those people—they're all I've got. That, and my reputation as an honest man. I can rebuild my family, but not my reputation."

Taylor watched his profile in silence. The set of his jaw was grim. Well, it was a grim business, murder, especially when the detective in charge of the case suspected you.

Growing up, she'd had only her uncle Mark to teach her about ethics and morals. Her father delighted in real estate and investment kickbacks that might have been technically legal but were basically dishonest. He'd also been a violent man—especially when he was drunk. Once he'd beaten both her and Bradley so badly that Children's Services would have intervened in a heartbeat, had anyone reported him. Bradley had inherited all their father's bad traits. No wonder Taylor had been in a hurry to get out of the house. She'd mistaken her husband Paul for a knight in shining armor, only to find him even more tarnished than the men in her family.

Nick reminded her of Mel Borman, except that Mel was a realist. This man had more than a little Don Quixote in him. Otherwise he'd never have promised to pay Pete Marley for the fake hippocampus. Taylor vowed this particular Don Quixote wouldn't suffer for his honor—if she could help it.

Ten minutes later they cruised slowly past the Eberhardt house. There were no other cars around, no sign of police activity. Apparently Vollmer had not yet identified Clara Eberhardt's body.

The Eberhardt house was a nineteen-thirties' Tudor, set high on a bank among aging trees along a winding road past Rowan Oaks, Faulkner's house.

Nick circled the block and drove back to park. Taylor directed him to a space two doors down from the Eberhardts's. "So how do we handle it?" he asked.

"Walk up to the front door and ring the bell. There could be relatives or friends staying there. Maybe someone missed her when she didn't come home last night."

"And if somebody answers?"

"We're tracing the carousel animals. We don't know anything about a murder."

"And if no one answers?"

Taylor shrugged and pulled a device that looked like a small cordless screwdriver from her satchel. "Mel tried to teach me to pick locks. He finally gave up and bought me this. It's a cordless electronic lock pick. Very handy." She reached into her glove compartment for another pair of surgical gloves and handed them to Nick. She wore driving gloves.

He slipped the gloves on. ''What's the sentence for breaking and entering in Mississippi?''

''Actually, we're not breaking anything—we're only entering. Besides, we won't get caught.'' She slid out of the car. Nick followed her to the front door and waited while she rang the bell. It echoed inside the house. When no one answered after several moments, Taylor fitted a pick into her little device and bent to the lock. As she rested her hand on the doorknob, it turned. The door swung open silently.

Taylor stepped inside and pulled Nick after her. He shut the door.

''Anybody home?'' Taylor called. Silence. Dust motes danced in the shadowy hallway. The whole place had a disused air, as though Clara Eberhardt and her husband had left months before. Taylor moved to the living room.

''Damnation!'' she swore.

''What?'' Nick asked as he came up beside her.

Taylor spread her hands. The place looked as though a tornado had swept through it. Chinese porcelain jars lay broken on the oriental rugs, books were torn from bookcases and from their leather bindings. Every piece of upholstery had been slashed. Feathers coated every surface like an early snow.

An antique lady's desk in the corner had been turned on its side, its fragile legs fractured as though a heavy boot had stamped them. ''Someone hasn't just searched this place, they've vandalized it.'' Taylor picked her way through the dining room and then to the kitchen.

The Eberhardts had owned lovely things. And someone obviously hated them for it.

Taylor's steps crunched the shards of delicate crystal goblets. She picked up half a dinner plate and turned it over. ''Lowestoft,'' she read, and sighed.

Someone—working like a centrifuge—had flung sugar and flour around the kitchen, then broken a jar of molasses on top of the mess. The room stank of it.

Taylor turned to find Nick standing in the doorway.

"This is sick," he said. He stooped to pick up a Georgian silver teapot in his gloved hands. Its lid had been stamped flat.

For the first time, Taylor felt afraid. Clara Eberhardt's murder had been savage, but swift. The destruction of this house had taken time, energy and boundless rage. She turned around slowly like a child in a game of blindman's bluff.

"I don't think they found what they were looking for," Nick said. He set the lidless teapot on the kitchen table.

They found more destruction upstairs. Ten minutes later, shaken by the devastation, Nick took Taylor's arm. "We need to get the hell out of here, Taylor." When she didn't move, he took her arm. *"Now!"*

He half dragged her to the truck and hoisted her into the passenger seat. He went to the driver's side, started the truck and drove away. At the first corner, he stopped and turned right into a residential area.

They both heard the sirens behind them. Taylor twisted in her seat. An Oxford police car slid to a stop in front of the Eberhardt house, and two uniformed policemen climbed out. Nick drove away well under the speed limit.

"Vollmer must have identified the body," Taylor whispered. "He must have found her purse."

"Come on, let's head back to Memphis," Nick said.

"THERE'S SOMETHING fundamentally wrong with me," Taylor said as Nick turned onto Highway 7.

"You sick?" Nick asked. "Want me to stop somewhere?"

She shook her head. "That's not what I mean. That house

affected me more than Clara Eberhardt's body did. How can I care more about things than about people?"

He dropped a hand on her knee. For a moment she considered removing it, but it felt comforting.

"The murder doesn't seem real. *That*—" he jerked his head back towards Oxford "—that's insane."

Taylor shuddered. "You felt it too? It wasn't just me?"

"Either we've got one murderer *and* one lunatic, or the killer did the searching. Probably last night while we were entertaining your friend Vollmer."

"You think the killer got angry because he didn't find what he was looking for?"

"No. That was personal. Who breaks the legs of desks like that?"

Taylor smiled. The destruction of wood affected him more than the destruction of porcelain or crystal, no matter how beautiful. "What was he looking for?"

"Could be a she."

"I realize that."

"Maybe evidence linking him or her with Eberhardt and the theft."

"I wish we'd had time to search. Mel's taught me some great hiding places even the police sometimes overlook."

"The last thing we needed was to get caught by the cops in that house."

"They couldn't blame you for the destruction. You were with me and the Homicide Division's finest until two in the morning." Even as she said the words, she realized their import.

So did he. "I could have driven to Oxford in an hour, spent an hour wrecking that house, driven home and still met you with plenty of time to spare."

"Yes, you could have. But I don't think you could have broken that desk."

"So what now?" he asked.

"Do you know where Eberhardt's shop was?" Taylor asked.

Nick nodded.

"Could we drive by? I don't know what it would accomplish, but it's stupid not to take the opportunity while we're here."

Nick turned right on the bypass. Taylor had expected the store to be near the center of town. Instead they drove four or five miles past the city limits before she saw the blackened building on her left.

The store had been housed in a large, low metal complex. The front half facing the road still seemed relatively intact. As they drove into the parking lot, however, they could see that the entire back half had melted and twisted like candle wax.

Nick pointed to the ruins. "The report in the newspaper said they found Eberhardt's body back there where he did his restoration."

Taylor opened the door of the truck. Surely after a week the stench should be gone. Was she imagining the odor of roasting flesh? She took a few extra seconds getting out of the truck.

A man came out the front door. He was wiping his hands on a filthy cloth. There was soot on his face, on his jeans and on the black T-shirt that stretched across his barrel chest. He was shorter and younger than Nick, but outweighed him considerably. His shoulders sloped down from his neck—or what passed for his neck—at close to a forty-five-degree angle. His arms hung down nearly to his knees. His body screamed "power-lifter."

"We're closed, man." He pointed to the sign, moving in a miasma of unwashed armpits and ash.

Taylor breathed through her mouth and handed him a card that said, Wendy Wright, Estate Sales. He took the card, raked Taylor with prurient eyes and pulled his short upper

lip down over a set of yellow teeth that would have bene-
fited from orthodonture and regular flossing.

Taylor did not offer to shake his hand. She smiled
brightly and asked, "And you are Mr...?"

"Eugene Lewis."

She heard Nick's low growl behind her. She continued
pleasantly, "I'm interested in carousel animals, Mr. Lewis.
A friend told me you might know where I could find some."

"I don't know who the hell told you that. We ain't got
no carousel crap now and never did have. I told you. We're
closed."

"How soon do you plan on reopening?"

"Who said we did?"

"Listen, friend," Nick said, "I know somebody who
bought a carousel animal here less than a month ago and I
know you've got more. Answer the lady's question."

"Shoot, I ain't answering nothing. Now y'all git or I'll
call the sheriff."

"For what? Asking questions with intent?" Taylor said.
"Who are you anyway? You own this place?"

"It ain't none of your business, but I work here. I'm
trying to salvage what I can. And I ain't found no animals,
alive or dead." He grinned as though he'd made a joke.

Taylor felt Nick close behind her and knew trouble was
imminent. She turned around and herded him back toward
the truck. "Come, dear, let's let the nice man get back to
his job." When Nick refused to move, she took his arm.
"Quickly, dear—" she wiggled her eyebrows at him
"—before Mr. Lewis has more company."

Nick nodded, climbed in, slammed the truck into gear and
spun rubber out of the parking lot.

"Son of a bitch," Nick snarled.

"Several generations back, I'd say," Taylor answered.
"Did you notice his shoes?"

"No. Why?"

"Our Mr. Lewis was wearing steel-toed work boots. He'd probably enjoy destroying china. The question is whether he'd enjoy destroying middle-aged matrons even more."

CHAPTER FIVE

"HELLO, MOTHER, SORRY I'M LATE." Taylor pulled out her chair without waiting for the maitre d' to hold it for her. She plunked her satchel onto the floor by her feet. She should probably have left the Glock in the car, but she didn't want it stolen, and recently there had been a series of thefts from the country club parking lot, much to her mother's chagrin.

"You look nice, dear," her mother said. "That's a very becoming shade of lipstick."

Taylor smiled and accepted the compliment. It would do no good to tell her mother that she had dressed to con The Peabody parking lot attendant.

Irene continued, "If you'd just let your lovely hair grow, maybe use some hot rollers, a few highlights in the front..." She reached out red-tipped fingers to touch Taylor's hair. Taylor drew back as though she were being confronted by a striking copperhead. Her mother dropped the offending hand and let out a small but perfectly audible sigh.

Taylor spoke through clamped teeth, "I like my hair, I like my clothes, I like my job, I like my life."

Her mother stiffened. "Why do you always attack me? I'm only trying to help. You used to be such a lovely woman. And you're still young. Well, youngish. It's not too late for babies yet. You could probably still have almost any man you choose. You got Paul, after all." She caught her breath. "Oh, dear, I didn't mean to open old wounds. I am a stupid old woman."

"You're barely sixty, you have an I.Q. of one-thirty, and why you persist in this Billie Burke imitation I will never know. It went out of style with the Eisenhower administration."

Her mother reddened and opened her mouth to retort.

Before she could speak, however, a shadow fell across the table. Both women looked up.

"Irene, darling, I haven't seen you for ages. And Taylor. How lovely of you to ask me to join you."

Taylor knew she'd been sandbagged. She'd figured her mother's luncheon invitation involved throwing Taylor at Irene's latest prospect for replacement son-in-law. Instead, here was CeCe Washburn, owner of the new antique shop. Another attempt to prune Taylor from her unsuitable employment with Mel Borman.

But this time her mother's plan might not be so bad. CeCe Washburn could be a plu-perfect source of information about Helmut Eberhardt, the business of fake antiques, and possibly Nick Kendall as well.

Taylor turned on a genuinely welcoming smile.

"CeCe, I couldn't be more delighted. Sit down, please. We're just about to order. Would you like a cocktail, maybe? Glass of wine?" Taylor rested her cheek on her hand and simpered. Out of the corner of her eye, she caught her mother's startled glance. Taylor smiled at her.

Irene narrowed her eyes.

CeCe drained her fourth frozen margarita forty-five minutes later, and fished around in her salad bowl for any stray shrimp that might be hiding under the arugula. Taylor drank her iced tea and wondered at CeCe's ability to suck up not only the alcohol but the calories without any appreciable effect on her fashionably skeletal frame.

"So you see, darling, I really do need an assistant manager for the new shop. And since your degree is in interior design, naturally your name popped right to the front of my poor little brain," CeCe said, and signaled to the waiter. The fifth frozen margarita appeared at CeCe's elbow.

"Sorry, CeCe, I have a job."

Taylor heard her mother's sniff. "But you'd meet the loveliest people with CeCe, dear."

"As opposed to the scum of the earth and the dregs of humanity with whom I presently associate?" Taylor said.

Irene tittered. "Dear Taysie, you get so prickly whenever I mention that nice Mr. Borman and his...clients."

"Sorry, Mother." Then the demons that invariably beset her whenever she was around her family began to dance a jig in her head. She leaned closer to her mother and whispered, "You'd be amazed at how many of those dregs are lunching in this room as we speak."

Her mother jumped and began to peer around myopically. Taylor sat back and smiled. CeCe had been too involved in licking the salt from the rim of her glass to notice their exchange.

"CeCe, did you ever run across a man named Eberhardt?"

CeCe's tongue stopped in mid-lap. CeCe took a sip and set her glass down. "Terrible tragedy. Of course I never did business personally with him."

Taylor nodded. "Not too savory a reputation?"

"My dear, the man was a crook. Sold overpriced nineteen-twenties' reproductions as eighteenth-century English. I've heard he even commissioned pieces to order. If a client was dying for a William and Mary dining table, Eberhardt would magically discover one."

"Did he ever fake a provenance?"

Again the darting tongue was still a moment before CeCe replied. She cleared her throat and shook the heavy gold cuff on her right hand. "Possibly. 'Course the man made a mint. Some people are so crass."

Taylor couldn't have said why she asked her next question, but the moment the words were out of her mouth she knew she'd hit pay dirt. "Did you ever work with a cabinetmaker named Kendall? He's dead now."

CeCe blinked at her and burst into loud laughter that grated like a flock of guinea hens running from a raccoon. "Oh, Lord, that man was a genius!" She looked around the room, leaned forward and lowered her voice. "I wouldn't tell just anybody this, but what with you possibly bein' in the trade and all. What old Nicholas Kendall didn't know about furniture hasn't been invented. He could fake fresh mahogany so you'd swear the worms ate on it in seventeen-fifty." She caught herself. "Not that he ever faked anything for me, you understand, but when you're replacing veneer and paneling and things, you have to make the new parts match the rest of the piece."

"Of course." Taylor smiled. "Did you like him?"

"What an odd question." CeCe took a hefty swig of her margarita. The four-carat diamond on her ring finger glittered in the light from the chandelier. "Frankly, I loathed the sanctimonious old fart."

Taylor stifled a giggle at her mother's horrified expression.

"Ever meet his grandson?"

"God, did I ever!" CeCe clasped a hand over her sternum—every inch of which was visible beneath her pebbled skin. "If I'd been five—well, maybe ten—years younger, I'd have bought him a closet full of Armani suits, chained him to my bed and screwed his brains out until neither one of us could stand up."

Taylor laughed out loud. She didn't dare glance at her mother.

CeCe blinked. "Whoo-ee, I am drunk as a skunk." She flipped her diamond-encrusted hand over her shoulder. "Armande! You'd better call the store and tell Felix to come on over and get me in the panel truck. That is, if I can walk.'' She struggled to her feet. Armande took one elbow, Taylor took the other.

''Lordy! I better go lie down in the ladies' room until Felix gets here. Thanks for lunch, Irene.'' CeCe minced off as though she were picking her way through a minefield. Both Taylor and Armande followed two steps behind, ready to catch her if she stumbled.

When Taylor resumed her seat, she bit her lip to avoid cracking a smile.

''Well, I never. Taylor, you egged that poor woman on. Obviously, she wasn't paying a bit of attention to how many margaritas she'd had. It's your fault if she gets sick all over the ladies' room.''

''Obviously.''

In her mother's world, women who wore big diamonds didn't talk like field hands and inhale margaritas like elephants at a watering hole. But Taylor was feeling much too good to be annoyed at her mother's arcane value system. She knew CeCe would have a doozy of a hangover by sunset.

Taylor reached for her satchel and stood. ''Thanks for lunch, Mother. I mean that. It's been very informative and a heck of a lot of fun, but I've got to get back to work.''

''Taysie, you can't go. You haven't told me anything that's been happening with you.''

For a moment Taylor's demons begged her to sit back down and regale her mother with tales of bloody corpses and long nights spent with homicide detectives. She smacked them back and prayed the newspaper wouldn't mention her name in connection with the murder.

Taylor leaned over and kissed her mother's silken cheek. On impulse she hugged her. ''I love you, old girl, I really do. And I'm fine. I wish you could believe that. I promise I'll call you.''

She threaded her way among the tables feeling a sudden

sense of sadness. Why couldn't families just accept one another? She tried to accept her mother and her brother, but neither made much attempt to reciprocate. At the doorway she turned. Her mother still sat at the table watching her, her eyes bright with unshed tears. Taylor felt her own eyes sting. She must be a terrible disappointment. She waved. Her mother waved back.

Now she knew why Nick's spotless reputation was important to him. He was living down the reputation that old scoundrel, his grandfather, had bequeathed to him. She'd have to do some further checking on Nicholas Kendall Senior. Did the old man's lessons in woodcraft include failsafe methods for faking antiques? And did those antiques possibly include carousel animals?

"YOU'RE EARLY," said Max Beaumont. He stood aside to let Nick into his front hall.

"Needed to talk to you before Josh got here." With an ease born of long familiarity, Nick walked to the sunporch at the back of the house and dropped into a white wicker armchair.

Max followed and took a seat opposite him. "Want a beer?"

"Later, maybe." Nick ran a hand down his face. "Vollmer thinks I killed that woman."

"You didn't, did you?"

"Hell! Of course not. I didn't know who she was until this morning."

Max picked up on his statement instantly. "This morning? Last I heard, the police didn't have any idea who she was."

"It's a long story. I'm sure it'll be on the evening news. She was Clara Eberhardt, Helmut Eberhardt's wife."

Nick expected a reaction, but not the one he got. Max

surged up from the couch as though he'd been shot out of a mortar. "Clara Eberhardt? Clara Fields Eberhardt?"

Nick looked up at him, puzzled at his distress. "Yeah. Car registration said her maiden name was Fields. How'd you know?"

Max dropped back onto the couch. "Last week when you asked me to check on Eberhardt, I found out he'd married Clara Fields."

"So?"

"She was at Ole Miss when I was there as an ROTC instructor back in the seventies. I not only knew her, I slept with her."

"God." Nick stared at Max. "You didn't identify her picture."

"When I knew her, she had bushy red hair to her waist and bangs to the bridge of her nose. She was twenty pounds overweight and still wore love beads—the last of the long-haired hippies. Apparently at some point she married Eberhardt, dropped the weight, and turned into a society matron. Before last week I hadn't thought of her in years."

"I thought you were married when you were at Ole Miss."

Max shrugged ruefully. "Clara is part of the reason I'm not married any longer. After Vietnam, I laid every female I could con into bed with me. Sarah tried to be sympathetic, but eventually she stopped forgiving me for post-traumatic stress disorder and blew her stack over straightforward marital infidelity. Can't blame her. That's when she took Michael, moved to California and divorced me."

In the week since he'd discovered the theft of his animals, Nick had made no connection between Helmut Eberhardt and anyone at Rounders. Here it was.

He knew how much Max had hated losing his family, hated the distance—emotional as well as physical—between him and his son Michael. He'd never even seen his grandson, Michael Junior.

Could Max have run into Clara after all these years? Met Eberhardt through her? He remembered the force and pinpoint accuracy of that thrust into Clara's throat. Max knew how to kill, no doubt had killed in the course of his twenty-five years as an artillery officer.

Max always said that his killing had been long-range, that he'd never had to see the faces or the bodies of the dead. But was that accurate? There'd been plenty of hand-to-hand in the jungles of Vietnam.

Nick and Max had often told one another that their military careers had made them more peaceable. But was that true? If Clara Eberhardt presented a direct threat, would Max have reverted? After all, he had thirty years of orchestrated violence in his background.

"I need a beer," Max said.

"Yeah, me too." Nick watched his closest friend, his nearest ally, walk out of the sunroom into the kitchen. Max was over sixty now, but still strong and straight. From the back he looked like a man half his age. His shoulders and arms were still muscular. He could have picked Clara Eberhardt up like a child after he'd killed her.

If so, he'd have been covered with her blood. What would he have done with the clothes?

Nick shook the idea way. This was Max, not Jack the Ripper! He took the long neck Sam Adams from Max's hand and drank deeply. Max sank once more onto the wicker couch and propped his feet, in their snow-white running shoes, on the glass coffee table between them.

"You going to tell the cops you knew her?" Nick asked.

Max shook his head. "Not if I don't have to. Why borrow trouble?"

"Tell Taylor."

Max snapped, "Surely you're going to dump her."

Nick stopped with the bottle halfway to his lips. "Dump her? Why would I do that?"

Max leaned forward and set his bottle on the table with a clunk. He began to draw circles on the glass with the condensation from the bottom of the bottle. "All right, all right." He raised his eyes and Nick was surprised to see anger in them and in the set of his jaw.

"I'm a little ticked off—no, make that mad as hell—that you went and hired that, that…uppity…woman without mentioning it to Josh and me." Nick started to speak, but Max held up a hand. "We're your partners, goddammit! You're treating us like suspects—like we could be the ones who stole those animals."

Max's sense of outrage seemed to be aimed more at Taylor than at Nick for hiring her. Nick felt a surge of irritation. "I wanted professional help because you damn well *could* have stolen them."

Max's eyes widened.

"All I know is that whoever stole those animals was familiar with Rounders. That includes all the carvers—and all my partners. And now that there've been two murders…"

Max gaped. "What two?"

"Hell, Max. Eberhardt's death can't be a coincidence. Somebody must have knocked the poor devil over the head and incinerated him to keep him from talking to me. You're no fool. You must know that. If you didn't before, Clara Eberhardt's murder should have convinced you. It convinced me."

Once again anger flared behind Max's eyes. Then he looked once more at the bottle on the table. He picked it up and drained it, then set it back carefully in the same wet ring. "Yeah." He sounded tired. "Goddammit, Nick, you think I could do something like that to Rounders? To you? To Clara?"

Waves of guilt swept over Nick. Not for the first time,

he wondered if he should tell Max about the ten-day limit before he had to cough up thirty-five thousand dollars to reimburse Pete Marley for his hippocampus. He was sure Max would offer him the money—if he had it.

Time enough for that if Borman and Taylor didn't come up with the answer. "Hell, Max, you've got to see that as long as we don't know who stole the animals, everybody's a suspect. Vollmer even suspects me. We're going to wind up hating each other unless we get this cleared up. We need Taylor. The cops aren't going to give a good goddamn about carousel animals, but I think they're the motive for these killings. Either they've all been sold, in which case sales records must exist, or they're out there waiting to be sold."

"They burned up in the fire."

"You guessing?"

Max glared at him. "Stands to reason. Marley bought the hippocampus at Eberhardt's shop, right?"

"Yeah, and according to him, it was the only one Eberhardt had. So either Eberhardt brought them all conveniently to the shop so his killer could destroy them, or they're stored somewhere, or they've all been sold." He leaned forward and let his forearms rest on his knees. He tried to relax, but he saw Max look at the cords in his hands. "Records exist. Even if the animals burned, records should be somewhere. If Eberhardt had them, he'd have kept them in a fireproof container. Or a bank box. Somewhere safe and secret. We've got to find them—and fast."

"Maybe the police already have."

"I doubt it." Nick longed to tell Max about the wreck that had been made of the Eberhardt's house. Again something warned him to keep his mouth shut.

Both men jumped when the doorbell sounded. "That's Josh," Max said, and rose. Nick handed him the empty beer bottle on his way by.

"My God, Nick, did you see the evening news? That

woman, the one who was killed. She was married to Helmut Eberhardt.'' Josh Chessman entered and collapsed onto the couch.

Max shook his head at Nick. He obviously didn't want Nick to tell Josh about his liaison with Clara at Ole Miss.

For twenty minutes, the three friends discussed the problem without coming to any conclusions.

Finally, Josh stopped in mid-sentence, peered at his watch, and headed for the door. "I've got to get home. We're meeting the vice president and his wife at Amaranthus for dinner. Margery's furious about all this, you know. She thinks it'll hurt my chances to become vice provost when Hawkins retires in December." He giggled. "You know Margery. Anything that 'endangers my career'—" he imitated Margery's syrupy southern society drawl "—is a personal affront to her."

"No doubt the woman got herself murdered at Rounders just to spike your career plans," Max said acerbically.

Josh looked at him in panic. "Oh, God, I didn't mean that. But you know the only reason Margery let me invest in Rounders was because she thought my having a hobby made me seem well-rounded and less of a university grunt."

"We know, Josh," Max said wearily.

Impulsively, Josh laid a hand on Nick's shoulder. "Don't worry, Nick. I'm sure the police will sort it all out. We're all behind you." He scurried out and slammed the front door behind him.

"Behind and well to the rear of the action," Max said.

"Is he scared of Margery or what?" Nick asked.

"Petrified is more like it," Max said. "Want another beer?"

"No, thanks. I thought I'd take my Harley out. Need to clear my head."

"Anyplace special?"

"Just out.''

"If you say so." Max uncapped his third beer. "I think your Ms. Hunt is in way over her head."

Nick bridled. "I'm paying Borman for her services. It's not coming out of Rounders."

Max raised his hands. "Okay, okay."

Nick stood, and Max followed. "Taylor's going to need to talk to everyone at Rounders about the animals. Can you see her tomorrow morning?"

"If I must."

"Why don't you like her?" Nick asked.

"I don't dislike her. She's possibly competent and intelligent in routine matters. You obviously find her attractive. That might cause problems."

"I don't see how. We have a professional relationship, period. Besides, she's got one thing going for her that I don't."

"Indeed?"

"Yeah. Her judgment isn't clouded by friendship."

MAX STOOD ON THE BACK STEPS and watched Nick unlock the garage door and roll out his Harley. It gleamed in the late-afternoon sunshine, a perfectly restored Flathead. A black fiberglass helmet with visor hung from the handlebars. Nick picked it up and slid it over his head, visor up. "I won't stop when I bring it back," he said. "I'll just take the truck and go."

"I'll probably be up working on those tiles in the living room. Why don't you ring the bell if the lights are on." Max sounded wistful.

Nick glanced up at the house—mansion, really—its two-story Corinthian columns soaring. It was meant for parties, large families, children. Max must rattle around in it like some kind of ghost.

"Maybe," Nick said, and flipped his visor down. The Harley kicked on with a saber-tooth's growl. Nick rolled up the driveway, accelerating sedately and well within the speed limit.

Reflected in the side mirror, Max stood with his shoulders slumped, his hands in his pockets. For the first time, Nick thought he looked every one of his sixty-one years.

the driveway, a distance behind, and went within the
street-front.

Behind him, she watched Max, troubled by the ugly
thought, let herself in the frail door for the threshold that
threatened to bar entry into his safe, own zone.

CHAPTER SIX

NICK REALIZED HE'D BEEN HEADING for Taylor's address
ever since he rolled the Harley out of Max's garage. Max
must have guessed. Apparently he resented any contact between Nick and Taylor.

Nick turned on his headlamps in the gathering dusk and
swooped along the sunken road Taylor had described. He
knew these roads well, had probably passed her place a hundred times without ever realizing it.

He hoped she was home alone. He knew she was a
widow, but he had no idea how, or with whom, she spent
her free time. She had a private life, after all. Vollmer or
some other man might be with her.

Why should he care about her private life? But he did
care, did not want her to have a lover, some faceless male
with every right to share her bed and her life.

He felt an intense flare of heat in his loins at the thought
of her face as it might look, staring up at him, eyes soft and
unfocused with pleasure as he made love to her.

The bike skidded on a piece of loose gravel so that he
had to fight for control.

At the rate he was going, he'd never make it to her house.
He forced his mind back to the problem of Max's attitude.

Max did not normally dislike people at first meeting, but
he certainly seemed to feel instant antipathy towards Taylor.
It was more than her inexperience. Almost seemed like jealousy. Or fear.

What was Max afraid of? A week ago Nick would have

said he and Max knew everything there was to know about one another. Now he felt as though he'd spent the last hour with a stranger.

He slowed for the curve, saw the small green road sign peaking out of a tangle of honeysuckle, turned left and began to search for Taylor's address on a mailbox. When he found it and turned into the drive, he was startled to meet tall, sturdy iron gates set in thick, concrete pillars. Barbwire fences led away on both sides. Beyond the gates, a narrow gravel drive wound down an incline and curved left into darkness. From the road he couldn't see the house. Loblolly pines festooned with wild vines pressed against either side of the drive. The whole area was thick with honey locust and old-growth oak trees. He wondered how Taylor's guests notified her they'd arrived.

He walked the bike close to the gates. Set into the left pillar was a sophisticated wireless callbox and keypad. Very impressive. He'd seen the same sort of thing on some of the executive mansions in Rivers Edge and Germantown when he was still doing custom cabinetry. He leaned over and tapped the intercom button. After a moment, he hit it again.

"Yes?" Taylor sounded tinny and distant.

"Hi. It's Nick. I need to talk."

A moment's silence, then he heard the buzzer sound on the gate. The two panels swung open softly. He put the bike into gear and rolled down the road towards her house. He splashed through a shallow ford, barely a trickle now after ten days without rain.

The gates should have led to a mansion. Instead he found a low cabin that looked as though it had been constructed completely of old barn timbers and salvage. None of the windows matched. Even in the failing light, he could discern three different colors of metal roofing. The front door was a massively carved antique that belonged on an Arizona monastery.

Taylor stood in the lighted doorway with her hands on her hips. Amazing, he thought. Not many women could look sexy in black sweats. Taylor managed.

He turned off the engine and slipped the flattened soda can he carried off his handlebars. He held the bike one-handed and slid the can under the kickstand so it wouldn't bury itself in the mud and pull the Harley over.

"Very impressive," Taylor said.

"Yeah, like those gates." He gestured over his shoulder. "Expecting an invasion?"

"My uncle Mark left me this place. He was an assistant district attorney. He had the gates installed after a guy he'd convicted drove in and tried to take him hostage." She shrugged. "At least I can count on my privacy." She pointed to the motorcycle. "Really nice bike."

"Bought it in pieces. Spent two years redoing it. It lives in Max's garage. There's no place to keep it at Rounders."

"Come in." She stood aside.

The cabin consisted of one large room, perhaps thirty-by-forty, floored in old brick varnished to a high sheen. The rafters formed the ceiling, the timbers the walls. Against the back wall stood a galley kitchen with mismatched cabinets painted Chinese red. In the corner a small fire burned in a stone fireplace. To his right a ladder climbed to a sleeping loft. The area underneath it had been walled in to create what he assumed was a bathroom. Bookshelves crowded the available wall space.

To his left, sat enough exercise equipment to start a small gym—weight bench, free weights, treadmill, stair climber—all top quality. No wonder she looked tough. She'd apparently been using them when he drove up. Under the light, he could see her hair was damp. He remembered that old southern adage his grandmother used to throw at him—men perspire, women glow.

Taylor glowed all right. She pulled the white gym towel

from around her neck and wiped her face. "Sorry," she said, "I wasn't expecting company."

He walked to the back of the room and stared into the darkness at the trees hugging the house. They might have been in the middle of the Amazon rain forest. No outside lights broke the darkness here.

He turned back to look at this woman who obviously enjoyed her solitude, and started as his own full-length reflection stared back at him. A tall, ornate gilt pier mirror, totally at odds with the rest of the room, sat against the wall in front of him. Beside the mirror, the door to the bathroom was open to reveal gleaming white tile.

He looked away from his reflection and spotted a computer in the shadowy corner beyond the exercise equipment. White desk, shelves, filing cabinets, scanner, laser printer and a big PC. Across its screen multi-colored fish swam languidly. "You use this as your office?" he asked.

She shook her head. "Not usually, but I can if I have to. I can modem into Mel's computer." She raised her shoulders. "Nice when we get an ice storm. I hate to drive in ice or snow. Getting up the hill to the front gates can be murder when the ford freezes over, even with four-wheel drive." She motioned to the only other visible furniture—an obviously aged maroon leather sofa and matching wing chair, a coffee table made from a fat slice of old-growth walnut, a couple of Victorian end tables rescued from somebody's attic, and a round claw-foot dining table with four mismatched chairs.

"Have a seat. You said you needed to talk."

"I've been sitting on that motorcycle for the better part of an hour. I'll lean, thank you." He grinned ruefully. "When you own a Harley, you have to swear to eternal discomfort. It's part of the contract."

"Suit yourself," she said, sank into the wing chair and propped her feet on the coffee table.

Except for the mirror, the room was about as masculine as any he'd ever entered. But Taylor wasn't in the least masculine. His pheromones snapped to attention every time he saw her.

He heard a yowl and looked down in time to grab a Siamese cat in midair. The cat walked up his chest, settled on his shoulder and began investigating his ear with its nose.

"That's Elmo," Taylor said without an apology.

Nick reached around and gently scratched behind the cat's ears. "Hello, Elmo," he said. The cat yowled directly into his ear and jumped lightly to the kitchen counter.

"I don't drink, but I can offer you a diet soda," Taylor told him.

He shook his head. "Sorry to come without calling. I didn't know I planned to until I was almost here."

Finally she smiled. Apparently, once Elmo accepted his presence, he was okay.

"Max slept with Clara Fields," he said without preliminary.

Taylor caught her breath and leaned forward.

He told her everything almost word for word. She hardly blinked during his recital.

"So that's it. Max doesn't want the police to know."

"I don't blame him." She thought for a moment. "Didn't you tell me Josh Chessman finished his Ph.D. at Ole Miss?"

Nick nodded. "He met Margery there. She was president of her sorority or something, and he got conned into chaperoning one of the dances."

"Then both Josh and Margery could have known her as well."

"Josh didn't admit it." He shook his head. "Why would he hide it?"

"Why not? Particularly if they were more than acquaintances." Taylor leaned back and began to knead her temples. "This gets more and more complicated. First we don't have any connection between Rounders and Eberhardt, now we've got too many. I think it's time I called Mel and got him over here." She looked up. "You had anything to eat?"

He shook his head.

That's when the pier mirror exploded before his eyes.

A nanosecond later he heard the crack of the rifle.

Nick flung himself sideways. On his way down he reached across the coffee table, hooked Taylor's wrist, dragged her off the chair, and rolled her beneath him.

"Damn!" Nick snarled.

"You're hurt!" She raised a hand to his cheek. Her fingers were red with his blood.

He checked. "Shard must have nicked me."

They were both breathing hard, and Taylor's eyes were wide with terror. This was crazy. Someone just tried to blow his brains all over the walls, and might be waiting to try again, yet whatever mind he had left centered on the warm woman smell of her, the feel of her breasts against his chest, and her long body beneath his. Their eyes locked. Her lips were parted, and her arms were wrapped around his shoulders. He could feel her heart beating against him, and for a moment nothing mattered but a terrible need to kiss her. He bent his head.

Suddenly he heard running footsteps on the gravel. Taylor flinched. The moment was gone. He let her go and was on his feet in an instant. "Don't move."

"Nick, for God's sake, stay down!" Taylor begged. She grabbed at his wrist and missed.

"He's getting away."

"Let him go!"

He dove out the front door low and fast, and slipped into the trees that lined the driveway. The grass would deaden the sound of his steps. A three-quarters moon illuminated the road but couldn't reach under the trees.

Ten yards along, he stopped. No more footsteps. The

sniper had either reached the highway or gone to earth waiting to ambush him. Nick felt naked without a weapon.

The cabin door opened again, and light spilled out as Taylor came toward him. He could see the gun in her hand. He wanted to send her back inside, but knew his voice might attract the sniper.

At the road, a car backfired and roared to life.

Nick sprinted to the top of the hill in time to see taillights disappear around the curve in the road.

A moment later, Taylor raced up with the gun in her left hand and a big black flashlight in her right.

"Are you crazy?" she gasped. "He might have had a nightscope."

"He didn't."

Her chest heaved. "And you knew that? How'd he get in here?"

Nick took her upper arms. "I told you to stay down. Why'd you follow me?"

"I've got the gun, dammit. And in case you've forgotten, you're the client." She pulled away from him. "Don't you dare try to teach me my job."

"Your job is to stay alive."

"No, that's my first priority. At least I've got better sense than to come out here *without* a gun."

They stood nose to nose. After a moment he grinned. "Yeah. Okay. Point taken."

She sniffed. "Fine. May I suggest we try to find footprints or tire tracks?"

"Not likely. No rain in a week."

"He'd leave prints if he ran through the mud at the ford." Suddenly she leaned over and put her hands on her knees. "I didn't realize I was this out of condition."

"You're not. It's from the adrenaline rush." He reached out to her, but she eluded him and edged along the barbwire fence to the right of the gate. After a moment she said,

"This top strand is broken. There's a piece of fabric caught on the wire."

"So he climbed the fence."

"Leave it for Mel."

"Right. Let's check that mud." He walked down the gravel drive, aware of her behind him. She might deny the moment they'd had, but he couldn't. He acknowledged now that he wanted much more from her than her professional services.

At the ford, Nick recognized car tracks—probably Taylor's truck—and the Harley's narrow tires. Prints from a pair of big running shoes side by side—must be where he'd landed. Smaller ones—probably Taylor's.

Then they spotted it. A booted foot, pointed toe, dug in hard, almost no heel marks.

"Somebody big," Taylor whispered. "Heavy. And running hard."

"Yeah."

When they were inside once more with the door locked, Taylor walked over to the mirror. She seemed utterly calm.

The glass lay in shining stilettos across the brick floor and mingled with clear glass from the broken windowpane. She stared down at the mess, then up at the wall. There was a round hole in the rough paneling. She began to chew her thumbnail. "Let Mel dig out the bullet," she said. After a moment she walked to the table and stuck her gun back into her satchel. Then she sank onto the couch.

"You okay?" Nick asked. He reached a hand towards her, but she brushed it away, bounced up and began to pace just beyond his reach.

"Fine. I am perfectly fine."

He watched her silently.

After a moment she glanced at him. "Okay. So nobody's ever shot at me before." She tossed her head. "Hey, I'm always up for new experiences, right?"

He wanted to take her in his arms, pet her, stroke her hair, do all the comforting things a man was supposed to do for a woman. But she obviously had no intention of allowing him near her.

So what was he supposed to do?

"Damn! That was my grandmother's pier mirror. It was the only thing I brought with me when I moved out here." She whirled on him angrily. "How come I can't stop shaking?"

He caught her in mid-pace, pulled her to face him, and wrapped his arms around her. For an instant she resisted fiercely, then she folded against his chest like a kitten.

Her head fit precisely in the hollow of his shoulder. Her hair felt damp against his neck. He drank in the sweet scent of her, closed his eyes and rested his cheek against her hair.

Her arms slid around his waist and she leaned against him, clung to him.

She had to feel that he was erect against her, but she didn't move away.

She wanted comfort. He wanted to offer much more. He could feel the pulse in his own throat throbbing against her, knew his own heart was racing. Not from fear. This was desire. Fierce, sudden.

Lousy timing.

Still, neither of them moved.

"The shooter didn't know you'd be here," she said softly against his chest.

He caressed her hair, slid his fingers down the nape of her neck. "Unless he followed me from Max's." He closed his eyes and moved his cheek against the top of her head. She sighed.

"If you hadn't been standing where you were…if you hadn't been reflected in that mirror…if he'd waited…" she whispered and turned up her face to look at him.

Her lips were very close, her eyes wide, pupils big and dark, eyes smoky gray in the light from the fire.

Softly he bent his mouth to hers. Her eyes closed, her lips opened. His tongue teased her and felt her answer him. She was setting his lips on fire. She made a sound deep in her throat. Her hips moved against him…

Without warning she broke away, her hands raised in front of her. "I can't do this. You're the *client*." She grabbed the telephone. "I'm calling Borman."

"Taylor."

She spun away. "No."

He sighed. "Shouldn't we call the police first?"

She grimaced. "We're in the country. They'd say it was some drunk poaching deer, or worse, they'd call Vollmer and he'd say you set it up yourself."

He knew she was right. He also knew damn well that she'd wanted that kiss as much as he had.

So he hadn't bedded a woman in months. So they'd both been through a dangerous experience. That couldn't explain the solar flare between them when he'd taken her in his arms. Even she couldn't deny the passion of that kiss any more than he could.

He watched her back straighten, her shoulders thrust back as she dialed the phone and spoke to Borman.

"Mel?" she said. Her voice sounded completely businesslike, much different from the throaty whisper she had used in his arms. "I think you better get over here. Somebody just put a bullet through my window. I think they were shooting at Nick."

Nick sat on the sofa, and Elmo dropped into his lap to have his belly rubbed. Nick lost the thread of the conversation with Borman as he watched Taylor thrust her hands through her hair, arch her back almost as though she could feel his eyes caressing her.

A tender woman disguised as a tough cookie. Why did

she lock herself behind iron gates in a house designed for fraternity parties? Was her heart locked away as well?

She obviously hadn't locked her heart away from Vollmer. Even though she'd told Nick that it was over between them, he felt a stab of jealousy that the man had ever been close to her. He desperately wanted to believe that Taylor was the one who had broken off with Vollmer, not the other way around. How the hell could anyone break away from her and stay sane?

"Fine. Oh, and Mel? Pick up the biggest pepperoni pizza you can on the way, will you? I'm starved." She dropped the phone into its cradle. "I always eat when I'm scared. You ought to see me load up before I get on an airplane." Elmo bounded out of Nick's lap and into her arms.

She set him on the kitchen counter and began to draw the café curtains across the windows. Nick started to get up, but she stopped him.

"Please don't help. I need to do this. Impose a little control."

He nodded.

She spoke conversationally as though they were discussing the weather, but in the kitchen light he saw that the vein in her throat still throbbed. "I've always felt completely safe out here," she said. "I don't even turn on the outside lights at night. You can't see the stars properly when they're on."

"Will you at least let me help you sweep up the glass?"

"No. Leave it until Mel gets here. Elmo's smart enough to stay away from it. Mel needs to see everything just as it is." She drew the remaining curtains, threw a log on the fire. Then she opened the refrigerator, took out a diet soda, opened it and drank deeply. She couldn't keep still.

She avoided his gaze and spoke as though he wasn't in the room. "I worried about people in cars breaking through the gates, not lone snipers on foot."

"Nobody is safe from a lone sniper, Taylor. Ask the Secret Service."

"I know, I know." She put both fists on the kitchen counter. Elmo oozed around her wrists in figure eights, chattering softly.

She picked him up and held him against her shoulder. Nick could hear his purr across the room.

She looked at Nick directly. "I've always been afraid of impersonal violence. That's what killed my husband. I've never even considered that someone might hate me enough to do me harm."

"Not you. Me. And probably not hate."

"What then? And for the love of God, why?"

"PIZZA MAN!" Mel called as he climbed out of his Lincoln Continental.

Nick had only met him once—when he hired the Borman Agency. In his office Borman had worn a beautifully tailored navy suit and a red power tie. Tonight he wore a crewneck sweater with the sleeves pushed up over powerful hairy forearms, and jeans that hung below his paunch. He was shorter than Nick by a couple of inches, and although he was probably close to Max's age, Nick bet that anyone who ran into Mel would bounce off. He moved gracefully on small feet, but the jeans stretched tight across barrel thighs. Under the flesh lay a thick layer of brawn. He looked like a good man to have beside you in a fight.

Taylor took the pizza box.

Five minutes later they sat around the coffee table and tore into the pizza.

Nick was amazed to discover he was ravenous. From the way she ate, so was Taylor. She spoke calmly of the shooting. Nick didn't think she felt as calm as she sounded, but he wasn't about to give her away.

"You'll move out of here tonight," Mel said. It was a command.

Taylor stopped with a slice of pizza halfway to her mouth. "Where is it written everybody makes decisions for Taylor but Taylor?"

"Somebody's trying to kill you, girl. If they succeed, you won't be around when I have to tell your mother."

"Nobody's trying to kill me. They're trying to kill him." She pointed a slice of pizza at Nick. "God only knows why."

"Because I'm the only person who can recognize the fake animals."

Taylor's head swiveled towards him.

Nick laid down his pizza and wiped the grease off his fingers. "Think about it. I had enough trouble recognizing the hippocampus myself. If I were dead, you think Max or Josh or anybody else is going to be able to say 'hey, guys, this is a fake carved twenty years ago by a guy named Nick Kendall'? Not a chance in hell. Whoever's got those animals would be home free. He'd wait six months and start peddling them again."

"But the provenance," Taylor said. "Didn't you say the carousel was a Stein and Goldstein? Were all your animals copies of Stein and Goldsteins?"

Nick sank back in the leather chair. "No. Far as I can remember, there were a couple of Illions, a couple of Philadelphia Toboggan Company, even a Denzel or two. The only animals I didn't copy were the Parkers." He shrugged. "I never liked them much."

"So the provenance wouldn't work for the others."

"You'd still be able to get fifteen or twenty thousand apiece for them without provenance, especially if you sold them in mint condition and advertised them as 'professionally restored.' Nice chunk of change with almost no risk. Better yet, forge the provenance."

"Whoever shot at you is likely to try again," Mel said. "Taylor, I want you out of this. I'll take over. You weren't hired to be a bodyguard."

"Mel, look at this man. Does he need a bodyguard? A bullet-proof vest, maybe, and somebody to check his truck for bombs before he starts it, but he *is* a bodyguard, for Pete's sake."

"What if I'm wrong?" Nick asked. "What if the killer thinks we both know something? He may come after you, Taylor. I'm not about to let that happen."

"Wait a minute, Nick. You client, me detective," Taylor said.

"No, you female, me male."

Taylor threw up her hands. "You sound like my mother! For pity's sake, Mel, this is the first job I've had that didn't involve hours staring at a computer screen or fighting off drunks in a bar!"

"You're the one who told me if things got dangerous, you'd run," Nick said.

"That was when I thought they wouldn't—get dangerous, that is." She turned to Mel. "Let's assume for the moment you're both right—I'm a target too. Do I take out a classified ad in the personals column? *Dear Killer, Taylor Hunt announces that she will no longer take part in the Clara Eberhardt murder case and promises to forget any information you may feel is dangerous to you.*"

Borman harrumphed.

"There's another problem. For some crazy reason Danny Vollmer has suddenly decided he wants me back. I can't assume he'll step out of the way of his libido long enough to look at suspects beyond Nick."

Borman set his pizza down carefully and asked, "How good a cop is Vollmer?"

"He found the men who shot Paul," Taylor said. Then she, too, stopped eating. "No, Mel. No. He wouldn't do something like this. I haven't seen Danny for almost a year."

"You say he wants you back."

"Well, yes, he made noises that he did, and I think it's colored his judgment about Nick, but he's not a stalker and he's certainly no killer."

"You think he could be the shooter?" Nick asked.

"I have no idea," Mel said. "But he's good with a gun, and he knows this place intimately."

"If he knows the place intimately, he'd know about that mirror, wouldn't he?" Nick asked.

Borman nodded. "Maybe that's the point. Maybe you weren't a target—not a real one, at any rate. Maybe this was Danny's notice to keep hands off Taylor."

Taylor sniffed. "Danny's probably had half a dozen girl-friends since the last time we saw each other, Mel. He's not likely to get back into my good graces by destroying my grandmother's mirror. You think he's going to risk his career for some dumb stunt?"

"Not sober," Borman said softly.

Taylor went still.

"He drinks?" Nick asked.

Borman nodded and pointed his pizza at Nick. "Come on, Taylor, tell the man."

Taylor got up and walked to the refrigerator for another diet soda. She leaned against the counter. Her half-eaten pizza sat abandoned on the coffee table. "Okay, okay. Nick, the real reason Danny and I broke up was that I can't stand drunks. My daddy was a drunk. Not all the time, just at home on Sunday afternoons watching football or at the club on weekends. I hated what it did to him. And I hated what it did to Danny."

Her face grew hard. A vein throbbed along her jaw. She ran her hand through her crop of hair and shook her head.

"I don't think Danny did this, Mel. I'm not backing off this case."

"I give up. Dammit, I've been giving in to you ever since the first day I met you, Taylor. I should never have hired you in the first place," Mel said.

"You don't mean that, Mel. I'm good. Not as good as I'll be in five years, but you trained me. Except with lock picks and power tools, I am not a fumble-footed southern belle. Admit it."

"Nobody ever said you had a second-rate mind, Taylor. But this independent streak of yours is going to get you into trouble you can't get out of. Trust me."

"I do trust you." She turned to Nick. "I also trust you. We're losing sight of the original objective. Nick, we're no closer to finding out who stole your animals than we were in the beginning, but we're starting to make somebody very uncomfortable. That's a good sign."

"Wait a minute, Taylor," Borman said. "How do we know that whoever stole the animals didn't sell them outright to Eberhardt, pocket the cash and walk away?"

Taylor turned to Nick. "Do you think that's what happened?"

He shook his head. "As much as I'd like to believe that, I don't. Eberhardt wouldn't want to tie up that kind of capital when he could only sell three or four horses a year without raising suspicion. Also, only the killer knew Clara Eberhardt was dead and unlikely to walk in while her house was searched. Must be someone connected with Rounders, otherwise Clara wouldn't have met the killer there." He dropped his head into his hands.

"We've barely begun, Nick. Once we know which one did it, you'll be free to trust your other friends again."

"The hell of it is, I trust them now."

"Stop it this instant," Taylor said.

"Taylor, the killer knows where you live," Borman said.

"The gate didn't stop him. You're damn isolated. That's not good."

"I won't move into a motel, Mel. I can't afford it and I have Elmo to consider."

"Nick's isolated too. That warehouse area after dark might as well be on Mars."

"You've defined the problem, glorious leader. What's the solution?"

"We don't own any bullet-proof vests, and I can't see Danny Vollmer loaning us any. So I'd say you two stick together after dark, either here or at Nick's. Stay away from lighted windows. Watch your backs."

"Who's baby-sitting whom?"

"You're baby-sitting each other until further notice. Kendall, we'll make some arrangement about the fee you owe us. I value Taylor's safety considerably more than I value money."

"Whoa! Stop the role reversal! I can look after myself and after Nick as well."

They both stared at her. She subsided. "Okay, maybe I'm not that great in a fist fight, but I know self-defense and I carry a gun."

"Let's hear it for Belle Starr," Borman said dryly. "Listen, Kendall, I know you were an Airborne Ranger."

"That was over ten years ago."

"You don't forget the moves. You're still in shape. Anybody tries for Taylor, you have my permission to beat the crap out of him."

"I don't need anybody's permission. Anybody goes for Taylor, I'll kill him."

"Thank you, oh, my knights in shining armor." Taylor sniffed disgustedly. "Can we please get back to the problem at hand. Who shot at Nick? And what do we do about it?"

"Since it's unlikely there are two killers kicking around, I would think whoever killed Clara Eberhardt—and possibly

Helmut—also shot at Nick. And we discuss what to do about it tomorrow. In the meantime, we clean up the mess, then I take that piece of cloth off the fence and the slug out of the wall, and go home to my solitary bed. And Nick stays here with you.''

Nick stole a glance at Taylor. She was looking from one man to the other with a mulish expression on her face. After a moment she relaxed and broke into a smile. ''Done.'' She laughed. ''And won't that annoy Danny big time!''

Nick reached across the back of the couch and picked up the phone. ''I have to call Max, tell him I won't be bringing the bike home tonight. If he doesn't hear me come in and then sees my truck tomorrow morning, he'll worry.'' He shrugged ruefully at Taylor. ''You have your mother hen, I have mine.'' He dialed. The phone rang seven times, then the answering machine kicked in. Nick left a message. ''Max swore he'd be home all evening.''

''Maybe he had to go to the store for more paint,'' Taylor said.

''Max hates going out in the middle of a job.''

''You thinking he might have taken a long drive in the country?'' Mel asked.

''No.'' He looked up at the pair of them, watching him with something like pity on their faces. He felt embarrassed for Max and then foolish for feeling that way. ''Even if by some crazy chance he did drive out here, he'd have had plenty of time to get home again. It's been over an hour since...''

''Since the sniper,'' Taylor said softly.

''It's not Max, okay? Drop it. He's probably in the shower.''

''Here's the answer to Taylor's question about what to do,'' Borman said. ''Go back to Oxford. Talk to Clara Eberhardt's people. See if they remember anything at all about Clara and Max Beaumont or Josh Chessman. In the meantime I'll start a computer check on the finances of everyone who was at Rounders the day Nick announced he'd discovered the thefts. They're our prime suspects. I'm going to try to find out if any of those people have had a fast infusion of cash recently."

"Can you do that?" Nick asked.

"You bet," Borman said. "Technology can do amazing things." He stood and laid a heavy broad hand on Taylor's shoulder. "Keep your curtains drawn and your door locked." He reached down with the other and scooped up Elmo, who had begun to stalk the remaining pizza. "And set your guard cat here on full alert."

"YOU GOING TO TELL VOLLMER we went snooping at Eberhardt's?" Nick asked as he helped Taylor smooth the sheets on the sofa bed.

"Not if I can help it." She looked up at him. "That Eugene Lewis guy who was at Eberhardt's—he look to you as if he could handle a deer rifle?"

"He looked like he could play tiddlywinks with anvils." Nick sat down on the edge of the couch.

"The Eberhardts had help moving those animals. If Eugene killed the Eberhardts, he may be clearing up loose ends."

"But all along I've thought somebody at Rounders was in on it."

"Somebody was, but possibly only peripherally. Neat little theft, nobody hurt, no connection between the inside man and the Eberhardts except when money changed hands. Then when you find out about the thefts, Eugene takes out Eberhardt and burns the store to get rid of evidence."

"And Clara?"

"Maybe all the evidence wasn't at the store." Taylor sat in the leather wing chair and propped her feet on the end of the sofa bed.

"Not at the house either."

"No, but this was." Taylor stood and went to her satchel. She pulled out a leather notebook that was the twin of the one in Clara's handbag. She shrugged, embarrassed. "I found it under that little desk while you were upstairs. If Anvil Man hadn't knocked it over, I might never have found the thing."

"You think Eugene did the house?"

"Don't you?"

"Yeah, I do. And maybe that as well." Nick pointed at the empty mirror frame. The shards had been collected and dumped into the trash outside. "What's in the notebook?"

"Not a hell of a lot that I can see." Taylor tossed it across the couch.

Nick caught it, slid down onto the bed and opened it. There were random notations of appointments running throughout. "Mostly meetings with clients, suppliers, dates of antique sales, auctions," Nick said after he'd paged through it. "Eberhardt saw his dentist two weeks ago."

"Look in the back," Taylor said.

The last page listed telephone numbers.

"Recognize any?" Taylor asked.

Nick shook his head. "Wait." He looked up at Taylor. "Why would Eberhardt have the Rounders number in his address book?"

CHAPTER SEVEN

TAYLOR SAT ON THE ARM of the sofa beside Nick to peer over his shoulder at the Eberhardt address book. He was painfully aware of her nearness. The smell of fear she'd carried earlier was gone, but the smell of woman was strong enough to touch. That's exactly what he wanted to do.

Before he could move or say anything, she slid away and stood up. "Maybe they wanted to call Rounders before they burgled it to be sure you weren't there. Who knows? I'm too exhausted to think."

He laid the book over his lap. His physical attraction to her was obvious. He couldn't remember being this blatantly responsive to a woman since high school.

"There's a new toothbrush in the medicine cabinet and a new razor in the cupboard. Sorry I can't offer you fresh clothes, but I don't think my underwear would fit you."

"Thanks," he said, and watched her disappear around the corner. A moment later the bathroom door closed.

It was definitely not going to be easy to keep their relationship professional—at least on his side. The thought of her climbing that ladder and going to sleep just above his head—just out of reach—tantalized him almost beyond endurance.

He prided himself on controlling his relationships with women. He could be romantic, charming, a nice guy. They told him he was a good lover.

But the women who climbed into his bed moved in and out of his life like carousel horses, arriving with trumpets blaring, giving them both an enjoyable ride, and then disappearing around the corner when the carousel stopped.

Five minutes later Taylor said good-night and climbed the ladder. Without much success, he tried to keep his eyes off her bottom and long legs.

He finished his own ablutions, sank onto the sofa bed and flicked out the light on the table beside him. He could feel the wire coils under the thin mattress. He'd be lucky if he got any sleep at all—what with the condition of the mattress and Taylor's soft breathing above his head. He felt a slight thud at his feet. Elmo wriggled under the covers and walked the length of his body before curling against his chest.

"Guess you'll have to do, cat," he whispered, and fell asleep instantly.

"OPEN THE GATE, TAYLOR, I need to talk to you."

"A little out of your jurisdiction, aren't you, Detective Vollmer?" Taylor asked through the intercom. She hesitated a moment, then sighed. "Come on up." She clicked the gate latch and went to open the front door.

Two minutes later Vollmer climbed out of his car, and said, "Your client's disappeared."

"No, he hasn't." She stood aside to let him in. "Coffee?"

"Yeah. You know where he is?"

"At the moment he's standing under my shower."

Vollmer scowled. His head swiveled towards the bathroom wall. The sounds of sluicing water were barely audible. "Damn, Taylor, I can't believe you'd bed a killer."

Taylor's hand froze on the coffeepot. "He's not a killer and I'm not bedding him—not that it's any of your business. What do you want him for?"

"I called him to come down and give us a statement, and got his answering machine."

"You could have asked me if I knew where he was over

the telephone. You didn't have to drive all the way out to my cabin at eight in the morning.''

"I wanted to see you, apologize for smarting off yesterday.''

"No problem.''

He glanced over at the wall again. The water sound cut off abruptly. He reached for the coffee, and, with his other hand, took Taylor's arm to guide her to the couch. She resisted. He dropped his hand, shrugged. "I haven't had a drink for six months.''

"That's wonderful, Danny.''

He turned away and walked to the front window. He sipped his coffee, pulled the curtain aside and stared out at the gray morning. "I wish I could say it was because of you. Maybe in a way it was. After that Sunday, I started drinking heavy. One morning I woke up two hours late for my shift and realized I didn't know where I'd been the night before.'' He looked back at her. "Wherever I'd been I'd driven home too drunk to be conscious. I checked the car for damage, checked for hit and runs, spent the day scared to death. That night I went to A.A.''

"Good for you.''

"One day at a time. What happened that Sunday won't ever happen again, Taylor. I promise you that. The soberer I got, the more I realized how much I'd thrown away that day. A hundred times I picked up the phone to call you, and couldn't. When I saw you the other night, I thought there might be a chance for us.''

Taylor smiled. "I'm glad for you, Danny, I really am. But, no. I'm afraid not.''

His face closed. "The Incredible Hulk in there?''

"There's nobody in my life right now.''

"Then I'm going to keep coming back like a bad penny, Taylor, until you trust me again.'' He smiled at her and held out his cup.

She took it and refilled it. "You still drink too much coffee, Danny."

"Keeps me going."

The bathroom door opened. Nick wore his T-shirt and jeans from the night before. He was barefoot. There was a one-inch scratch high on his right cheekbone. His sweater was draped over his arm. When he saw Vollmer he stopped dead.

"Morning, Mr. Kendall," Vollmer said with suspicious mildness. He sipped his coffee and leaned casually against the kitchen counter as though he were in his own home.

Nick got the message. "Morning, Sergeant Vollmer."

"Need you to come down to the station for a little talk this afternoon. Couldn't find you—" Vollmer raised an eyebrow "—thought Taylor might know where you were."

Nick nodded.

"That woman you...that was killed. You said you didn't know her, right?"

Again Nick nodded.

"Guess who she was."

Before Nick could answer, the gate intercom buzzed again. Taylor frowned at it. "For Pete's sake, it's barely eight o'clock in the morning," she answered.

"Open this gate, Taylor," a peremptory male voice commanded. "Your mother and I want to talk to you."

Taylor threw up her hands. She punched the button harder than she might otherwise have done. "That's all I need. Attila the Hun and Mother."

"Want us to get out of here?" Vollmer said, and glanced over at Nick. "We can continue this downtown."

"Stay." She opened the door and, leaving it open, went to the sink to put on another pot of coffee. "Must look like a parking lot out there," she said over her shoulder to the two men.

Gravel crunched, doors slammed, and Bradley Maxwell marched in. Irene trotted behind him.

Taylor sighed and turned to face them.

"Have you seen the papers?" Brad Maxwell shook a folded newspaper at her, then slammed it down on the side table. "You're a suspect in a murder!"

Danny picked up the paper and opened it. He burst out laughing and handed it to Taylor. The headline read, Homicide Detective Questions Investigator in Death of Woman.

Taylor grinned. The picture showed Danny holding Taylor's upper arms and snarling into her face. She was scowling back. It had been taken under the front awning at Rounders. "So the bum with the grocery cart had a camera as well as a notebook. I thought we'd been too lucky with reporters."

Brad Maxwell was tall and thin, with a fast-receding hairline and Taylor's features—distorted by testosterone and bad temper. "Dammit! This could have serious repercussions for my career."

"You're a lawyer, Brad. Lawyers get mixed up in murder all the time."

"I am a *corporate* lawyer!"

Taylor's eyebrows went up.

"I want you to resign from Borman, pack your things and stay with Mother until we can find you a suitable townhouse in a decent neighborhood. And a respectable job."

"Get out, Brad," Taylor said pleasantly. She was still smiling. Nick didn't know about Vollmer, but he found that smile chilling. He hoped Brad Maxwell had the sense to leave. He doubted it.

"What?"

"My only invited guest is Mr. Kendall."

Brad's gaze whipped around to stare at Nick, then to take in his state of dress—or lack thereof.

Irene Maxwell's hand flew to her mouth.

"Please leave, Brad, you're not welcome here." Still reasonable, Taylor sauntered toward him. He took a step back.

"As head of this family—"

"I am the head of my family," she said, her voice steely, "not you."

Irene said, "Brad, let's go, please."

Taylor spoke to her mother. "Mother, I told you, I'm fine. You mustn't worry. I can take care of myself. At least you care about me. All Brad cares about is his image. Go on home, I'll call you later."

"Now you listen to me, young lady," Brad said, but his voice lacked resonance.

"I'm not young and I'm probably not a lady. Why don't you just tell people I've been disowned?"

Irene dragged him backwards out the door and toward the car. He seemed uncertain how to proceed. Taylor followed, matching Brad step for step.

Brad helped his mother into the car and stalked around to the driver's side. "Oh, and Brad?" Taylor called. "Don't take this out on Ellen and the boys."

Brad threw her a malevolent glance, and whipped the car around. Taylor stood on the porch with her hands on her hips until he drove out of sight around the curve.

"Ellen's his wife?" Nick asked.

"Yeah." She closed her eyes a moment. "Brad inherited Daddy's temper. That's why I don't have anything to do with him. My mother refuses to see it, and Ellen says she has to stay with him because of the boys."

"He hits her?"

"I have no proof, but she runs into too many doors. She swears she and Brad are in counseling. I've tried every way I know to help, but she won't let me."

"You're there for her. That's more than plenty of women have," Nick said, and his eyes took on a faraway look.

"Many women stay with men who beat them—sometimes all their lives."

"I know."

"Look, you get any proof of abuse, you give it to me. I'll handle it," Vollmer said, then he turned to Nick. "And you, Kendall. Two o'clock, my office. East Precinct. Homicide. Be there."

"Should I bring a lawyer?"

"Only if you've got something to hide," Vollmer said, reached down to stroke Elmo, and walked out without a backward glance.

The moment he was gone Taylor closed her eyes and leaned against the wall.

Nick reached her in a moment, whirled her around and drew her into his arms. She clung to him.

He held her tight and stroked her back. He felt her shiver as though she'd been left all night in a refrigerator.

After a moment she pulled away and dove for the bathroom. The door slammed behind her and a moment later he heard water running. "Taylor?"

"Please," she called out, "let me be."

She came out five minutes later. Her hair was damp at the edges and her skin seemed transparent. Her gray eyes looked enormous. Her nose was suspiciously pink.

"Sorry about that," she said flippantly. "How come I always break down in front of you?"

He reached out to take her back into his arms, but she avoided him and walked over to the computer. She began to run the mouse along the mousepad in tight little circles. She refused to meet his eyes.

"Confrontations with my family give me palpitations and heartburn. I was sure Brad was going to hit me."

"He would have regretted it." His voice was grim.

She flashed him a misty smile, and his heart turned over. "Vollmer would have loved arresting you for assault."

"Would you have bailed me out?"

For a moment she stared at him silently, then whispered, "With my last dollar."

"Taylor..."

"Let's stick to business, okay?"

He went to her. "That kiss last night wasn't business."

"I was scared. You were handy."

"It was more than fear."

"Please, Nick. I'm trying so hard to get my life together, and every time I care about somebody I screw it up. It's the wrong time for this to happen."

"It's the time we have."

"It's not fair."

"What is?"

"If you really care about me, then please let me do this thing, solve your problem, find your animals, keep my head on straight while I'm doing it."

"It's that important to you?"

"Yes!"

"After last night—kissing you, holding you, and then lying awake half the night wanting you down here or me up there—avoiding bankruptcy or jail for a murder I didn't commit doesn't seem quite as important."

She began to laugh. "Oh, Nick, I don't think any man has ever paid me that big a compliment in my life." She touched his cheek. "Be serious. Both those things could happen, and I couldn't bear it. Please, give me some space."

He sighed. "I am a nice guy, and at the rate I'm going I'll be crazier than Vollmer before this is over."

"I didn't make him crazy."

"I doubt that. Maybe you better tell me about the two of you before I have to sit down with him this afternoon."

She pointedly sat in the wing chair, not on the sofa. He poured himself another cup of coffee, picked up Elmo—a poor substitute—and sat on the couch opposite. He shrugged. "See? Space."

"Danny says he's been sober for six months."

"You believe him?"

Taylor shrugged and drew a shivery little breath. "The last Sunday I saw him he came out here for brunch. We'd planned to maybe take in a movie. Instead he showed up drunk and belligerent. He'd just arrested a man who'd raped and murdered his three-year-old daughter and buried her body in the backyard."

"God."

"I tried to be sympathetic. He didn't want that. We ended up in a big fight and he slapped me."

Nick wasn't surprised. He'd recognized the violence in Danny just as he recognized it in himself.

Taylor continued, "I grew up thinking daddies were supposed to whop their children with leather belts. I swore I'd never have an abusive relationship. The only time my husband Paul hit me, I told him that if he ever did it again, I'd call the newspapers, the police and his boss—not necessarily in that order. I must have scared him badly, because he decided psychological abuse was safer. It didn't leave telltale bruises and isn't, so far as I know, illegal."

"Still hurts."

"Sometimes worse." Taylor shifted uncomfortably. "I don't know why I'm telling you this. Even Danny doesn't know." She looked down at her hands.

Nick waited without moving, almost without breathing.

"I finally saw a divorce lawyer. When I told Paul, he flipped, not because he cherished our marriage, but because it would hurt his precious career."

Her head dropped back against the wing chair and she closed her eyes. Nick saw a tear squeeze out between her lashes and slide down her temple to land in her ear.

"He got control of himself finally, and started being really lovey-dovey. Apologized for the umpteenth time. Said he'd go into counseling. Then he said he'd go get us a pizza and a bottle of wine, the way he used to when we were first married.''

"Would you have stayed?"

Taylor heaved a sigh. "I honestly don't know. He could be so sweet when he wanted to be... Anyway, he didn't have any cash, so he stopped at an ATM on the way. Three teenagers shot him. He died on the spot." She shook her head. "He'd taken out twenty dollars. That's what his life was worth to them."

"So when Danny hit you that Sunday?"

"Same old, same old. I thought after Paul died that I had quit trying to be Daddy's perfect little girl, and here I was afraid all over again."

"Is this..." Nick waved his hand at the masculine room "—a better fit?"

"Absolutely. But Daddy's little girl is still lurking inside me, telling me that if I'm sweet and pretty, Prince Charming will make me happy, and give me multiple orgasms and an unlimited charge account at Neiman Marcus.''

CHAPTER EIGHT

"MEL SAID I HAVE TO FOLLOW YOU to Rounders," Taylor said. She stood on the front porch of her cabin with her hands on her hips, car keys clutched in her fist. "I do as I'm told."

"When it suits you," Nick added. "All right, but not to Rounders. I left my truck at Max's when I picked up the bike."

Nick climbed aboard the Harley and stamped the starter. After three tries the engine exploded into raucous life with a couple of thuds and bangs for good measure.

"Wait for me at the gate," Taylor yelled over the noise. Nick nodded, dropped his visor and drove slowly down the lane and across the ford.

She kept close to Nick, and watched for cars following, or suspicious parked vehicles by the side of the road. She had no idea what to do if she actually spotted a possible sniper. Knock Nick off his bike, probably, on the theory that a busted shoulder or kneecap was preferable to a high-caliber rifle bullet through the brain.

He rode well. He balanced the several hundred pounds of Harley between his thighs as casually as if it were a Schwinn. She envied him the sheer freedom of flying around curves in a welter of noise.

It was harder to keep close to Nick in city traffic. Once she wound up beside him at a traffic light. He smiled over at her, and she found her heart doing flops and her fingers tightening on the wheel. She'd recognized the danger in that smile the instant she met him. Now it seemed all too knowing.

At Max's, she waited in her truck while he put his bike away. He came over to her and leaned into the car. ''I want to check on Max. See where he was last night. Want to come?''

She shook her head. ''I'll wait here.''

He nodded, and went to bang on the door. After what seemed an interminable time, Max came to the door. He was wearing pajamas and a robe and was still unshaven. He exchanged a few words with Nick, and then, somewhat preemptorily, Taylor thought, shut the door on him with barely a glance at her.

Nick came over. ''Says he went out for some beer. He does that sometimes—'' He shrugged. ''Now that, I can believe, especially when that damn house of his feels too big and too empty. You planning to follow me to Rounders?''

''Your friendly neighborhood bodyguard at your service.'' Taylor snapped him a salute.

He grinned and walked over to his truck.

At Rounders he parked in front rather than going down the alley to the loading dock. He opened his door, saw that she hadn't gotten out of her truck and came over to her. ''Coming in?'' he asked.

She shook her head. ''I'm going back to Oxford to locate friends or relations of the Eberhardts. I also need to talk to the cops about the fire. See whether they're still treating Eberhardt's death as an accident.''

''You taking Borman with you?''

''Why would I?''

''Eugene Lewis probably shot at us last night. I don't want you running into him in Oxford.''

''He's not likely to shoot at me at high noon on the square.''

"You're the one who said 'me detective, you client.' Me client wants you detective alive and kicking."

"Me detective wants the same thing." She glanced at her watch. "You don't have to talk to Danny this afternoon, you know."

"I know. While you were in the shower, I called Rico Cabrizzo and asked him to represent me. He's meeting me. At least now that the paper's printed Clara's name, I don't have to pretend not to know who she was."

"Watch Danny. He's single-minded and smart."

"So's Rico."

She continued as though he hadn't spoken. "And don't let his patient act fool you. He has a hell of a temper when he's crossed."

"I have no intention of crossing him."

She sighed. "You cross him just by being alive." She turned on the ignition.

He reached into the truck and laid a hand on her arm. "Look, Taylor, come back here after you go to Oxford, please. Before dark."

"I was planning to." She smiled up at him. "I'll be fine. See you this afternoon. Good luck with Danny."

For a moment she thought he was going to lean into the car and kiss her. She wanted him to, no matter what she'd said earlier. Instead he reached over and ran his rough index finger down the curve of her jaw. She felt disappointed that apparently he'd decided to take her at her word and let her get on with her job unencumbered by emotional entanglements.

"Anybody ever tell you you've got a great jaw?" he said.

"Just like granite."

"Granite shatters. Don't put it to the test."

TAYLOR STOPPED AT THE Chamber of Commerce on the square in Oxford to locate the best mortuary. Five minutes later she walked into the Holcroft-Nevins Mortuary and found that it was handling the funeral arrangements for Clara Eberhardt.

"Lord, wasn't that a terrible thing? Both of 'em in less than a week. My, my." The receptionist sat behind an expanse of cherry desk and in front of an arrangement of fresh bronze chrysanthemums and eucalyptus leaves.

From somewhere down the shadowy hall, Taylor heard the strains of an electric organ playing the opening bars of "He Walks With Me."

"Have they released the body yet?"

"No, ma'am. S'posed to be here sometime tomorrow or the next day." The secretary shook her head and set in motion a cap of tight little curls so heavy with henna that they had taken on a greenish tint. "We don't have the visitation book out yet so you can't sign you've been here and all. You family?"

Taylor shook her head. "Just a friend."

The receptionist's eyes narrowed. "You one of them Memphis reporters?"

Taylor smiled. "No. I'm not a reporter. Is any of Mrs. Eberhardt's family here at the moment?"

The receptionist glanced toward the office doors down the hall opposite the "organ" room. "Why, I do not rightly know."

Taylor smiled at the secretary and took a seat in one of the tall damask wing chairs in the reception area. If she waited long enough, someone would come out and would have to walk past her.

"You gonna stay?"

Taylor nodded. "It's been a long drive. I just need to sit down a minute."

The receptionist reached for the multi-buttoned telephone on her desk, then changed her mind. She pushed her chair back. Taylor smiled innocently.

At that moment the door of the end office opened and a man and woman came out.

Taylor knew instantly that the woman was someone genetically close to Clara—perhaps a younger sister, though not by much. The bone structure was identical, but this woman's hair was a pale pinky blond, and she dressed with a flair Clara hadn't shown.

Taylor stood to intercept her. She put on her best smile and stuck out her hand. "Good morning, I'm Taylor Hunt. I'm so sorry about your sister."

The woman smiled weakly and took her hand.

"Were you a friend, Ms. Hunt?" The woman's accent was southern but overlaid with something else. Chicago, maybe?

Taylor shook her head. "I'm a private investigator working on her murder."

The woman blinked and frowned. "What on earth for? Who hired you?"

"I was hired on another matter." Taylor glanced at the tall thin man standing behind Clara's sister. He and the receptionist were entirely too avid. "Do you mind if I take five minutes of your time?"

She was sure the woman was going to refuse. But she opened her mouth—probably to say no—and suddenly began to cry. Taylor reached out, and felt the woman grasp her hand.

"Get me out of here, please," the woman whispered.

Taylor led her out and put her into the front seat of the truck.

"I don't cry in public." She hunted in her bag, came up with a tissue and blew her nose. "That unctuous man! He was dying to gossip about Clara's death. God, a murder." She leaned back against the headrest of the truck and closed her eyes. "Nobody you know gets murdered."

"These days they do." Taylor started the truck and drove

away. "How about coffee on the square?" She glanced at the woman beside her, whose cheeks were laced with a fine network of tears running down to the grooves on each side of her mouth.

"Please." The woman sat up and laughed shortly. "I'm sorry to do this to a total stranger. This is the second time I've been at that funeral home in a week. It just got to be too much. I'm Estelle Grierson." Her head dropped back against the seat again. Her hands worked in her lap. Taylor could see her left hand smoothing and re-smoothing the black wool of her skirt as though she wanted to wear away the nap.

"After my father died," Taylor said, "my family sat around the funeral home for two days telling each other stories about him. We did more laughing than crying. It's tough not to have anybody to talk to."

"That's the problem. There's nobody left who knew us both."

Taylor heard the catch in Estelle's voice.

"There were just the two of you?"

"Estelle and Clara. Names out of the twenties. Clara was a menopause baby and two years later I was a real shock." Estelle laughed. "Our parents were foot-washing evangelicals. Maybe that's why we went hog-wild once we got to Ole Miss."

"I've heard a couple of things about Clara at Ole Miss, but not about you."

"Really?"

"From someone who knew Clara back then."

Estelle showed little interest.

It was too late for the farmers to be meeting for breakfast and too early for the ladies to be having lunch. The coffee shop was empty. They slid into a booth. Estelle ordered coffee, Taylor, iced tea.

"I just flew back to Willamette on Saturday," Estelle said

as she stirred two packets of artificial sweetener into her coffee. "Clara's husband was killed in a fire last Tuesday."

Taylor nodded. "I know."

"What would a private investigator want with Clara?"

"Not with Clara. My client thinks her husband was also killed."

Estelle sat up and stared at Taylor. "The police said it was an accident. No. I can't believe it was anything else. Lord, you should have seen that shop of his. Just waiting to burn down."

"Tell me about you and Clara at Ole Miss."

"You think it goes back that far? That's crazy."

"Maybe."

"All right. If it'll help find the devil who killed her." Estelle began to cry again. She pulled a paper napkin from the holder on the table and wiped her eyes and nose, then balled it up in her fist. "There's nothing, really. Neither one of us was a good student. We were having too much fun."

"My source says Clara was a rebel. Were you involved in the civil rights movement?"

"We weren't mixed up in anything that noble. Our particular brand of rebellion involved sex and drugs and rock and roll."

"Drugs?" Taylor repeated.

"Not the hard stuff. Pot, you know. Bell bottoms and ironed hair and parties that started on Friday and wound up Monday afternoon."

"Did you know any of the men Clara dated?"

"I knew 'em all. Well, most of 'em anyway." Estelle sipped her coffee and looked past Taylor into a shadowy past.

"Ever remember a man named Max Beaumont?" Taylor asked.

She shook her head. "What year was he?"

"He was teaching ROTC."

''Oh, *that* Max. I'd forgotten his name. Lord, he was the most gorgeous man. He was older, had been to Vietnam and all. Married but not working at it. If Clara hadn't started sleeping with him, I'd have gone after him myself.'' She laughed. ''Does that sound too awful?''

Taylor smiled back and shook her head.

'''Course, Clara used to say there wasn't a nickel's worth of difference between us and those women—we always referred to them as the prissy bitches—at the sorority houses except that we didn't do it with white gloves on.'' She laughed again, but it turned quickly into gulps and then into sobs. She propped her head in her hands. ''We didn't see each other much these last years, what with me being in Chicago and all, but she was all the family I had.''

''I am so sorry. Did you get along with her husband?''

''Helmut? Yes, yes, I did, even though he was ten years older, and I always thought he wasn't a hundred percent certain whether he ought to be married to a woman at all, if you know what I mean.''

''Why did Clara marry him?''

''Respectability and money. Clara liked living high. And Helmut was about as respectable as you can get. Talk about getting back at the prissy bitches! Helmut sold 'em half the furniture in their fancy houses and had things in his they could never have afforded. The greatest rebels are the ones who long most for respectability, didn't anybody ever tell you that? I'm married to a CPA.''

''They didn't have any children, did they?''

''Never wanted any.''

''You?''

''Two sons and a daughter.''

''You said you were here last week for Helmut's funeral?''

''More like a memorial service, really. There wasn't

much left of him to bury.'' Estelle wrinkled her nose. ''Sad.''

''Clara didn't want you to stay down here with her for a while? Help her get the estate settled?''

''I had to get home. Nels—that's my husband—had a big function in Chicago on Saturday. Clara swore she'd be fine. Nels told her he'd come down and work with her on probate once she found all the paperwork on the estate. Get the death taxes done, the final tax report, you know, those things.'' She stared at Taylor. ''My God, I've got to do it now, haven't I? For both of them?''

Taylor nodded. ''Have you been by the house?''

For the first time, Estelle looked at Taylor with suspicion. ''Yes.''

Taylor shook her head. ''I didn't have anything to do with the destruction at the house.''

''Then how come you know about it?''

''I have friends on the police force.'' Perfectly true.

Estelle seemed to accept her statement. She relaxed and waved to the waitress for a refill. ''Why would anybody destroy everything that way?'' Her eyes began to brim once more. ''Or kill Clara?'' She ran her fingers across her cheeks under her eyes. Her fingers came away shiny with moisture.

''Everything was insured, wasn't it?''

Estelle stared at her as though the idea had only now entered her head. ''Why, yes, I suppose so.'' She frowned. ''But probably not for anything like full replacement value. Helmut kept the most beautiful things around him. He couldn't bear to part with them.''

''Still, in the long run, insurance may make closing the estate easier for you.''

''I hadn't thought of that.''

''Did you find Clara's will?''

''It was in their lockbox—hers and Helmut's.''

Lockbox. Taylor caught her breath. If there were any clues about the person who had set up the theft of the animals, they might well be in that lockbox. Pushy was one thing, even with a woman as garrulous as Estelle Grierson, but demanding to know the contents of her dead sister's lockbox went way beyond pushy. "Was there an inventory? Polaroids? Sometimes people take videos of their things. Might make it easier to claim the insurance."

Estelle tilted her head. "You know, there were some Polaroids, but I don't know whether they were of stuff from the house or the store."

"What kind of stuff?"

"Crystal, china, some silver, some antique jewelry, mostly art-deco. I figured they were things from the shop, but I suppose they could just as well be from the house."

"If you can match the pictures to the broken china and crystal, your insurance company might pay up much easier, particularly if Helmut took out riders on his home-owner policy."

"Thanks…Taylor, was it? That may really help."

"If you'd like me to help you, I'd be more than happy to." *Please,* Taylor thought, *you have no idea how much I want to check those pictures!*

"The police won't let me in the house until tomorrow at the earliest." Estelle shook her head. "But I don't even know you, I couldn't ask you to help me."

"Sure you can."

Estelle laughed. "Well, maybe. If you're available."

Taylor felt both annoyed with herself for her duplicity and elated at the ease with which she'd insinuated herself into Estelle's life—and Clara's house. She decided to push her luck. "I've heard Helmut sailed kind of close to the line sometimes."

She'd expected Estelle to be incensed at her implication. Instead Estelle broke into laughter. "That man loved to brag about all the people he put things over on. I suppose most antique dealers fudge a little, but Helmut was a real old fraud. I think that's what attracted Clara, really. In his own way, he was a rebel too. He seemed so stuffy and correct on the outside, and on the inside he was having fun at the expense of all those fancy decorators and rich folks.''

"Did Clara help out much?"

"Oh, my, yes! She and Helmut were like a couple of kids sometimes. He found Nels and me some wonderful things— real bargains. I have a beautiful house.''

"Did he keep everything at the store?"

"I don't know what you mean.''

"Did he have another workshop or storage facility?''

"Not that I'm aware of. Why would he?"

"Maybe to do his faking in private, away from the prying eyes of his customers.''

"It's possible, but if so, neither of them ever talked about it.'' She sipped her coffee in silence.

Taylor watched her closely. Her eyes were far off. Taylor wondered whether she was thinking about the contents of that lockbox. She cleared her throat, ready to ask something, anything, that might get Estelle to talk further.

Estelle didn't give her the chance. "You know, it is possible,'' she said.

"I beg your pardon?''

"I was just thinking back to the last time Clara visited us. Meg—that's my daughter—was having a really fancy sweet-sixteen party complete with a band and all. Clara got a little drunk at the party, and afterwards we drove up to the lake, just the two of us.'' Her eyes began to tear. "It was the last time we really saw one another...to really talk, I mean.''

Taylor nodded encouragement.

"We were laughing about Helmut and Nels—how we both married kind of right-wing republican types, you know—and Clara said that the only differences between

Helmut and a big-time fence were his right-wing convictions, and how he and she had enough stuff stashed—that was the word she used, 'stashed'—to keep them in European vacations until the twenty-third century. Clara loved going to Europe with Helmut. They stayed in the best places and got the red carpet rolled out by all those bankrupt lords and barons, dying to unload the family heirlooms.''

"Far cry from love beads at Ole Miss."

"Maybe. I always just followed her lead, you know, but Clara was a real outlaw. She just learned to cover it up better.'' Estelle said this with pride in her voice.

"I assume she left everything to you."

"Nobody else left. Helmut left it all to her, and she left it to me.'' Estelle set down her cup and narrowed her eyes. "You're not thinking I might have a motive for killing her, are you? My very own sister that I loved?"

Taylor shook her head. "Not at all. Besides, you were in Willamette when both she and Helmut were killed, weren't you?"

"Yes, I was, and I can prove it.''

"I'm sure you can. I just thought that if there is another location with their stash, then, as executrix, you need to know about it.''

"I suppose.'' She reached across the table and touched Taylor's hand. "Say, you could find out, couldn't you?"

"Sorry, I already have a client, but if I do find out anything, I'll be happy to let you know.''

"Would you?'' Estelle dug into her black crocodile handbag, pulled out a gold Waterman pen and reached for another napkin. "I'll be at the Holiday Inn until after the funeral. Nels and the children aren't coming. What would be the point? But after I go home, you can reach me here.'' She wrote on the napkin and shoved it across the table to Taylor, who looked at it, folded it and stuck it in her wallet.

"You could do one thing,'' Taylor said. "Check Helmut

and Clara's bank statements. See if they paid rental on any property you don't know about.''

"Could I get in trouble? If they've done anything funny, I mean.''

Taylor shook her head. "You had no way of knowing. But it might help in the long run. Will you do it?''

Estelle pursed her lips. "I'll have to, won't I?'' She reached for the check.

"Please, let me,'' Taylor said. Estelle gave in gracefully. As they stood up to go, Taylor asked, "One more thing. Did either of you know a Josh Chessman at Ole Miss?''

Estelle froze halfway out of the booth and hung there a moment in a semi-crouch. "That bastard! Of course I knew Josh Chessman.''

Taylor sat down again, and after a moment Estelle did the same.

"Tell me.''

"That son of a bitch. He got Clara pregnant and wouldn't marry her. Then she lost the baby and almost died. Had to sell her car to pay the hospital bill because there was no way we could tell Momma and Daddy. After that, she and Helmut couldn't have had kids even if they'd wanted to. How does Josh Chessman come into this?''

"He may not. But both he and Max Beaumont are partners in Rounders—the place in Memphis where they found Clara's body.''

TAYLOR'S NEXT STOP was the police department. After several false starts she connected with Tom Owenwald, the officer who had investigated the fire at Eberhardt's shop.

Owenwald was a compact man who looked as though he'd be more comfortable in jeans and a camouflage vest than in his uniform. His hair was so fair and cropped so short that from a distance he looked bald, and his green eyes were made for staring down the sight of a deer rifle. A photo on his desk showed officer Tom holding up a nine point buck. "You know anything about arson?" he asked.

"Some. Was there any suspicion of arson?"

"Problem is that with most fires if you find evidence of an accelerant—gasoline, say, or kerosene—you know you've got arson 'cause the damn stuff was where it had no business being."

"Not at Eberhardt's."

"Hell," Owenwald said, "that whole storeroom was one big accelerant. There were gallon drums of paint stripper and denatured alcohol and lacquer thinner and I don't know what all. Miracle the man didn't blow himself up sooner. Plus he had a bunch of ventilation fans in the ceiling, so once the fire got started it had a real nice source of fresh air to keep it going."

"Still, he must have been careful about fire. I mean the man didn't have a death wish, surely?"

"Might as well have. What we think happened, he was there all by himself stripping something using a heat gun." He raised his eyebrows.

She nodded. "I've never used one, but I've seen them. They're like big hair dryers. Make paint blister up so you can scrape it."

"Right. Anyway, Eberhardt was using this heat gun. No idea what on. All the wood burned smack dab up along with Eberhardt, who probably got sick from the fumes or else had a stroke or something. Fell with the heat gun, and after a couple of minutes of resting against one of those cans, the whole shebang went up."

"Was he alive when the fire started?"

"Yeah. The body was what we call a crispy critter—not enough skin left on his face to see whether he breathed in any soot, but there was enough lung tissue left to see he'd been breathing when the fire started."

Taylor gulped, but persisted. "Could somebody have knocked him out, put the heat gun against one of the drums, and left?"

"Sure. Taking an awful chance, though. Whole thing could have blown up too soon and trapped whoever did it."

"Did Eberhardt show any evidence of head trauma?"

Tom laughed. "We think he fell and hit his head, so even a fractured skull wouldn't be evidence of murder."

"You do know his wife was found dead yesterday morning? Murdered?"

"Yeah. Weird coincidence."

"Coincidence—my aunt Fanny."

"Who'd want to get rid of both the Eberhardts?"

This was the one question Taylor couldn't answer even if she wanted to. "What do you know about that guy who worked for them? Eugene Lewis?"

"Oh, yeah, we know old Eugene all right." Tom grinned. "Mean drunk. Likes to fight in bars." He shook his head. "One of these days I'm gonna have Eugene's ass."

"Could I possibly have a copy of the arson report?"

"Why not? Case is closed."

Next, she checked the city directories. The Eberhardts had only two properties listed—the store and the house. When she finally walked out onto the front steps of the courthouse, she realized it was sunset. She'd never make it back to Rounders before dark.

As she drove onto the highway, she noticed a dark Toyota pickup behind her. It was still there in Holly Springs, but by the time she'd turned onto the expressway, it had disappeared. In any case, she couldn't see Eugene Lewis driving a Japanese pickup. He looked like one of the "America—Love it or Leave it" types.

CHAPTER NINE

BEFORE TAYLOR REACHED THE SOUTHERN SUBURBS south of the Mississippi line, darkness closed in with a threat of rain. Even driving against the caravan of homebound commuters, traffic into town was heavy.

She paid no further attention to the shifting headlights in her rearview mirror, but as she reached the downtown fork of the interstate, a Toyota pickup accelerated past her and disappeared over the hill as though the driver had suddenly decided he was late for an appointment.

At sixty-five miles an hour, Taylor didn't dare take even one hand off the wheel long enough to call Nick on her car phone. A twenty-minute wait was preferable to winding up under an eighteen-wheeler.

Instead she concentrated on reaching downtown as soon as possible. Mel expected her to be with Nick after dark for his protection as well as her own.

Mel would be proud of what she had learned from Estelle and Owenwald. She was a pro, dammit. It was about time these men admitted it.

She allowed herself a moment of worry about Nick's encounter with Danny, then dismissed it. Danny was on a simple fishing expedition, looking for an easy solution. Nick and his Boston-bred lawyer would have been able to handle Danny.

She felt like celebrating. She'd make Nick and Mel take her out for a steak before she and Nick went home to feed Elmo and circle the wagons for the night.

She thought about spending another night with Nick below her on the sofa bed. She'd been as aware of his breathing as he'd said he was of hers. Every time she woke—and she woke often—she watched him in the dim light that spilled from the bathroom—the way the muscles of his back rose and fell gently with his breathing, the way his hair curled over his ear. Fickle Elmo had spent the whole night curled against his back.

Lucky Elmo.

By the time Taylor pulled down the dark alley to the square in front of Rounders, her wipers beat an intermittent thwack against the mist that formed on her windshield. The place looked even more deserted and forlorn than it had—had it only been two nights ago?

She pulled up, slung her satchel over her shoulder, opened her car door, ducked her head against the drizzle, and sprinted for the front door of Rounders without waiting for Nick to spot her and buzz the door open.

She felt the change in atmosphere and heard a shoe scrape a second before a hand covered her mouth and stifled her screams. The man's other arm pressed across her breasts, pinned her arms to her sides. She felt herself lifted off the pavement.

Terror burned her body like a blowtorch and sucked the breath from her lungs like a bellows. This was it!

She heard the soft grunt of laughter and the voice whispering, "You and me's gonna take a little ride, sweet thang."

She was carried backward in a paroxysm of terror. She struggled, but the arms that held her felt thick and powerful. She smelled stale sweat and day-old Brut.

She'd had the courses. Self-defense for women, lesson one: *Get in the car with him and you're dead.*

It had to be Eugene, all two hundred and fifty body-building pounds of him. She couldn't see him, but she knew his stench. That Delta drawl chanted from beneath white sheets with eyeholes cut out, snickered from behind broken beer bottles and over broken women. Oh, yeah, she knew that voice in her soul.

She struggled.

She might as well have been an eland in the jaws of a lion.

She tried to open her mouth to bite the filthy hand across her face, but she could barely breathe. His palm forced her lips hard against her teeth, and she tasted her own blood. His thumb pressed against her cheekbone under her eye so hard that tears welled.

He pressed her against him, and the cut steel of his belt buckle etched a pattern into her spine. Below his belt he was urgently erect.

She kicked back at him. He chuckled. God, he was loving this.

She was being carried farther and farther from Rounders, from light and safety and Nick…into darkness, towards the waiting Toyota pickup that had dogged her from Oxford.

Her nine-millimeter lay useless on the front seat of her car. Her satchel hung just as useless from her shoulder and swung against her legs with every step he took.

Yeah, she'd had all those damn self-defense courses, all right. She'd fought the guys in the protective gear and yelled the words. But it wasn't like this. Then there had been light and air and an instructor urging you on, and the guy in the protective gear was a guy you went out for coffee with after you kicked him in his well-protected balls.

This was for real. Eugene didn't want coffee. He wanted her body, and when he was through with that he wanted her dead.

"Settle down, sweet thang," he whispered, his rough cheek close to her ear, his breath rank with nicotine and beer. "You gonna like it. We got us a lawwwng night."

One chance. Remember the lessons. Let him think he's won. God! He had won!

Taylor whimpered and let herself go limp.

He hadn't expected that. The hand across her mouth slipped two inches, the one beneath her breast loosened for an instant to get a better grip.

"No!" she screamed, and bit him.

He howled.

She twisted free and landed with both heels on his right instep. He yelped.

Every instinct screamed *run*. But if she ran he'd have her again in a second, and this time he'd deck her.

She whipped around, came into him at a crouch, raked his face with her nails, and, with every ounce of strength she had left, brought her knee up into his crotch.

Only then did she spring back and kick out at his kneecap. She heard the thunk of rubber on cartilage. If she'd worn boots she'd have broken his goddamn leg.

He was down, but far from out. She grabbed her satchel by the strap and swung it at his face. It struck him in the throat.

He gurgled.

Light flooded from the third-floor windows of Rounders. Taylor turned and raced for the entry. She flung herself at the door as the buzzer sounded. Behind her she heard footsteps.

They were limping, but they were leaving.

She slammed the door behind her and leaned against it. A moment later she heard a car door slam. An engine started and roared away down the alley.

Her breath sobbed in her throat. She felt the artery under her chin. Not quite atrial fibrillation, but close. She felt slimy with her sweat and Eugene's. She sank to her heels with her back braced against the door.

"Taylor? You okay?"

Nick's voice. She pictured him standing as he had on Monday evening, silhouetted in the open doorway of his apartment.

She wanted to run up those stairs and fling herself at him. She wanted to rip off her clothes and scrub her body until blood ran from her pores.

She cleared her throat and called back, "Sure, Nick. I'm fine. Just let me brush off this rain." She sounded remarkably normal. She cleared her throat again and dragged herself up using the doorknob.

The whole thing had lasted no more than a minute, two at the most. She'd fought for her life outside, while inside Nick heard nothing, saw nothing.

Even now he knew nothing.

And she couldn't tell him. Not if she wanted to keep this job.

One hint that she'd nearly been dragged off by that Neanderthal for an evening of rape, probable torture, eventual murder, and Mel would chain her to her computer terminal until the twenty-third century.

Nick would demand that Mel replace her immediately.

She ran her fingers through her hair, wiped her mouth with the back of her hand and squared her shoulders. She pulled down her sweater and prayed Eugene's dirty paw hadn't left traces. She took a deep breath and walked up the stairs.

She'd been monumentally stupid. Eugene should never have been able to get to her. And she'd make sure he wouldn't get another chance. Somehow she'd make certain that Mel and Nick understood how dangerous Eugene was. Somehow she'd get the word to Danny that Eugene was the key to this whole mess.

But she wouldn't tell anyone about Eugene's attack. Not now. Not ever.

CHAPTER TEN

TAYLOR TOOK A DEEP BREATH and managed to run up the stairs to Nick's apartment. She sauntered past him casually and hoped he'd put her rapid breathing down to exertion. She must not let him touch her. He was too quick to catch the scent of her fear. More important, he might catch the scent of Eugene.

"You were supposed to check in before dark," Nick said. "I was worried."

"You sound like Mel," Taylor answered with what she hoped was insouciance. "I call him Papa Bear. Oxford took a little longer than I thought."

She realized they were not alone. The smallish dark man who leaned against the kitchen counter scaled the heights of dandified spiffiness that Danny Vollmer never quite attained. "Hi," he said in a broad Boston accent that could have doubled for Teddy Kennedy's. "Rico Cabrizzo." He smiled a sleepy, seductive smile and extended a neat, manicured hand.

He held hers a moment too long. The navy suit he wore had been tailored for him. His dark, wavy hair was nearly the same texture and length as Nick's, but Nick probably had his lopped off whenever it caught on his collar. Rico must have his razored once a week by an expert. Even now in November, his face was tanned and taut.

Even if she hadn't just kicked and bitten her way out of attempted rape, she wouldn't have responded to Cabrizzo.

Beside Nick, every other man seemed to blur around the edges, like a copy of a copy of a male.

Rico tilted his handsome head and smiled at her quizzically, then glanced at Nick with a smirk and a nod. Taylor felt her face flush. Her attraction to Nick couldn't be that obvious, surely.

All at once Taylor's knees began to shake. She gulped away her now-familiar post-traumatic-stress nausea, then sank onto the sofa and set her satchel on the seat beside her. She didn't want either of these men getting too close. "I could use a drink," she said brightly.

"Nonalcoholic, right?" Nick said.

She forced herself to look squarely at Nick, smiled reassuringly and shook her hair back from her face. "The road was slick. Tough driving."

He nodded, unconvinced.

She licked her parched lips and nearly gagged as she tasted Eugene's palm on her mouth. "Diet soft drink if you've got one. In the can will be fine."

Her throat was so dry that she thought her voice sounded choked. When he handed her the soda, she willed her hand steady. She drained half the can at one gulp.

"You okay?" Nick pulled one of the dining chairs across from her, swung it around and sat down with his arms across the back of it. Rico still leaned against the kitchen counter, and she felt his eyes assessing her.

"Sure." She drained the soda and set the empty can on a carousel magazine on the table beside her. "How about you? How'd it go with Danny?"

"He's mad because I hadn't reported the theft or told him about Eberhardt's death. He tried to build that into a motive for me to kill Clara Eberhardt."

"Ridiculous."

"So I informed him," Rico said, and chortled.

"I'll sic him on Officer Tom Owenwald in Oxford," Taylor said. "I had a lovely chat with him this afternoon about arson."

"Good," Rico said. "Maybe he won't drag you in tomorrow morning and demand you drop the case for your own good." He shoved off from the counter and walked over to the sofa. He shifted her satchel to the coffee table, arranged his trousers and sank beside Taylor with the grace of a premier danseur. "Not a bad idea. You dropping the case, that is."

"Fat chance." Taylor felt the tension in her neck relax. She'd probably have hysterics later when she was alone.

"I'm pretty sure it was Eugene who shot at you last night," she said to Nick.

"You found out something today?"

She hesitated a moment too long, then said casually, "The Oxford cops say he's a real bad boy. No doubt the Eberhardts kept him around for cheap muscle. He must have helped move the animals from the storeroom. Either he's doing this on his own—taking up where they left off—or more likely he's set up another connection."

"With whoever organized the theft," Nick added sadly. "You think he killed Clara?"

"Not Eugene's style. Whoever killed Clara was neat, competent, and ruthless. Eugene may be ruthless, but..." She wrinkled her nose at the memory of Eugene's touch. She shuddered, took a deep breath and said in what she hoped was a normal tone, "Can you see Clara Eberhardt meeting Eugene at The Peabody? Or driving down here with him after dark?"

"If she hired him, she wasn't afraid of him," Rico said reasonably.

"Even after Eberhardt's death?" Taylor shook her head. "Nope, Eugene would have bashed her over the head and left her where she dropped."

"You think he's got the animals?" Nick asked.

"Makes sense," Taylor answered. "And probably whatever records exist about the thefts. That would give him a real hold over the Rounders connection."

Rico turned towards her. "I have just spent twenty minutes trying to convince Nick that he has absolutely no liability in the thefts. He doesn't owe Pete Marley or anyone else money. *Caveat emptor*—Let the buyer beware. He didn't turn the animals into convincing frauds, he didn't sell them, he didn't furnish the fake provenance. If Pete Marley was stupid enough to hand over thirty-five thousand dollars to a dealer he didn't know, that's his lookout, not Nick's."

"How successful were you?" Taylor asked.

Rico shrugged. "Guess."

"You got nowhere."

Nick shifted on his chair. "I have a moral obligation."

Rico waved him away. "Moral, my ass. Marley is blackmailing you, and you're too dumb to see it. Tell him to publish and be damned."

"Better yet," Taylor said, warming to the idea, "put ads in the carousel magazines explaining what happened and warning buyers to be on the lookout for the fakes."

"Not unless I have to," Nick said. "People would always wonder if I had a hand in the whole thing. If I stood to gain." He shook his head. "Unless they find out who killed the Eberhardts, I'll never be entirely free of suspicion."

"My dear Nick, people will always gossip," Rico said. "At least let me talk to Marley. He needs to hit Eberhardt's estate with a suit, so he gets his thirty-five thou from them, not you. That way you stay out of bankruptcy court until we can trace the remaining animals. Then we sue the Eberhardt estate too for the additional losses, plus pain and suffering. Could cop a bundle."

With a pang of guilt Taylor thought of poor Estelle Grierson. Still, Rico was right. Even Nick had said he'd probably end up suing the estate, and there was probably plenty in it to pay off Marley and any others. She nodded in agreement.

Nick sighed. "Not yet. And don't expect Marley's lawyers to cooperate. He doesn't want anyone to know he got taken."

"Tough. I think we can keep it quiet, but my responsibility is to you, not only because I'm your lawyer, but because, I hope, I'm your friend."

He might also be a thief and a double murderer, Taylor thought. She needed to talk to him alone.

Rico turned to Taylor. "And now, we have an extraspecial treat for you."

Taylor looked at him suspiciously.

"Rico, don't be a jerk," Nick said, then turned to Taylor. "We're invited to Josh's to talk strategy."

Taylor looked from one man to the other. "What am I not picking up on here?"

"Margery does not entertain anyone except celebrities and society *chez* Chessman," Rico said with an exaggerated sneer. "Even I have never been invited, and I am—I kid you not—a remarkably presentable bachelor who makes a hell of a lot of money. Unfortunately, I have a weird Yankee accent and I can't advance Josh's career one iota."

THE CHESSMANS LIVED IN A NEW, very expensive one-story house on the outskirts of Germantown. The style was what Realtors called "mansion architecture"—brick veneer with plenty of windows and little character. Margery opened the door herself.

"You're late." Margery stood aside grumpily. She wore a navy turtleneck sweater tucked into taupe wool gabardine slacks. Taylor wondered whether that perky bosom and flat tummy had been achieved with the help of Jane Fonda—or plastic surgery.

Around her neck Margery wore three heavy twisted gold

chains, each with a different pendant—a broad white jade disk, a sixty carat citrine, a three-inch gold reproduction of an antique hypodermic needle. No doubt an award from one of her hospital boards. She wore heavy gold hoops in her ears and a three-inch gold cuff on her left arm.

The inside of the house wasn't nearly as cozy as the mortuary in Oxford. No magazines, no books, no family photos. No antiques. Two beige sofas, so overstuffed they looked as though someone had pumped them up like truck tires, sat on either side of a black marble fireplace. The sofas were piled thickly with down pillows the shape and color of raw ravioli.

On second thought, Taylor decided it looked more like an upscale conference center than a funeral home. Even the dining-room table seemed designed for board meetings. Taylor peeked to see whether the chairs were on casters. They were.

Josh came to meet them. Max struggled out of one of the sofas. From the other end, Veda smiled and waved her glass of white wine in their direction. Then she glanced up at Max. She looked worried.

Max swayed slightly and sat down as far from Veda as he could on the same piece of furniture. "Ah, the main event." He held up a half-full highball, dark enough to be straight bourbon. He spoke with the exaggerated care of a man who refuses to slur and knows he's drunk enough to do just that.

"I'll leave now, Josh," Margery said and kissed the air in the general area of his cheek. "I have an opera board meeting."

Chessman opened his mouth to protest, but by that time Margery was through the archway into the kitchen without a backward glance or acknowledgment of her guests. He shrugged. "Drinks?"

Nick took a beer; Rico scotch-and-water; Taylor, diet ginger ale.

Taylor, Nick and Rico sat on the second sofa. Taylor realized that she was ravenously hungry just about the time she found there wasn't even a bowl of salted peanuts on the glass coffee table between the sofas.

She watched Max over the rim of her glass. He smiled sardonically into his highball, and she felt waves of antipathy from him. She had no idea how she'd managed to antagonize him so quickly or so completely, but she knew an enemy when she met one. Were his feelings personal, or did he fear she'd discover he was a thief and a killer?

"So," Max said, "the suspects are gathered ready for the great detective to do his—pardon me, *her* stuff." He bowed in Taylor's direction. "What has our junior Miss Marple come up with?" He snickered.

Taylor bit back a reply and glanced at Nick. He stared at Max with his eyes narrowed and his jaw set.

Veda reached for his glass. "Max, honey, don't you think you've had enough?"

Max held it out of her reach. A few drops sloshed onto the leather couch. Josh yipped and leaned over to wipe them away with a cocktail napkin. Max sneered and took another swig.

"Tonight is a special occasion, Veda," Max said. "Not every day my best friend accuses me of murder."

"Come on, Max," Nick said, "nobody's accusing anyone of anything."

"Good. Because if she says I did it, I shall sue her and her precious agency for slander." He glared at Taylor.

"*She* hasn't accused anyone," Taylor said. "And I'm not going to." She set her drink down. "Not tonight. I thought this was a council of war. Now I see it's a lynching and I'm the lynchee."

"Max," Nick said, "knock off the bull or let me drive you home right now. Your choice."

Max raised his eyebrows. "My, my, aren't we protective of little Ms. Hunt's sensibilities? You don't seem to give a damn about mine."

"Crap," Nick said, still amiable. He leaned back. "I'd forgotten what a lousy drunk you are."

Max's chest heaved. Taylor was certain that he'd walk out, but Nick seemed to know the right note to hit with him. For a moment no one spoke, then Max waved his drink in Taylor's direction and laughed. "Oh, all right." He nodded to Taylor. "Sorry. Rude of me."

"No problem," she said.

Veda said quickly, "So tell us, Taylor dear, what have you learned?"

Taylor looked at Nick. "Is it all right? I only work for you, you know."

"Sure."

She took a deep breath and gave them no more information than she thought they should have. When she mentioned talking with Estelle Grierson, she saw Josh Chessman stiffen, but he said nothing. Somewhere during her speech Max stopped frowning at her and switched his attentions to Josh. His smile widened as the level of liquid in his glass lowered.

Veda didn't take her eyes off Max. Taylor tried to read her look. Earlier, she'd appeared worried, but seemed to be growing more annoyed with Max's every swig.

"So, that's where we stand at the moment," Taylor said. She set her empty glass on a pewter coaster on the coffee table.

"Ha!" Max said. "The woman hasn't found out a damn thing worth knowing." He stuck his nose in his drink. "Pay her off and send her packing. Let the police handle it."

"I haven't found proof that you or Dr. Chessman stole

the animals, if that's what you mean,'' Taylor said. "Not yet.''

"Ah, pussy has claws.''

Nick opened his mouth, but Taylor raised a hand to stop him. She could fight her own battles. For a man whom Nick had characterized as a gentleman, Max was being insufferably rude. But only to her.

She glanced from Max to Nick. Maybe it was fear—simple, straightforward terror of being found out. Or was he jealous?

Had he caught on to the chemistry between her and Nick? They might deny it even to one another, but it was there, all right. Was it that obvious to everyone? Surely not.

She caught Veda's eye. Oh, boy. Max wasn't the only one who was picking up the vibes.

"Do you expect Josh or me to confess? Or do you plan to get out your little truncheon and beat it out of us?'' Max asked.

"Stop it, Max,'' Josh snapped.

"I keep my truncheon in my other bag,'' Taylor said lightly. "All I've got with me is my little old blackjack. Will that do?''

Max slammed his drink against the table so hard that Taylor was afraid the glass would fracture. "I'm damned if I'm afraid of anything this smartass girl can throw at me.''

"Shut up, Max. Now. I mean it,'' Nick snapped.

Max's mouth dropped open. "You've never spoken to me like that.''

"You've never deserved it.'' Nick leaned forward. "What you deserve is a broken jaw. You probably won't remember any of this tomorrow morning, but that doesn't excuse your actions tonight.''

Max struggled to his feet. He stood ramrod straight, every muscle taut. "I'm leaving.''

"The hell you are. Sit down, apologize to Taylor and the

rest of us, and stop acting like a prize jackass before I forget *my* manners.''

Max hesitated.

''Do it,'' Nick said. ''Now.''

Max sat and stared at his knees morosely.

Josh paced in front of the fireplace. ''It doesn't matter whether she found out anything or not. This affair is still going to have serious repercussions for all of us, but for me most of all.'' He turned to them. ''I mean, who are you people, really? But I'm important in this city. It's too late to pull out, but I wish to God I'd never gotten involved with the place.''

''Now who's being snotty?'' Max said, rousing himself with difficulty. ''*Important* in this city?'' He whined in perfect imitation of Josh. ''You sound like Margery's ventriloquist's dummy. Rounders is the only remotely human thing in your life.'' He dropped a piece of ice from his glass into his mouth and sucked on it noisily. ''Except for bedding the coeds, of course.''

''What the hell are you talking about?'' Chessman bleated.

''Is it still two girls a semester? Or has your aging prostate cut you down to one?''

''This is ludicrous! Get out, damn you!''

''Is that why you stole the animals?'' Max continued. He seemed to have reached that lucid stage often attained by drunks just before they pass out. ''Did you need money to buy yourself the playmate of the month? Or possibly to buy *off* the playmate of the month.''

Josh gave a strangled cry and rushed at him. Veda stuck out her hand and caught him as he went by.

''Ignore him,'' she said.

''You can't ignore all those harassment charges, though, can you?'' Max asked. ''One more and I hear you can kiss that provost job good-bye. And kiss Margery good-bye if they hire someone else.''

Taylor reached across and laid her hand heavily on Nick's arm as he began to stand. She shook her head. She wanted them to keep talking. Rico nodded at her in agreement.

"I never stole anything in my life," Chessman snapped.

Max seemed suddenly gleeful. "I suppose you had to kill Clara to get her off your back. She probably just wanted a new car to replace the one she had to sell to pay for her miscarriage."

The room went dead quiet.

Chessman gulped as though he'd forgotten how to breathe. Max lay back amongst the cushions and smiled into his drink.

"I knew about your affair, Josh. Of course I knew. But murder?" He shook his finger and clicked his tongue as though Chessman were a child misbehaving. "Surely there was a better way."

"Oh, God!" Chessman sank into an overstuffed club chair and dropped his head into his hands. After a moment he looked up with hope shining in his red-rimmed eyes. "I didn't kill Clara. I can prove it!" He stared around wildly. "I was working in my office. Margery called."

"Margery might have mistaken the time. Not that she'd stick at lying to keep your chairmanship."

"No, not alone. I had someone with me. A student."

Max roared with laughter. "Josh, you dirty old man, you were having some poor coed on the couch in your office?" He wiped his eyes, then sobered. "That's not much alibi. Poor little twit's in love with you."

"She hates my guts!" Chessman's voice thrummed with hope. "She's been threatening to go to the president about me if I don't pay her off. She wouldn't lie to save me from the fires of hell."

"What's her name?" Taylor asked.

Chessman turned to her as though he'd forgotten she was there. "I can't have you talking to her. Margery might find out."

"Then tell Sergeant Vollmer."

Josh shook his head.

Taylor opened her hands to him. "Look, if Vollmer has one less suspect, he can concentrate on finding out who really did kill Clara Eberhardt. You'll be off the hook, no suspicion, no harm to your reputation."

"That makes sense," Veda said. "You should call him, Josh."

"Ah, little Miss Veda, the voice of reason," Max said. "How about you for the role of first murderer?"

"What?" Veda stared at him.

"Come now. A nurse practitioner like you would know precisely the right place to jam that chisel into Clara's neck for maximum bang for the buck." Max gestured toward Veda. "Josh has plenty of money, Rico's coining it, and God knows, Marcus Cato does. I have my pension and my investments. But who knows how much little Veda's widow's mite is?"

Veda set her drink down. "Probably more than yours, Max." She looked at him as though he were a total stranger. "I've been making excuses for you ever since the first day I met you. You're a real jerk, Max, you know that?"

Max laughed. "Oh, I can't bear it! A jerk!"

"Yes, Max, a jerk. And after watching your little exhibition tonight, I've finally figured out that you have about as much real sex appeal as an aardvark with a bad case of herpes." She stood. "I'm damn hungry. I'm going home."

The conference broke up.

Nick half carried Max—who had passed into maudlin semiconsciousness—to his truck. "I'll drive him home and put him to bed," he told Taylor.

As she said good-bye to Josh, she whispered, "Can I see you in your office tomorrow about ten?"

He shrank from her and stammered, "I don't want to talk to you."

Taylor smiled ingratiatingly. "If you talk to me, I can smooth your way with Detective Vollmer."

"I can give you five minutes before my ten o'clock class. You know where my office is?"

"I'll find it."

Rico waited for her outside the front door. He'd been so quiet she'd almost forgotten he was there.

He slipped his arm through hers. "Thank God, Max wound down before he got to me and Marcus. How about lunch tomorrow? I'm not in court. "

Taylor glanced at Nick, who was wrestling Max's car keys out of his hand. "I'll call you."

Nick dropped Max's keys into his pocket and walked him down the steps toward the Rounders truck. Over his shoulder he said to Taylor, "Can you take Veda home? She came with Max."

"We're not supposed to separate after dark, remember?"

"I'll be careful if you will. Wait for me at Veda's."

"Then can we please get something to eat?"

Nick grinned. "Promise."

Rico climbed into his Mercedes and drove away.

Max stumbled against the hood of Nick's truck. Nick caught him and steered him around the door and into the front seat.

Veda stood watching until they drove away, then climbed in beside Taylor. They drove off behind Nick.

Taylor's Glock lay on the seat between them. Veda poked it with a small index finger. "Some gun."

"Does it bother you?" Taylor opened the center console and slid the gun inside.

"Lord, no. I'm good with guns."

Taylor checked her rearview mirror. No Toyota trucks behind her. With luck, Eugene was home nursing his injuries. Taylor realized she was so tired and hungry that her eyes were starting to cross. "Does Max get like that often?" she asked.

"I've never seen it quite that bad before, but then I've never seen Max under pressure."

"Murder creates pressure."

Veda shook her head. "I don't think Max is a killer. But something has frightened him badly." They drove silently for a while, then Veda said brightly, "I'm bored to death with Max. Tell me about being a detective. Turn right here."

"It's an ordinary job. All those tough-talking female P.I.s in the books get into more trouble in a day than I'm likely to get into in ten years." Taylor laughed. "Mel says the main thing the fictional P.I.s have to be is fast-healers. They get beat up, break ribs, and five pages later they're making love."

Veda laughed. "As a nurse I can assure you nobody with broken ribs is interested in making love."

"I break the occasional fingernail, period. Even surveillance cases are just plain boring. You can't run the heater in the winter or the air conditioner in the summer because you'll mess up the car. So you freeze or bake, and try to stay awake with regular jolts of caffeine."

"Doesn't sound very glamorous."

"It isn't. Or dangerous, as I keep assuring my mother."

"But Clara Eberhardt got murdered," Veda reminded her.

Taylor sighed. "True. This is my first murder. And I'm not really in the line of fire." Her hands tightened on the wheel as the memory of Eugene's hands swept over her.

"You can park here under the light," Veda said. Taylor watched to see whether she'd been followed. Apparently not. She took a deep breath and followed Veda into her townhouse.

"I'll bet you could use some nibblies while you're waiting," Veda said. "I make a hell of a cheese straw."

This small house had all the grace and charm that the Chessmans's lacked. A cockatoo in a bamboo cage squawked and raised his crest the moment the door opened. Veda opened the kitchen door and a big ginger cat stalked out. "This is Denzel," she said.

Taylor scratched his ears.

"I moved here after my husband, Bill, died," Veda said. "My son wanted me to come live with them, but I'm happy here. I know this place is cluttered, but I can't get rid of all my memories. I am desperate for more space, not fewer memories. I like living in the Garden District, but so far I haven't been able to find a place I can afford to buy."

Taylor picked up a photo in a silver frame. A much younger Veda hung on the arm of a cheerful mustached man.

Veda handed Taylor a glass of iced tea and set a plate of cheese straws on the coffee table. "That's my Bill. We had a heck of a marriage."

"Are you retired?"

"No. Why?"

"You have so much free time," Taylor said.

"Bill left some money, and I do private-duty nursing whenever I want to do something special, like travel to Michigan to see my grandsons. Yech! I hate snow."

"You're awfully young to be widowed," Taylor said. "Have you ever thought of marrying again?"

"I could ask you the same. You're widowed and considerably younger than I am."

"The few men I meet come equipped with ex-wives, delinquent stepchildren, alimony, child support, and all the psychological problems that made the ex divorce them in the first place.''

"Nick doesn't have an ex," Veda said.

"Why not? At his age, most men have been married at least once."

"He's had two live-ins since I started working at Rounders, but they left because he spent too much time with the carvers. He can't—what's the word I'm looking for?—invest himself in any woman the way he does with us."

"Why?"

Veda raised her hands. "I'm no psychologist, but his mother deserted him and his grandmother died on him very suddenly. There never was anyone else."

"I thought his mother died."

Veda shook her head. "Nope. Just vanished. You like him, don't you?"

"He's a client."

"He's a man. A great big, sexy man."

"I don't generally go for men like Nick, no matter how big and sexy they are."

"Why ever not?"

Taylor took another cheese straw, leaned back and put her feet on the ottoman. "For the same reason you're in love with Max."

"I beg your pardon?"

"Max is your prototypical star bastard," Taylor said. "I have been falling for star bastards since Freddy Colbert knocked me off my skates in the second grade and I had to have three stitches in my bottom lip—" she touched the thin white line that ran from her lip like a minute hand pointing to twenty-five minutes after the hour "—but point me at a decent, caring, gentle man and I run screaming in the other direction. The psychologists say it's low self-esteem. We think we deserve to be mistreated," Taylor said, and sipped her iced tea. *Until now, she thought.*

"Horse pucky," Veda said and gulped hers. "I've got self-esteem up the wazoo, and even after tonight I'd probably still go to bed with Max if he asked me. Which he won't."

"Hasn't he given you any sign that he's interested?"

"I'm twenty years too old for him," Veda said bitterly. "He's got a string of women my son's age and younger. He takes them to dinner, beds them. They help him with that benighted house of his, but nobody stays long." Veda leaned back against the sofa and closed her eyes. "After Bill died I didn't think I'd ever want another man. Then I walked into Rounders and there's Max. God, what did I see in the man?"

"Maybe some of the same things I saw in my husband Paul."

"Nick's different."

"But he doesn't keep his women around long either."

"They always part friends. Max's women always leave in a huff." Veda raised her head and Taylor saw that her eyes were filled with unshed tears. "Tell me about your Paul."

"Handsome as Lucifer, Law Review at Harvard, slated to be a named partner in his firm before his fiftieth birthday, married Taylor Maxwell, perfect consort and hostess, in a society wedding with twelve bridesmaids and a reception at the country club. Cinderella gets her fella. Happily ever after."

"What was the problem?"

"I'm not Cinderella, although I didn't know that until after he died. We both got cheated."

After a moment Veda said softly, "You think Max is guilty of this, don't you?"

"Assuming that Josh's alibi checks out, he's starting to look better and better," Taylor said.

"I could tell from the way you looked at him. You don't like him."

"He loathes me."

"He's afraid you've taken Nick away from him."

Taylor said nothing.

Veda nodded. "Oh, yes, he is. Nick is the son he never knew. Nick respects him. The other women in Nick's life were unimportant adjuncts, but you're different. I've seen the way Nick looks at you."

"How?"

"Like you're a shiny new Illions King Stander with the original park paint."

Taylor laughed.

Veda took her hand. "No, I mean it. When he looks at you he's—I don't know—hungry. I used to wish Max looked at me that way."

"Why don't you tell him how you feel?"

"If he said he wasn't interested—and he would—we'd never be easy with one another again. I'd have to give up Rounders. God, I can't imagine life without Rounders!"

"Is the carving that important to you?"

"I was a floor nurse for twenty years. Everybody said how competent I was and how caring. I didn't want to be competent, I wanted to be creative! I can't play an instrument or draw a straight line, or act, or dance—but the day I walked into Rounders I found out that I could carve. I'm damn good at it."

"I know you are, I've seen the frog and Harvey."

"They rely on me at Rounders; they like me—not as a nurse, but as a colleague. I won't give that up, not even for Max!"

"You shouldn't have to." Taylor regarded Veda with compassion. "It doesn't get easier, does it?"

"With age, you mean?" Veda laughed without humor.

"Harder, if anything. On top of everything else there's the pressure of time and the pull of gravity."

"You still look great."

"Not naked I don't. Or not that great." Veda set her glass down on the side table. "Hell, Taylor, I don't want to die without ever making love again."

"And you want to make it with Max."

"I don't know anyone else."

"Somebody will look at you the way you want Max to."

"I probably won't look back." Veda shook her head. "I know he's bad for me, but if you think the pickings are slim at your age, you ought to try them at mine."

The two women sat silently for a moment, then Taylor asked, "Veda, does Max need money?"

Veda drew in her breath shortly and began to shake her head in a gesture that was more denial of the question than an answer to it. "I don't know. That house is a money pit, and I know he's sent his son money a couple of times. He feels so guilty about losing the boy—hell, he's no boy, Michael's a grown man with a son of his own."

"A grandson? Does Max see him?"

"I don't think he's ever laid eyes on him."

"Do you have any idea when the animals were stolen?"

"The last time I was in that storeroom was when I finished my Death and Glory Frog—you know, the one in the red waistcoat. That was in June—no, July. Just before the Fourth, I think. I didn't pay much attention, but the room seemed as full as usual."

"Why didn't you take the frog home?"

Veda laughed and waved a hand at the clutter around her. "And put him where?" She shook her head. "Nick is determined we're going to start a carousel museum. There's a lower floor that's not in use. It was rented out for a while to a man who did ornamental ironwork, but he moved out to his own building."

"What's down there? Nick told me Rounders only uses the second floor. I assumed there was another tenant on the ground floor. There's no access from the foyer."

Veda shook her head. "Nick had the door blocked off. The iron person had a side door put in. It's always locked." Veda raised a hand to her mouth. "Taylor, you don't think someone moved those horses down there, do you? That they've been there all along and nobody's even checked?"

The doorbell rang. Veda went to let Nick in.

"Sorry it took me so long. I had to put Max to bed. He gets like this sometimes."

The moment she heard his voice, Taylor felt her skin tingle. Was she finally growing up? Resonating to a man like Nick instead of to the insensitive louts she'd hankered after since the second grade? She wanted to run into his arms, taste his kiss once more. Instead she sat where she was and waved a cheese straw in his direction.

"Nick," Veda said excitedly, "could the animals be stashed downstairs at Rounders?"

Nick grinned. "Sorry, Veda, I checked. Empty."

"Well, damn," Veda said.

"You want to join us for dinner?" Nick asked.

Veda shook her head. "Thank you, no. I am going to take a glass of wine and a salami sandwich up to bed. It's been a hell of a long day."

CHAPTER ELEVEN

NICK BARELY SPOKE OVER DINNER. Taylor made a couple of attempts at chitchat, then gave up and concentrated on her steak.

Over coffee she said, "The only suspect I haven't met is Marcus Cato. I'll try to see him tomorrow. Veda says she thinks the animals were all there in July, but that's four months ago. We need to narrow down the time of the theft."

"I can do that," Nick said.

Taylor blinked. "I beg your pardon?"

"I said I think I know when they were stolen."

"Well, would it be too much for you to enlighten me?"

He looked up at her and shook his head. "I've been sitting here going over things. That's why I haven't been decent company."

Taylor leaned her elbows on the table and propped her chin on her hands. "Okay. Give."

"Not going to be much help."

"Try me."

"I helped Veda move her frog Fourth of July weekend. I know everything was there because I had to move some things around to find space for it."

"Go on."

"Most of the time, I stick pretty close to Rounders. I haven't had a vacation in three years."

Taylor nodded.

"Whoever took them would want to move other animals to fill in the gaps so the room would look okay."

"I'm with you, so far."

"The freight elevator's not that wide, so I figure it would take several hours to move ten animals, especially if Eugene was doing the grunt work by himself. I don't see Helmut Eberhardt or Clara as the kind to get their fingernails dirty, do you?"

"Not from what I've learned, no."

"Eberhardt took a couple of weeks, minimum, to age the hippocampus, but he probably didn't start aging it or the others immediately. He'd want to know whether the thefts had been discovered and reported. Then there was lag time in his shop. I doubt Pete Marley stumbled on the hippocampus the first day Eberhardt brought it in. That leaves a space between the Fourth of July and, say, October first."

"Go on."

"There were only two spans when they could count on getting into Rounders without getting caught. I went to a carousel convention in Sarasota the first week in August. Josh and Veda looked after Rounders during the day, but nobody stayed overnight."

"And the second?"

"I went to an auction in Louisville over Labor Day. Left Friday afternoon, came home Monday evening. Rounders was closed the entire time."

"That's probably when they were stolen," Taylor said. "In August there was always a possibility somebody would stay late or arrive early. How come you just figured this out?"

"I guess I didn't want to analyse it. The only people who could have known about my absences were the regulars—my friends. I wanted to believe that it could have been someone from outside Rounders who cased the place and got in touch with the Eberhardts."

"Not likely."

"I know, I know. In the end the only real suspects are

the people who were at Rounders when I called from Seattle to tell Max about Marley's hippocampus—correction, my hippocampus.''

"So where were all of them over Labor Day weekend?''

Nick shrugged and shook his head. "Does it matter? Whoever set the thing up didn't have to be physically present. If it were me, I'd arrange to be halfway around the world.''

"Was Max with you in Sarasota and Louisville?''

Nick sighed. "Both times.''

TAYLOR SAW NO SIGN OF EUGENE outside the restaurant. As she walked to her truck, Nick called after her, "Leave your truck here. I've got something to show you.''

She shrugged and climbed into the Rounders truck beside him. As usual, the moment they weren't actually discussing the thefts, she started thinking of Nick the man, and forgetting Nick the client. Not good. She slid as close to her door as she could.

"Where we going?'' she asked.

"Wait and see,'' he said mysteriously.

Ten minutes later they pulled up before the guard shack in front of the amusement park. Nick left Taylor sitting in the car and walked over to talk to the guard. Several times Nick pointed at Taylor. She saw the guard hand Nick a heavy key attached to a tag by a chain.

"Come on,'' he said and opened her door. He unlocked the entrance gate in the chain-link fence, held it open for her and locked it behind them, then led her through the turnstile into the park.

Old-fashioned gas lamps spilled red-gold light on the curved concrete walk that meandered between shuttered concession stands. The moon was nearly full and the night was warm for early November.

They turned a corner and reached the big circular enclo-

sure around the carousel. The park was still open on weekends from Labor Day to Thanksgiving, so the sides of the
enclosure were open. Inside, Taylor saw the looming shape
of the dozing carousel.

Nick stepped inside and flicked a switch.

Lights blazed. Taylor blinked in the sudden brilliance.

Nick turned around with a wicked grin on his face. "Welcome!"

"How did you manage this?" Taylor said.

He waggled his eyebrows. "Hey, lady, I got connections." He took her hand and drew her inside the enclosure.
His eyes lit with pleasure. "This is my baby. Max and I
helped restore it a few years back. I know you think carousels are kind of dumb, but I thought maybe if you saw a
really fine one in action…"

"It's lovely," she whispered, staring in awe.

She hadn't seen the carousel since she rode it as a tiny
child, and had never appreciated its beauty. The horses were
strong, lifelike, and yet appealing with their gentle faces and
large eyes. They had been painted to be so perfectly lifelike
that she felt as though their tossing manes would blow in
the breeze the moment the carousel started. How could she
have forgotten how much she had loved it as a child?

She turned to Nick. He looked like a young boy who'd
presented her with a shiny box and couldn't wait to see her
face when she opened it.

"So what do you think?"

For the first time she saw him as he must look when he
wasn't weighed down with worry, saw the laughter in his
eyes. He grinned down at her, no longer with a wolf's grin,
but with the smile of a joyous sixteen-year-old boy showing
off his first car to his girl.

"Isn't it great?"

"It's wonderful," she replied.

His big rough fingers intertwined with hers.

She felt her heart turn over, a flash of longing tingle from her fingertips along her nerve endings. She looked up at the curls around his ears and the crooked smile that she'd known from the first moment she'd met him would get her—sooner or later.

Oh, he is a nice man, she thought, *a good man, a gentle man. I want him to smile like this always. I want to be the one who fixes things for him. And I want to hold him and love him and feel his body against me and his lips on mine. I want him above me and inside me and smiling down at me. I want to feel his hands and his tongue and his body. I want to cherish him and have him cherish me.*

I want him to smile at me the way he smiles at the carousel. Forever.

No more casual lust. No more simple sexual attraction. He'd carried her across a threshold into magic. Under the benign gaze of the wooden horses, she felt a lingering chill break loose inside her, as though the last remnants of a glacier had tumbled and melted into a warm green sea.

She was terrified.

Alone was safe. Nick wasn't safe. She needed to stay on her guard, keep her distance, enjoy and be enjoyed without opening herself to the possibility of pain.

She'd been as armored as the horse she'd chosen to carve. Her protective shield was as impregnable as a bullet-proof vest. Cupid's arrow hadn't a chance of piercing her heart.

But Nick was peeling off that armor like layers of park paint. Underneath, she was naked and raw.

He turned to smile down into her eyes, and she nearly choked. She was certain that he could read her feelings in her face. All her instincts for self-preservation snapped to rigid attention, and, just as surely, this new vulnerable self kicked the stew out of them.

The moment passed. She hadn't leapt into his arms or

torn his clothes off or attached her lips to his mouth like a limpet. Although she'd wanted to. She gulped.

Maybe he hadn't noticed. *Please God,* she prayed, *let me not make a total idiot of myself.*

"Come on," he said and pulled her onto the platform.

They wove through the sleeping carousel while Nick explained about the horses—the outside row standers with three or four legs anchored firmly to the ground, the king stander—the largest lead horse. "They don't move up and down," he said.

She nodded. She didn't trust her voice. She watched Nick, not the horses. She tried to concentrate on his words, but the feelings that swept over her when she looked at him were so new, so scary that she kept losing her train of thought.

"The inside rows—the prancers with both forefeet in the air, the jumpers with all four off the ground—they move up and down," he said.

"There's not going to be a quiz later, is there?"

He laughed and patted a saddle. "I'll have you picking out Illions and Philadelphia Toboggan Company and Denzel and Parkers before you know it."

"Not in the next millennium."

Nick slid his hands down the bodies, legs, under the hooves, all over the horses, as though he had eyes in his fingertips. Taylor watched him, the sensitivity with which those long, callused fingers delved into the furrows in this one's mane or under that one's saddle. His face wore a gentle, secret smile as though he'd come home to long lost friends. She visualized those fingers delving into the secret places of her body, and couldn't breathe.

Suddenly he froze. His eyes popped open. His languid hands suddenly became urgent, sliding up over the ears of a second-row prancer. Then he began to shake his head. "No. It can't be. My God, it can't be."

"What?" Taylor went to him. He moved to the next horse in the line, and then he began to weave through them almost at a trot, reaching out to touch the left ear or right foreleg of each horse in turn. She held on to the pole and watched him until he disappeared around the curve, then heard his footsteps echo as he strode across the wooden planks until at last he came up behind her.

"What is it?" she asked. "What's wrong?"

"Taylor." He sounded sick.

"What?"

He pulled her roughly away from the gray prancer. "Look at the left ear."

"So?"

"My God, Taylor. It's mine."

She stared at him openmouthed. "But that's impossible." And then after a moment, "How can you know?"

He sank into the chariot behind her. His head dropped into his hands. She sat beside him and touched his arm. "Tell me." She wanted to cry out against whatever had lost him that smile, that peace.

Without raising his head he spoke. "I told you I instinctively recognized the hippocampus in Seattle as mine. That was only part of it." He raised his head to look at her and his eyes were frighteningly bleak. "I carved these things when I was twenty-five and arrogant as hell. I knew damned well they were good, and I knew a hell of a lot about how to fake anything valuable. I didn't want anybody to be able to do that, so I carved an identification into every one of my animals, Taylor. A mark nobody else knew about." He pointed. "That prancer has my mark. Somehow, God only knows how, a real antique horse has been replaced by one of mine."

"No way," Taylor said.

Nick nodded.

"Only one?"

He nodded again.

"What mark? This one doesn't look any different from the others." She stood, went to the prancer and ran her hand over the ears. Then she came back to him. "They're old. They've been restored dozens of times. It's just a coincidence."

"No. It's mine."

"That's what you were checking? For a nick in the wood?"

"Yeah. Left ear or right foreleg, sometimes both. Not a big nick, but big enough so that I could feel it when I touched it. My nick. My mark. The hippocampus had one on the tail fluke. My God, Taylor, somebody's stolen a real Denzel and replaced it with mine."

"How? When?"

Nick sank onto his haunches at the edge of the carousel platform. Taylor sat beside him, not daring to touch him.

Finally he spoke. "This carousel has been protected from the weather. It's in great shape, but there's wear and tear, and the damn thing is old. We pulled some of the horses off and took them to Rounders to repair—new mane carvings, belly pieces, even a leg or two. That's when it must have happened."

"Who helped?"

"Max. Only Max."

"But how could he swap off a horse without your knowing?"

"Very easily. The first horses I carved were modeled after these. It was the carousel I knew best. Max stayed late plenty of nights after I'd gone home. I was still living in Granddad's house and trying to get it ready to sell. All he had to do was wait until one of the real horses was ready to paint, swap it for one of mine after I left for the night, spray mine with a white gesso undercoat, take the real horse home and hide it somewhere so he could work on it in private.''

"But you recognized the nick tonight. Wouldn't you have seen the same thing then?"

Nick shook his head. "We worked on different horses once we got to that stage. The painting is where the real art comes in. You get proprietary about your horse. You just wait until you've got your first horse on its feet. You'll see what I mean."

"What would be the point?"

"Money. A real antique with a real provenance sold underground to a crooked collector would be worth big bucks."

"Couldn't someone else have done it?"

"No. Only Max." He turned to her, his face bleak. "Well, I guess we've solved our little puzzle. It's Max after all. Max from the beginning. My friend Max." The last was spoken with a wrenching bitterness. "No wonder he got so drunk tonight."

Her heart went out to him. "We have to go talk to him. Maybe he can explain all this."

"We're not just talking about carousels here. There have been two murders, remember. How about we go talk to him and he decides to get rid of us too?"

"We'll tell Mel first. There's no reason to kill us if it won't buy Max anything." She pulled herself up and reached down a hand to him. "Come on. Let's go find a phone."

Wood exploded from the platform two inches to the left of Nick's heel. He fell back and rolled across the platform towards the nearest chariot. "Down!" he yelled.

Taylor flung herself flat and began to wriggle towards Nick as the second bullet pinged against the metal pole a foot above her head.

The chariot was built of wood old enough and thick

enough to be as strong as steel and covered with layers of gesso and paint. Hit straight on, it would probably stop a bullet.

But they were trapped. All the shooter had to do was work himself around to get a clear shot at them as they hunkered down behind the chariot. They wouldn't see him or hear him. They were sitting ducks in a shooting gallery, spotlighted under the purple, gold and green lights of the carousel.

"Stay flat," Nick commanded. Taylor needed no urging.

"What do we do?" Taylor whispered. Her body felt hot with fear and her pulse throbbed in her throat.

"We're sitting ducks. I've got to get to the controls, give him a moving target," Nick whispered. "Stay here."

"Nick, no! He'll kill you!"

"Not if I'm lucky."

He began to wriggle across the floor towards the hole in the center that led to the controls.

Taylor's mouth was too dry even to pray aloud.

Nick dropped into the center well and slid towards the door of the control booth. A shot pinged against the metal door frame.

"Hell!" he snarled. His hand snatched at the handle. He dove inside. Taylor couldn't see him, but she heard him.

The band organ wheezed into life with a cheerful rendition of "In the Good Ole Summertime." The carousel began to turn. Lights blinked. Taylor felt as though she were trapped in a kaleidoscope.

She grasped the edge of the chariot with both hands and held on as the carousel picked up speed.

She couldn't get to Nick across that open space of gears and struts that held the platform. He couldn't get to her.

Taylor grabbed the nearest steel pole and felt herself jerked up. As the jumper's pole rose, so did she. As it sank, a bullet struck the pole just where her head had been a moment earlier.

She let go and slid behind the second chariot.

The music was loud above the whirring of the mechanism. The carousel spun faster and faster.

She could feel the centrifugal force thrusting her out towards the edge of the slippery floor. She lay flat, pressed her face against the wood, held on to the edge of the chariot, and prayed. Her stomach heaved.

A spurt of shots hit the wheelhouse. A mirror exploded into shards. Taylor cowered under the chariot seat.

She raised her head a moment later to try to spot a silhouette...the flash of a rifle barrel...anything. If Nick had been hit, she'd ride until she died or spun off onto the concrete.

Nick must live. She couldn't lose him now.

At first she wasn't certain whether the carousel slowed or whether she was too dizzy to care. Then she realized the strains of the "Tennessee Waltz" were becoming identifiable. The ponies moved up and down in an easy rhythm.

Finally the carousel jerked to a halt and rocked gently like an ocean liner moored at dockside. Edges of moonlight filtered through the enclosure windows. Had the thing run out of gas or had Nick stopped it? How did he know they were safe?

She heard shouts and running feet.

A moment later six guards with drawn pistols erupted into the enclosure.

"Please, don't shoot!" Taylor said, but she stayed prone just in case.

The door to the engine room opened. Nick stepped onto the platform.

"What the hell, Nick?" one of the guards shouted.

"Someone was shooting at us."

The guards hesitated a moment, then ran into the darkness.

Nick dropped beside Taylor. She threw her arms around his neck and buried her face against his shoulder.

"Oh, God, Nick, you're all right."

"I couldn't tell whether he'd hit you." He began to check her all over.

She clung to him.

"Come on," he said, and pulled her to her feet. "They won't catch him now."

"Whoa! I'm dizzy."

"I've got you, baby, I've got you. Hold on to me."

A large guard came into the enclosure and holstered his sidearm. "Whoever it was is long gone. What the hell happened?"

"Damned if I know, Jack."

"What I don't know is how anybody could miss." Jack snorted. "Must be one hell of a lousy shot."

"Not necessarily." Jack's partner, five feet ten and whipcord thin, leaned on the edge of the door frame. "You lock the gate behind you, Nick?"

Nick nodded.

"Must have been trying to hit you from the delivery lot."

"The angle of that first shot was down. Hit the platform." Nick pointed to a V-shaped groove in the wood.

Jack shrugged. "Stood on the hood of his car, maybe. Man, what you been up to?"

"Pissing somebody off big time," the smaller man said as he moved into the enclosure. "We're supposed to call the cops if anybody shoots off a firearm in the city."

"Yeah, yeah," Nick said.

"Ask for Detective Danny Vollmer," Taylor said.

VOLLMER DIDN'T SHOW UP to take statements, and by the time the police released Nick and Taylor, the clock on the tower of the amusement park had tolled twelve.

Nick suggested that they spend the night at Rounders. "I've got a sofa bed too," he said.

"You don't have Elmo," Taylor answered. "He's never going to speak to me again if he's run out of cat food. Besides, I don't intend to let anyone scare me out of my home."

"I was afraid you'd say that," Nick told her. He pointed to a gym bag on the backseat of the truck. "I came prepared this time." Wearily, he considered the misery of another night on that sofa bed, his body tormented not only by the springs under the thin mattress by but the vision of Taylor so close and yet so far above him.

"Eugene's probably through for the night," Taylor said, "but we can't count on that."

"We can't be sure it's Eugene."

Oh, yes we can, Taylor thought, shuddering at her memory. *But I can't tell you how I know.*

"Leave your truck at Veda's. We'll pick it up in the morning," Nick continued.

"Is that a good idea? Won't Veda worry when she finds it in the morning?"

"She'll just think we spent the night together."

Taylor closed her eyes. "Oh, great." *I wish.*

At her cabin, Nick reconnoitered before he let Taylor out of the truck. She realized she'd left the Glock in the console of a truck that sat twenty-five miles away. Should they be attacked, they were unarmed. "Great," she whispered.

Elmo's fury evaporated at the sight of a can of his favorite cat food. "If I ate the way Elmo does," Taylor said as she dumped the can into his dish, "I'd be the size of one of those chariots."

Nick watched her taut rear end as she bent over the dish. She was more like Elmo than she realized. Sleek and tight-muscled. He'd never found muscles sexy before. In fact, a woman like Taylor shouldn't be able to stir his blood, but she did. She'd done nothing but mess him up since the moment she walked into Rounders. He should kick her intrusive sleek rear end out of his life, out of his troubles, and out of danger.

Unfortunately, the best way to assure her safety was to keep her right by his side.

There was a moment tonight—after he'd turned on the carousel lights—when he'd thought she'd looked at him as a man rather than as a client.

He was fooling himself. What could a high-class, college-educated woman see in a guy like him? He wasn't much except a halfway decent wood carver with sawdust in his hair on his way to bankruptcy and, possibly, prison.

"You think they'll pick up Eugene for questioning?" he asked, to keep the conversation going. "I'd like to know for sure whether he's the shooter."

Taylor shrugged. "Who? Mississippi state police? Tennessee state police? Shelby County sheriff? Memphis police? Or even, for that matter, the police in Oxford? The way bureaucracies work he's probably safe until he dies of old age, or unless he wanders into some station house and demands to be locked up."

"He's going to keep trying to get us."

Taylor dropped onto the sofa. "I know. And sooner or later the law of averages will kick in." She leaned forward and looked at Nick, who leaned once more against the sink. "You weren't the only target tonight. He was after both of us."

"Yeah. You gonna call Borman?"

Taylor shook her head. "Not tonight. Should we sleep in shifts the way they used to do in Comanche country?"

Nick shook his head. "Unless Eugene has scored a rocket launcher I'd say we're safe enough."

"Good." Taylor stood. "Then I, for one, am going to bed. This day feels as if it started in September."

Nick couldn't sleep, and not because of the mattress, or even because of Taylor. He dreaded the coming of morning as much as if he were facing the gallows at dawn. Morning meant confrontation with Max.

He'd never known who had fathered him. His grandfather wasn't even a halfway decent role model, much less a friend. Max had needed a son, Nick had needed a father. They'd been a perfect fit.

Now, it seemed as though he'd never known Max at all. Had he projected his own needs onto Max so completely that he'd never recognized the weakness in the man? The viciousness he'd shown tonight with Josh Chessman couldn't be excused simply because Max was drunk. And Max seemed to be drunk often lately.

Could Max be trying to drown his guilt?

Max was a supreme pragmatist. If he needed money, he'd steal the animals and assume the thefts would never be discovered. Nick could carve more, couldn't he? Nick would never find out; therefore Nick would never be hurt.

But Nick had found out. And Helmut Eberhardt had died. Suddenly a simple business transaction had exploded into murder and arson.

Had Clara Eberhardt tried to blackmail Max? Tried to threaten him about her husband's death? Tried to get him to steal again?

Clara Eberhardt would have come to Rounders with Max without a qualm.

Would Clara have come with Josh? Maybe.

She'd have come with Veda. And Veda was an expert with chisels and she knew where a blow would be the most devastating.

Rico? Clara might be flattered by his attentions. He was not above seducing any woman he wanted.

Suddenly Nick sat up. He remembered the underwear in Clara's luggage. Had Clara been coming to meet a lover and had that lover been Rico? He realized they'd never checked to see whether there was a reservation at The Peabody in her name. Maybe Rico was the one registered.

Finally, there was Marcus Cato. Nick couldn't see Clara agreeing to join Cato in a darkened warehouse alone at night.

Unless Eugene Lewis came with her.

Maybe Eugene was a party to the murder. Maybe they'd been wrong about Eugene not having the brains to work a scam like this. Maybe he'd killed Clara himself. He knew his way around Rounders. He'd been there to help the Eberhardts steal the animals.

But he didn't have a key.

Or did he?

Nick's brain felt infested by a hundred white rats lost in a maze. He heard Taylor moving around in the loft above his head. Great. He'd never get to sleep at this rate.

He had two additional problems—maybe even more immediate than the murders and the recovery of the animals. First, he had to either get Taylor Hunt *into* his bed or *out of* his heart. Second, he had to keep them both alive.

CHAPTER TWELVE

"Ms. HUNT? This is Estelle Grierson. I hope I didn't call too early."

Taylor rubbed her eyes and glanced at the clock on the sofa beside Nick's sleeping form. Seven-thirty in the morning. She'd gotten up to go to the bathroom and had planned to go straight back to bed. She'd caught the phone on the first ring. Nick lay with his back to her and the sheet pulled up to his shoulders. "Of course I remember you, Estelle," she said. "You hanging in there?"

"As well as can be expected. The police released the body yesterday. We're having a small memorial service this afternoon."

Nick rolled over on his back and opened his eyes sleepily. He stretched, and the sheet slipped down to his waist. His naked chest rippled with muscles delineated by a thick mat of dark hair. Taylor turned away before he could see her flush.

"You know you said you'd be willing to help me go through some of Clara's things?" Estelle continued. "I was wondering if you'd have time this morning. I found another lockbox key with a tag to a different bank. A bank officer has to be with me when I open the box, but I'd kind of like to have somebody—you know—on my side."

Taylor snapped to attention. "Of course, Estelle." She turned around and nodded vigorously to Nick. She spoke as much for his benefit as for Estelle's.

"It'll take me—" she mouthed "us" silently at Nick

"—a couple of hours to get down there to help you open Clara's lockbox." She glanced at the clock again. "Say ten o'clock? Then maybe we could go by the house and the store afterwards. What time's the service?"

"Four this afternoon." Estelle sighed. "I'll pay you for your time, of course."

"That won't be necessary. I'll be glad to help." She hung up and turned to Nick. "Yes!"

He grinned at her.

"Come on," she said. "Up and at 'em. We'll pick up some breakfast on the way."

"Me too?"

"I'll tell her you're an expert in antiques. You are, aren't you?"

Nick grimaced. "I can fake it."

"Great." Taylor turned towards the bathroom. "Do me a favor? Call Josh Chessman and tell him I can't see him this morning, but for heaven's sake don't tell him why." She smiled. "You mind making a pot of coffee while I shower? I'll be dressed in ten minutes."

Nick watched her pad to the bathroom. She wore an oversize black T-shirt that ended just below her crotch and barely covered her bottom. He glimpsed a flash of white cotton panties and was suddenly fully awake and fully aroused. She didn't even realize how sexy she looked.

She treated him as casually as though he'd been one of her sorority sisters. He must have imagined the sparks between them last night.

He'd finally fallen into a deep sleep sometime in the early hours of the morning—so deep that he hadn't heard Taylor climb down the ladder from the loft. Only the ringing of the telephone had dragged him to consciousness. Sighing, he shoved Elmo off the sofa bed, straightened the bedclothes, closed up the sofa and slid the pillows back into place. He called Josh, but got Margery instead. With ill grace she promised to pass along the message.

Elmo jumped up on the kitchen counter and protested loudly that he was starving. Nick filled his dish and water bowl, took coffee beans out of the freezer, ground them, and made coffee. Two days and he was as integrated into Taylor's routine as into his own.

But not into her life. Damn. He found the gym bag with his change of clothes and razor under the dining-room table and sat down to wait for the coffee and the shower. He wondered what Taylor would do or say if he were to open the shower door and join her. She'd probably deck him.

A dozen feet away, Taylor stood under the shower with her nipples at full salute. Okay, so she'd experienced truly flagrant desire for Nick at the carousel. No way could she act on it. Still, this morning when he'd rolled over and smiled up at her with those big brown eyes, it was all she could do not to leap on him and ravish him right then and there.

There wasn't a nickel's worth of difference between her and CeCe Washburn.

She turned the shower gradually colder and colder until she began to shiver. Goose bumps covered her arms and shoulders. Her nipples shriveled, her groin tightened. Her teeth began to chatter.

Suddenly she revolted. No man was worth this kind of torture. She turned the shower back to hot, stood under it for another minute, then shut it off.

As she dressed, she began to wish she'd spent more time shopping at Victoria's Secret and less at K-Mart. Not that she and Nick would ever get to the point of stripping, but if—just if—they did, she'd prefer to show off something black and lacy rather than white cotton panties and a sports bra. She blew her hair dry and wondered if maybe she needed a little eye shadow and a softer pink lipstick.

One more day with Nick and she'd check in to the nearest spa for a fashion makeover and a body wrap. She gave her hair a vicious brush and curled her lip at her reflection. Then she pulled on the bulkiest black sweater she possessed, grabbed a pair of tube socks and went to find her shoes.

NICK LEFT HIS SPARE SET of Rounders keys inside Veda's storm door with a note that said they'd be gone all day and that she could open Rounders if she wanted to. Estelle Grierson might be suspicious of the Rounders truck.

A rime of frost lay heavy on Taylor's windshield. Nick scraped it while Taylor waited in the warm cab. On the one hand, she felt grumpy that he'd appropriated the job simply because he was the guy. On the other hand, she loved watching the muscles in his big shoulders and arms work across the windshield. If only she could appreciate him aesthetically, the way she would a Greek statue... Greek statues, however, did not have big brown eyes or gentle grins. And marble fingers would be cold, whereas Nick's...

Drat! She closed her eyes to shut out the sight of him.

On the drive down, Taylor called Mel and gave him a much-edited version of yesterday's encounter with the person they assumed was Eugene on the carousel. She also left a message at Rico's office about lunch, and managed to catch Marcus Cato on his way to surgery.

They picked up breakfast at a fast-food place, and Nick drove one-handed while he ate. The day shone with the pale gold clarity of a fine Chablis. There was no sign of Eugene. If he was still stalking them, he was being cleverer than usual about concealing himself.

"Dr. Cato will see me at four this afternoon at home," she said with an exaggerated British accent.

Nick sipped his orange juice and set it back into the holder on the console. "Tell me what you think of the house."

"Why?"

Nick chuckled. "You'll find out."

"Won't you be with me? Mel wants us to stick together."

"Eugene doesn't strike during daylight hours. I've got to see Max."

"Now wait a minute," Taylor said and set her coffee down so hard it spattered. "Don't you go bopping in alone."

Nick took his eyes off the road long enough to give her a long look. "I will tell Max first off that several other people know what I know."

"Oh, great. He picks you off and then he comes looking for me and Mel."

"He's not crazy." He pulled out to pass a silver four-horse trailer. "This morning I'm not even sure he's guilty."

Taylor snorted.

"Maybe Eugene killed Eberhardt and set the place on fire. No finesse required."

"I'll grant you that," Taylor said.

"Maybe Clara Eberhardt's death was accidental."

"Nick," Taylor said quietly. "With a chisel?"

Nick shook off her words. "Maybe he went into the front room for something, picked it up—"

"Nonsense."

For a moment Nick concentrated on his driving. Then he said, "If he's guilty, I'll persuade Max to turn himself in, get Rico to plead him down to voluntary manslaughter or something. I'll stand by him, whatever happens."

"You are crazy! He's a murderer, he sicced his damn junkyard dog Eugene on us, he's stolen from you, compromised your reputation, even stolen a valuable horse from a public carousel, for God's sake. What does it take to make you see reason?"

Nick shook his head stubbornly. "I don't abandon my friends."

Taylor made a sound halfway between a snarl and a groan.

"Listen, Taylor," Nick said, "I know what it's like to be abandoned. I'll make certain he can't do us any harm, but even if he's guilty, I'm not walking away from someone I love."

TAYLOR PRESENTED NICK AS A FRIEND with some expertise in antiques. Thereafter Estelle addressed herself to him exclusively.

Estelle left the thick stack of stock certificates and CDs in Clara's lockbox, took all the other papers, and followed them to a café on the square for lunch. After they were seated, Taylor began to sort through the papers.

Almost at once, she said, "Estelle, this is what you need." She held a sheaf of six or seven slick yellowing pages from an old-fashioned fax machine. "Listen to this: Lowestoft service for twelve, Georgian chocolate pot circa seventeen sixty... It's an insurance rider."

"How does that help?"

"After lunch we'll go to the house and match up the broken stuff with this list. You can show the insurance company that the things were destroyed and not sold."

Estelle squeezed a slice of lemon into her iced tea. "That's nice," she said absently.

Taylor glanced at Nick and shrugged.

"I could use some good luck," Estelle said. She buttered a slice of French bread and held it halfway to her lips as though she'd forgotten it was there.

Taylor laid her hand on Estelle's right arm, the one still holding the butter knife. "Estelle, you saw those stock certificates. I know you can't replace Clara, but just think, you can send your kids to Harvard if you like. Take a cruise. Redo the house."

Estelle set the bread down. "No, I can't. My husband

will reinvest everything he can and sit on it like a broody hen on a nest."

"But Estelle, it's yours, not his."

"He won't see it that way."

Taylor felt like shaking her. "What matters is the way you see it." Estelle turned empty eyes towards her. Taylor gave up for the moment, but vowed that whatever money was left after the Rounders problem was solved, Estelle would hang on to, by God, even if she went out and bought herself a gigolo and a cruise to Aruba.

"Don't worry about that now," she said. "Eat some lunch. You look exhausted."

Estelle smiled wanly, not at Taylor but at Nick. He smiled back. Taylor rolled her eyes and dug out more papers. She found the Eberhardt's marriage certificate and a life insurance policy on Helmut. With double indemnity it would pay Estelle as residuary beneficiary a quarter of a million dollars. Not bad for somebody who hadn't fitted into the local sorority scene at college. Taylor wondered how many of Clara's "prissy bitches" were doing nearly as well.

Taylor studied Estelle.

What did they know about the woman anyway? Somebody hired Eugene. Why not Estelle? She stood to make a considerable fortune from the Eberhardts' deaths. Much more, in fact, than whoever stole the animals would make.

Taylor made a mental note to check Estelle's whereabouts on Monday evening. The flight from Chicago took a little over an hour. Clara would have picked her up at the airport. No—that wouldn't do. Then they'd have gone to Rounders in Clara's car. Besides, Taylor didn't think Estelle had the gumption to kill anyone. She seemed genuinely fond of her sister.

But maybe CPA Grierson wasn't.

The deeper she got into this thing, the more suspects she uncovered.

The waiter brought salads crisp with radicchio and some sort of flower petals. Nick wrinkled his nose, then picked up his salad fork and gamely dug in.

Taylor shoved hers out of the way. "Bingo!" she said. "I think this is an inventory of the stuff that was in the shop." She ran her eyes down the first sheet of a computer printout. "It's dated the first of this month. Probably close to accurate. Eberhardt can't have sold many pieces on a day-to-day basis."

The list was single-spaced and ten pages long. The first column listed the item and its date of creation; the second, the amount paid to purchase it and the date it was bought; the third, what Eberhardt intended to rename the article; and the fourth, the asking price. Presumably there was another list toting up the actual sales.

"Whew!" Taylor said. "Listen to some of these. 'Armoire, Pennsylvania, nineteen-twenty, fifty dollars.' Sell as Amish country cupboard, late nineteenth century, five thousand dollars.' My Lord!"

Estelle turned to Taylor. "I told you he liked to rook people." A small smile played across her lips. "He always said it was their lookout if they didn't know any better."

Taylor glanced across the table at Nick. He was no longer smiling, but staring out the front window of the restaurant.

"Nick?" she said, and when he did not respond, "Nick!"

His head jerked back. "Sorry."

"Take a look at this." He sighed and ran his eyes down one page after another. He looked up at her and shook his head. No carousel animals listed. Maybe there was another list somewhere devoted entirely to stolen goods.

"You can probably salvage most of the stuff from the store itself," he said to Estelle. "Most of the furniture that was burned was in the storeroom at the back—stuff he hadn't finished aging. Upholstery will have to be redone and some of the wooden stuff will have to be cleaned, but he had a great stock of toys and small things. Listen to this: Uncle Sam children's bank, excellent quality. Waterford crystal bud vase. Gold and amethyst art deco pin. Twenty-four carat gold lady's pencil. Twenty-two-inch, triple-strand cultured pearls. Even some sets of baseball cards and an ivory chess set.''

"What should I do?" Estelle asked.

"I know somebody in the business," Taylor said, thinking of CeCe Washburn. "I'll call her for you, get her down here. She'll give you a decent price for everything that's left."

"Oh, would you?" Estelle put her hand over Taylor's. "I can't take much more of this." The waiter put a plate of Cajun pasta with shrimp in front of Estelle, and she burst into tears.

"Ma'am," he asked, "Is there something wrong?"

Estelle shook her head and waved him off.

ESTELLE UNLOCKED THE WRECK OF A STORE. The wind had finally blown away the stench of burned flesh, but in its place the reek of moldy upholstery and soggy wood leapt out at their senses. Nick opened the glass front door and held it for the two women.

"Please," Estelle whispered. "I can't." She turned away. "I'll wait in the car."

Taylor nodded to Nick. Better that way.

The fire wall between the workshop and the store proper had kept the flames from leaping across, but the smoke line lay only two feet above the floor. The water that had run across the concrete floor had soaked the threadbare Orientals and turned them into mud pies. Taylor coughed.

Nick walked down the aisle to the left, moving slowly among the armoires, chests and tables, each one covered with an assortment of grimy accessories. Taylor stood and watched him. He kept his hands in his pockets, and shrank away from touching any of the wood.

At the far back corner—closest to the wall of the workshop—stood a long glass display case. Beside the case sat a doll carriage, melted and twisted by the reflected heat and covered with shards of glass from the broken display cases. Taylor walked back to it and looked at the contents. There was the art deco pin, a beautifully elaborate piece constructed of angular bits of amethyst. The pearls were there as well, but blackened and scarred. She was able to identify several other bits—a beaded evening bag, and a broad piece of woven hematite that would have fit into the décolletage of a lady's bodice in nineteen hundred.

Nick came up behind her so quietly that she jumped when he spoke. "No carousel animals. Nothing but ashes behind the wall." She moved to the door, but he put a hand on her arm and shook his head. "Don't look. It's like a terrorist bomb hit the place."

Taylor shivered.

"Come on."

Taylor followed him outside. He locked the padlock on the front door and walked over to lean on the window of Estelle's car. Taylor heard him whispering to her without being able to catch the words.

Estelle nodded and drove off.

"We're going to follow her to the house," he said.

Ten minutes later Estelle opened the Eberhardts' front door to them. She had been crying. "It's so hateful," Estelle said.

"I know." Taylor sat her down in the front hall on a prayer bench that had survived the onslaught nearly intact. "Do you mind if I go upstairs?"

Estelle nodded and waved her hand at the staircase.

"I'm going to start clearing up the kitchen," Nick said.

All the upstairs rooms had been attacked, but without the single-minded ferocity Taylor had seen downstairs.

Apparently the Eberhardts had slept in separate bedrooms. The third bedroom was obviously a guest room, the fourth a study-library with floor-to-ceiling bookshelves and walls that had been sponged to look like aged leather. The books were mostly leather-bound editions bought by the yard for their decorative value. All had been struck from the shelves.

The desktop computer lay on the floor behind the desk, screen smashed, case cracked, cables ripped, keyboard broken. Whatever the Eberhardts had kept on that computer was long past restoring. She dug through the desk drawers searching for backup diskettes and found only bootlegged software.

She set the computer back on the desk and began to replace the books one by one, checking the pages and spine of each as she progressed. She found no notes or inserts.

The pictures had been thrown from the walls and lay half out of broken frames. She picked them up, checked to see that nothing had been slipped between frame and picture, then set them in a neat pile on the desk. They were probably valuable prints. Most of the glass had remained intact on the thick Oriental carpet, or had broken into large pieces.

An hour later the books were back on the shelves and the room was relatively neat. Her back hurt from all the stooping and she had a couple of nasty paper cuts on her fingers.

She went downstairs to find Nick and Estelle.

They were both in the kitchen. Nick wielded a mop on the last of the molasses. Estelle sat at the kitchen table sorting bits of china and crystal.

She was laughing.

Taylor felt a stab of jealousy.

A moment later Estelle saw her and gave her such a welcoming, happy smile that Taylor felt horribly guilty. Nick had managed not only to clean up the horrific mess but to cheer up Estelle while he did it. Most of the men Taylor knew would have set Estelle to the scrubbing while he made certain she worked to his specifications. Nick did it himself.

"Oh, Taylor, I can't thank you enough," Estelle said, and turned shining eyes toward Nick.

"I've only managed the study," Taylor admitted. "It's after two. Shouldn't you be getting back to the motel to get ready for the memorial service?"

Estelle's hand flew to her mouth. "My Lord, yes!"

They followed her to her car. "You will call your dealer friend?"

Taylor nodded. "Absolutely."

"I hate to ask you, but could you, maybe come back?" When Taylor hesitated she shook her head. "Not tomorrow. I know you're busy. But I can't go home until next week anyway. Maybe in a couple of days?" she asked shyly.

Taylor smiled and nodded. "I'll see what I can do."

TAYLOR PULLED INTO THE CIRCULAR DRIVEWAY beside a silver four-door Mercedes and climbed out. Marcus Cato's house looked as if someone had adapted the plans for the Parthenon into a single-family dwelling. Taylor climbed the wide marble stairs to the double front door and rang the prosaic twentieth-century doorbell. From deep within the recesses of the house she heard a muted bong. Almost at once the door opened.

The man who stood in the doorway had built the house to his scale. He stood four inches taller than Nick and outweighed him by perhaps a hundred pounds. His thick gray hair stood straight up above a broad glowing face the color of coffee with double-thick cream. His face was pocked with deep acne scars.

Taylor smiled and stuck out her hand. "Dr. Cato? I'm Taylor Hunt. Nick called you about me."

Even in jeans and a cotton sweater, Marcus Cato smelled of money. And sex. His impact was as physical as a blow.

He grinned hugely and stuck out a hand like a Smithfield ham. Taylor shook it and felt the soft, feminine skin of a man whose hands are his livelihood. His fingers felt long and fine, as though the hands of a concert pianist had been grafted onto the body of a linebacker.

"Come in," he boomed.

Across a broad deep-green marble foyer, a large atrium opened up under a colonnade that ran around all four sides. A fountain chuckled in the center under skylights that let in light but didn't trouble the conditioned air. It was like stepping back two thousand years into Pompeii or Rome.

"Wow!" Taylor exclaimed.

"Looks like an ordinary house from the outside, doesn't it?" said Cato.

"It looks like an ordinary house the way a railroad cottage resembles Blenheim Palace," Taylor said.

He slid a large hand under Taylor's arm and propelled her through the atrium and around the fountain. "Come on. You want to see the carousel stuff? It's in the den. That's where we really live." He opened French doors and stood aside for Taylor to enter an opulent room with maroon leather couches and a fireplace big enough to roast an ox.

Catty-corner to the fireplace stood an oversize armored carousel horse. Taylor was beginning to recognize the things. "Oh, nice," she said appreciatively. "A Muller?"

"Mine." Cato went over to it. "Sit. Drink." He reached out a hand and popped open the belly of the horse. The inside had been fitted out as a bar.

"Not for me, thanks."

Cato looked hurt, then brightened. "Soft drink, then?" Taylor suspected it would be easy to overlook the formidable intelligence in those eyes and the obvious skill in those hands, to get caught up in the sheer exuberant size of the man. She laughed. "Sure. Diet."

He dumped ice cubes into a heavy cut-crystal glass, reached deep into the neck cavity of the horse, pulled out a soda and handed both glass and drink to her. He poured himself an inch of straight Chivas. On the way to the couch across from her he casually brushed her shoulder. She caught her breath. A very sexy animal indeed, and he knew it.

"As Nick told you, I'm interviewing everyone who was at Rounders the day Nick called about the theft," Taylor said.

"Not guilty."

"I beg your pardon?"

"I didn't do it." Cato stretched his arms across the back of the sofa, balancing his glass on his open palm like a juggler. "Whoever stole those animals did it for money. I don't need money."

"There could be other reasons."

Cato shook his head. "Nope. Money."

"Are you really as rich as you look? My daddy always told me that doctors are lousy businessmen."

He laughed. "Your daddy was talking about his generation of doctors. My generation all have hotshot business managers."

"I've heard rumors that you had been having some marital trouble lately."

The balanced glass trembled a moment. Cato curled it into his palm and brought it to his lips. Taylor flushed. It had been a rude question, but maybe rudeness was the only way to get through Cato's impeccable veneer.

When he removed the glass from his lips, he grinned. He was back in control.

"Charlene and I have been married thirty-two years. We have no intention of divorcing each other. Neither of us could live this well on half of what I make and Charlene hasn't worked since I got my degree."

"No gambling, no drugs, no women?"

A smile played across Cato's wide mouth and the lids on his eyes drooped. "Oh, yeah, honey, I got the occasional woman. You interested?"

Taylor gulped. "Not at the moment, thank you."

Cato threw back his magnificent head. His laughter boomed across the room. "Child, you sound positively prim."

Taylor knew her face was flaming. "Women can be expensive extracurricular toys."

"The women I play with are ladies. They can mostly afford to play better than I can." He sipped his scotch. "Charlene and I have an arrangement. I don't mess with her charge accounts, she chooses not to see my ladies."

"I see."

"Now listen here, child. I didn't steal those animals and I sure as hell didn't kill that woman."

"You could have. You'd know right where to stab. It was either an expert job or a darn lucky one."

"Nope. I don't consort with the enemy."

"I don't understand."

"Don't let anybody tell you there is such a thing as a benign brain tumor. Anything that's in your pretty little head that God didn't put there to start with is going to kill you if I don't get it out. Death is the enemy. Makes me madder'n hell every time I lose to the bastard. I sure as hell wouldn't go killing some little bitsy woman over a couple of carousel animals."

"So where were you Monday night?"

"Elbow-deep in somebody's brain from four in the afternoon until two in the morning."

"Did you win?"

He grinned. "Damn straight I won. Death is going to have

to wait a few years for that one unless the guy gets hit by a truck.'' He rubbed his big hands over the glass as though warming them. ''I like winning.''

Taylor laughed. ''I bet.'' Then she sobered. ''How did you know Clara Eberhardt was little?''

Cato set the drink on the glass coffee table with studied casualness. ''Newspapers?''

Taylor shook her head.

He blew out a breath. ''Okay. Charlene went through a period when she doted on antiques. She bought stuff from Eberhardt before she got smart and started going to New York and London.'' He leaned forward with his elbows on his knees. ''I saw Clara Eberhardt at the shop a couple of times.''

''I got the impression she didn't have much to do with the shop.''

Cato shrugged. ''Sure she did. At least in those days. That's probably ten years ago now.''

So Cato knew the Eberhardts too. As she was forming another question, he leaned back and slapped his long hand against the leather of the sofa.

Taylor jumped.

''Dammit, woman, I want you to get whoever did this. Rounders matters to me.''

''I wouldn't have thought Rounders would be anything to you except a casual pastime when the weather's too sloppy for golf.''

''Don't you believe it. I hate golf. Stupid little white ball that doesn't ever go where you hit the goddamn thing.'' He wrinkled his nose. ''You ever hear the only difference between doctors and God is that God doesn't think he's a doctor? I've got more faith in me than in God, and I got plenty in Him. If I'm standing over your brain, you better pray I got that faith in myself. I walk that hospital like I own the place. Patients and nurses look up to me. But at

Rounders, all they care about is that I can carve a fur saddle pad so perfect you'd swear the buffalo just stepped out of it. I wouldn't screw that up for all the money in the Chase Manhattan National Bank.''

"Do you have money in Rounders?"

"No." He frowned at her. "You think Nick's in trouble financially?"

"He could be. It's odd that Max and Josh are investors when you're the one with the big bucks."

"Yeah, but Rounders was already up and running when I discovered it." He gestured at the oversize Muller. "'Course, everybody except Nick turned up their noses when I turned it into a bar. But hell, it works and I like it." He grinned at her. "And what I like, I do."

CHAPTER THIRTEEN

"I KNOW ABOUT THE CAROUSEL," Nick said. He walked into the sunroom, but this time he didn't sit down.

Max stiffened. "What carousel?"

"Last night I took Taylor to look at the carousel. I found the horse you substituted."

Max went still. A muscle worked at the corner of his mouth.

"Why'd you do it?"

Max turned away. "I don't know what you're talking about."

"Don't give me that crap. I never told you, but every one of my animals has a special mark on it. I found that mark. You were the only one who could have substituted the horse."

"You had more opportunity than I did," Max said coolly.

"You must have had a good reason."

Max's shoulders sagged and he sank onto the wicker sofa as though his legs wouldn't support him. "Why does anyone do something like that? For money."

Nick shook his head.

"Sit down, my naive friend."

Nick sat warily on the edge of the wicker chair.

"It was all very innocent—at first." Max leaned his head back and closed his eyes. "I was filling surface cracks on one of the Denzels, and I started thinking how closely one of yours resembled the one I was working on. I checked yours in the storeroom and couldn't tell the difference. That might have been the end of it, except that night after I got home—that very night—Michael called me from California. Mike Junior had been diagnosed with osteomyelitis and a resistant staph infection. Michael was crying. He wanted to try a new surgical technique and some experimental drug not covered by insurance. I couldn't believe I'd never seen my grandson and now he might be dying.''

"You just got a card from him. I saw it."

"He's fine now, but it was close." Max looked Nick full in the eyes. "Christ, Nick! This was my grandson we were talking about!''

"So you stole the horse."

"The next day I went to my bank for a loan, tried to take out another mortgage, cash in my life insurance—anything. Everyone was sympathetic but not helpful." Max sounded bitter.

"You never let on to me. I thought I was your friend."

"You were. You are." Max reached out a hand, then drew it back as though he'd realized he had no right to the gesture. "But you were struggling. I couldn't ask you for the money I'd put into Rounders."

"I'd have given it to you."

"How? It was spent. The place was barely making a profit, you didn't have enough money to pay the utility bills on time. I decided to take your horse and sell it."

Nick moved restively.

"Not the Denzel, but your copy. I knew I could get five or six thousand dollars for it quickly. That would pay the immediate bills. Then when I started spraying the Denzel, I thought how much more money I could get for a real restored Denzel with provenance. You know there are collectors who don't ask questions as long as it's authentic. Hell, we could both name half a dozen off the tops of our heads right this minute."

"So you called one of them."

"I'm not proud of it, but yeah." Max shrugged. "He offered me twenty thousand cash on the front end, no questions asked. I wired the money to Michael the same day, then I took the Denzel home and hid it upstairs while I painted it. I damn near gave myself a heart attack living on coffee and no sleep for a week, but I finished it and shipped it." He stared defiantly at Nick. "And by God, given the same circumstances, I'd do it again."

"Did anyone know?"

"Of course not. Why?"

"You said you had it here for a week. Where?"

"Upstairs in the back room. When people were here, I hid it in the closet."

"What people?"

"On top of everything else, that was the week we had the Rounders end of the year party. There must have been fifty people in the house that night."

"Did anyone go upstairs?"

Max snorted. "Everyone who wanted to use the bathroom. It was the only one I had working at the time."

"Was the closet locked?"

"Hell, no. Who goes snooping in other people's closets?"

"But someone could have seen the Denzel and recognized it."

"Why wouldn't they say something?"

"Maybe it meant nothing at the time. Max, did you steal the other animals?"

"That's the only time I've ever stolen anything in my life."

"Uh-huh."

"It's the truth."

"Did you kill Clara Eberhardt?"

Max came off the sofa in one swift lunge. "Of course I didn't."

"Because if you did," Nick continued as though his

friend had not spoken, "turn yourself in. We'll get Rico to work out the details with the police."

Max gaped. "You really think I did it?"

Nick shook his head miserably. "I don't want to, but you've admitted to stealing one horse and lying about it."

"To save my grandson's life," Max said with growing hysteria. "Nick, Nick, my boy, I didn't steal your animals, and I swear I didn't kill Clara."

Nick sat back and watched his old friend in silence. After a moment, he said, "How are we going to handle the Denzel?"

"I don't know what you mean."

"You'll have to go to the management, tell them about the substitution."

"No! They don't know the difference."

"But I do," Nick said quietly. "Maybe they'll want to let sleeping dogs lie. I hope so. The publicity for Rounders could be pretty bad. But if they don't, you're going to have to give up the person who bought it and repay the money. Even then, they may still press charges."

"Nick, I'm too old to go to prison."

"I think Rico can get them to let you repay the money. We'll find it somehow." Nick thought with near despair about the thirty-five thousand dollars he owed Pete Marley, now topped by an additional twenty. Even if the Eberhardt estate paid off, getting the money would take years.

"You'd send me to prison over a goddamn Denzel horse?"

"You've got to tell the truth."

"And if I refuse?"

"Then I will."

"I need a drink," Max said. He went to the kitchen and came back with a beer. He didn't offer Nick one.

"The police will think I killed Clara," Max said when he sat down again. "You do."

"I think you're responsible even if you didn't use the chisel."

"What do you mean?"

"I think that during the party somebody found the horse stashed in the closet, and that led to the rest of it."

"Nonsense."

"Is it?"

"Christ, Nick, I hope it's nonsense." Max drained his beer. He seemed to have aged fifteen years in fifteen minutes. "Give me some time before we deal with the amusement park. Give me until the police find who killed Clara. Then I won't be on the hook for that as well."

Nick thought about it. "Yeah. Okay." He smiled sadly at his old friend. The smile turned to a look of deep concern. "You won't do anything dumb will you?"

"Like kill myself?" Max laughed ruefully. "No. I haven't lived a particularly honorable life, but I'm not going to put a forty-five to my head in the officers' club for the good of the regiment."

"I REFUSE TO SLEEP on that damn sofa bed again tonight," Nick said.

For a moment he thought Taylor had broken the telephone connection, then he heard her sigh. "I understand. Take the loft."

"After dinner we'll feed Elmo, you pack a bag and come to Rounders for the night. I have a futon."

He heard her laugh. "You got a deal. Wagons in a circle?"

"And triple-lock the doors."

"Mel says to meet him at Veda's right now. He's got some financial information and I want to hear from you how it went with Max."

"Yeah."

"Nick, are you all right?"

"Not really. See you in a few minutes."

He pulled into the parking space right beside Veda's compact just as Taylor pulled in on the other side. Mel's land yacht sat two spaces down.

The front door of Veda's townhouse opened before either of them could get out of their cars. "Get in here," Mel said. Veda peered from behind his shoulder the same way she'd first peered at Taylor from behind Harvey.

"What's the urgency?" Taylor asked.

"I'm hungry," Mel rumbled. He shut the door behind them. He held a cup of coffee in his left hand and seemed thoroughly familiar with the place. "I've been talking to Veda for the last hour and hoping you two weren't dead in a ditch somewhere. I thought I told you to stay together after dark."

"It's not dark," Taylor answered.

"Good as."

"So where are we dining, master?"

"Right here," Veda said. "Just chicken and a green salad."

Nick turned to Taylor. "Veda's a hell of a cook. She brings me brownies all the time."

During dinner Taylor and Nick reported on their day.

Taylor watched Veda's face drain of color when Nick told them about the theft of the animal. "I would have given him the money," she whispered. "Why didn't he ask me?"

Taylor noted she didn't say "lend" but "give."

"And I'll bail him out now if it comes to that," Veda continued.

Mel harrumphed like an angry bull and helped himself to his third piece of chicken. Taylor caught him looking at Veda and wondered if there was something going on between them. Mel hadn't looked at another woman in the eight years since his wife walked out on him to marry an engineer from Phoenix she'd met on a camping trip. If he was falling for Veda, she was going to break his heart. She watched Nick and thought the Borman Agency was batting zero for two: Nick was probably going to break her heart as well.

They moved into the living room for coffee. Mel settled in the leather recliner that had probably been Bill Albright's, and groaned with pleasure. "You want to hear what I found?"

"Give."

"First, Chessman makes eighty-five thou a year in salary and half again as much in consulting fees. Margery brings in about forty thou, tax free, from a trust fund she inherited when her mother died. She pays for the parties and the charity balls. She's mounting quite a campaign to get into society and get Josh a cushy job."

"Nothing unusual?"

Mel shook his head. "Not that I can find. They live up to their income, but Josh could well afford the money he put into Rounders three years ago. It doesn't make much money, but it's a good tax write-off."

Nick nodded. "I'm the only one who takes a salary, and I don't take much."

"Max Beaumont has some investments, his army pension, and not much else. He's way overextended on that money pit he lives in. He's got a second mortgage and pays off the interest on his credit-card debt without making much of a dent in the principal. I can see why he wasn't a good risk when he needed money for his grandson. If he told the truth."

Nick raised his head. "What do you mean?"

"How would you have reacted if he'd said he stole the Denzel to get enough money to take some twenty-year-old floozie to Vegas for a week?"

"Max wouldn't do that!" Veda said.

"Tomorrow I'll find out. If the boy was treated, there

will be records." He leaned back in his chair. "Rico Cabrizzo is no tough little Boston hood. His family runs canning and bottling plants all along the northeast coast. He was born with a silver spoon in his mouth, went to a fancy prep school before he went to Harvard."

"So he never ran away to join a carnival?" Nick asked.

"He worked at Old Orchard Beach amusement park a couple of summers while he was in high school."

"So does he need money?"

"He plays the ponies, drives a Porsche. He could use the money. Thing is, I don't see any sign that he's getting an infusion of capital from anywhere."

"How about Marcus Cato?" Taylor asked.

"He and his family spend money like water, but he makes megabucks in his practice. I doubt he's hurting for cash."

"Great. We've learned nothing."

"Not quite," Mel said. "The one who needs money the most is you, Nick."

"Now wait a minute," Nick said.

"Rounders pays you a subsistence salary, gives you a place to live and lets you write off most of your expenses. You have less than a thousand dollars in your checking account and less than five thousand in savings. If Rounders stays closed because of this, you could lose everything."

"I will anyway if I have to pay off Marley. Selling my remaining animals and getting another mortgage on Rounders may possibly keep me from bankruptcy if I can unload them quickly. Are you saying that gives me a motive for the murder?"

"Maybe somebody wants Rounders to close. Say you liquidate everything. Josh, Max, and even you could walk away with twenty or thirty thousand apiece. A developer would probably pay a pretty penny for that building."

Taylor threw up her hands. "I don't buy it."

"Me neither," Nick said.

"The point is that nobody's excluded," Mel said.

"And then there's Eugene," Nick said.

"I talked to Vollmer about him today," Mel said. "He seems to have dropped off the face of the earth."

"That doesn't mean he's gone for good," Taylor said.

"No. So be careful."

"Would you two like to stay here, dear?" Veda asked.

Taylor looked around the small living room. "Thanks, Veda, but I think we'll be safe."

"Nick, are you opening Rounders tomorrow?" she asked.

"Why not? Yeah, sure." Nick smiled at her. "Let's try to act normal. Besides, as Mel discovered, I need the money."

NICK AND TAYLOR MADE THE TREK to feed Elmo, and the return trip, with no sign of Eugene.

"Want a drink?" Nick asked as soon as they'd reached his living room.

Taylor shook her head. She felt uncomfortable here with Nick. From the way he stood uncertainly by the refrigerator, he wasn't too comfortable either.

"So, you want to go to bed early or what?" he asked.

"What?"

Nick flushed. "I mean, it's been a long day, we didn't get much sleep last night." He pointed at the futon.

"I'm not sleepy." Taylor prowled the bookshelves. A few paperback thrillers, stacks of books on cabinetmaking, antiques and carousels. Some of them looked very old and very fine. "You told me your grandfather taught you about carousel horses, Nick. How old were you when you carved your first one?"

"Twenty-two."

"Really? I don't know why, I thought—"

"Drop it, okay?"

"Certainly. I didn't mean to pry." She knew she sounded huffy.

"No, I'm sorry." He sank into the prairie armchair across from the futon. "I want to thank you for the work you've done."

"That sounds like a pink slip."

"No, but I don't think we're going to find out who stole the horses and killed the Eberhardts."

"Wow, you are down," she said.

"Yeah. I guess. I keep finding out things about my friends I'd rather not know."

"I warned you there'd be a price to pay."

"Even if we find the horses, I may come out of this with no friends left. Max and I can't ever get back to where we were."

"Maybe you can. Besides, there's Veda. And me."

"Yeah. Thanks."

She watched him a moment. There was no sign of the joy he'd shown last night when he looked at the carousel. He seemed far away in a lonely, unhappy place. She ached to take him in her arms. Instead she said gently, "Truth can sometimes hurt."

"Truth always hurts." He shifted in his chair.

She dropped down on her knees beside him. She wanted to shake him. "Stop that! We've found out a lot, Eugene is safely outside the wagons, we're alive, we're healthy. Anything else we can deal with."

He smiled. His hand slipped up the back of her neck to ruffle her hair. "Tough cookie."

She felt her breathing lurch at his touch. "Right." For a moment they stared at one another. Then he bent and kissed her gently.

Her body seemed to have developed a mind of its own. She moved closer to him and felt his other hand against the small of her back, drawing her deeper into the kiss. She felt his tongue tease her mouth and answered it with her own. Flame ran along her nerve endings to converge deep in her belly.

She drew away breathless and stumbled to her feet. "Oh, God, I can't."

He stood. One arm slid around her, bringing her against him from knee to breast. She felt him hard and demanding.

Her head dropped back, unresisting. He kissed her eyes, her ears, leaving trails of heat and desire wherever his lips found her skin.

"You're a client," she choked.

He kissed her again. "You're fired," he whispered.

Her eyes snapped open. "What?"

He grinned down into her face lazily. "Fired, pink slip, kaput."

"But—"

He stopped her mouth with another kiss. She resisted.

He broke the kiss and held her away from him. "I can always hire you back tomorrow morning," he said and grinned.

She laughed. She ran her hands up his back and felt the muscles work beneath her fingertips. She felt him shiver as she caressed the nape of his neck, then curl her fingers in his hair. "That's harassment," she whispered as his lips inched down to the hollow at the base of her throat.

"Uh-huh," he mumbled. His left hand slid under her sweater. She felt the snaps on her bra open. Then that oh-so-educated hand slid around beneath her bra to capture her breast.

As she felt her body sink into his, she whimpered, "Blackmail."

TAYLOR WAKENED BEFORE DAWN, stretched lazily and registered that she ached with the sort of pleasurable pain she hadn't experienced in ages.

She gazed at Nick, who slept with his back to her. Everything she had feared in that first moment she saw his lopsided grin had come to pass, only worse than she could have imagined.

Last night he'd needed a woman, the comfort she provided, the physical release, perhaps even the ecstasy.

She felt as though she'd been blindsided.

Because last night was much more than physical release or comfort for *her*. Before last night she'd never known the *meaning* of ecstasy. She'd never guessed she was capable of the passion, the abandon, that Nick had evoked. He seemed to know things about her body that she'd never realized herself before he caressed her, joined his body to hers. Nick had wrested control from her and accepted nothing less than total surrender.

She'd never again be willing to settle for less. And that presented problems.

Irene Maxwell had had kittens over the unsuitability of Danny Vollmer, a homicide detective who wore Nicole Miller ties and boasted a master's degree in criminal justice. She'd have a stroke over Nick, a man who actually had calluses on his palms.

Irene would never understand that the lunk in the dusty jeans was one of nature's true gentlemen—something Paul Hunt had never been for all his fancy clothes and his fancy career.

At the memory of the heights of pleasure Nick's callused fingers had coaxed from her, Taylor wriggled and felt her body awaken to full-blown desire all over again.

Nick sighed and turned over. He smiled at her lazily and touched her arm. He did have the most beautiful brown eyes. She bent to kiss him.

"Am I rehired?" she whispered.

"Not yet," he whispered and rolled over on top of her.

CHAPTER FOURTEEN

"I CAN'T COOK, but I can manage breakfast," Nick said as he flipped rashers of bacon in a hot iron skillet. "After last night I think we can probably handle the cholesterol."

Taylor wrapped her arms around him from behind and leaned her cheek against his shoulder. Her hair was still damp from the shower.

"Hey, woman," he said, "you're getting me all wet."

Her hand slid down the front of his jeans. "So are you complaining?"

He caught his breath. "I'm liable to do myself an injury here if you keep that up."

"You haven't rehired me yet. I'm holding you hostage until you do."

He quickly slipped the bacon slices onto a paper towel and the skillet onto a cold burner. "Now," he said, turning around and pulling her against him, "about this hostage situation we've got growing here..."

"*Big* hostage situation," she whispered.

His hands slid down to cup her bottom and raise her against him. He nuzzled her neck softly. "Be a shame to let a really great negotiating ploy go to waste."

"Ploy?" She laughed and tilted her head back to smile up at him. "Never heard it called that before."

"Works for me."

"Thought you wanted breakfast."

"You taste a hell of a lot better than bacon." He picked her up and carried her back to bed.

Twenty minutes later she lay curled against him, his arm around her shoulders, her fingers playing with the dark hair on his chest.

"Am I rehired or do I have to do some more negotiating?"

"Damned right you do. But not right this minute."

"Nick!" She bit his shoulder.

"Ow!" He turned and wrapped his arms around her. "Okay, you convinced me. You're rehired." The smile left his face and his eyes. "For all the good it'll do."

Taylor raised herself on one elbow. "I promise we will fix this."

He caressed her hair. "I didn't want this to happen, Taylor."

"Thanks so much."

He shook his head. "That didn't come out right. I wanted—want—to make love to you, but not if it means I have to worry about you even more than I do now."

She sat up. "Mel worries enough for both of us. Don't you start with me." She stood and began to search for her underwear.

"Taylor…"

"No. I'm rehired. You're the client again."

"Forget last night happened? I can't."

"Don't forget it. Just ignore it. For the moment. Okay?" Taylor asked.

"Maybe you can keep business and pleasure in separate compartments. I can't."

"Well, one of us has to." She sat on the edge of the bed and kissed him. "Please, Nick."

He sighed and began to dress.

When they finally sat down to bacon and muffins, Nick said, "You asked me last night about my grandfather and the carousel horses."

Taylor nodded.

"It's time I told you."

"So tell. I must admit I heard he was something of a rapscallion."

"And a hypocrite. He was a deacon in his church. He practically kept my mother chained in her room. First chance she got, she went hog-wild and came up pregnant. He wanted her to tell him who the father was so that he could force the boy to marry her. She wouldn't. I still don't know. The only name on my birth certificate is hers."

"Poor girl."

"He kicked her out and forbade Gram to see her. She was just a kid herself. It was tough. I got all this later from my gram."

"But you said your grandfather raised you."

Nick picked up the wooden pear from the center of the table. "My grandmother really raised me—" he paused "—after."

His voice remained unemotional, but his hands gave him away. That first night Taylor had watched him caress the wood. This morning his knuckles were white as though he wanted to crush it to sawdust.

"My mother used to get her dates to bring us to the park so I could ride the carousel, and after I got old enough to ride alone, they'd give me tickets to get rid of me, get her alone for a while. I knew what they were doing, but I didn't care. The carousel was bright and noisy and beautiful, not shabby and dirty the way it was at home. I felt I like a knight in armor. Nobody could hurt me. Nobody could even catch me." He stared at his hands and seemed to realize what he was doing to the pear. With a sigh he set it back into the bowl of wooden fruit and clasped his hands tightly in front of him.

For a moment he sat silent, then leaned back, closed his eyes, and began to speak again, "One day she stuck an envelope in my pocket, handed me the biggest fistful of tickets I'd ever seen, kissed me and put me on my horse to ride until the tickets were gone.''

Taylor felt a shiver run up her spine. She didn't think she could bear to hear what was coming.

"By the time the tickets were gone, so was she." He opened his hands like a magician making a dove disappear.

"What did you do?" she whispered.

"The letter was to my grandfather and grandmother, asking them to take me in. Her latest man didn't want me as part of the deal. The security guards or somebody must have called them, because my grandfather came and took me to his house. It was the first time I ever saw him."

"Oh, God, Nick."

"My grandfather couldn't let his precious church know he'd shirked his duty. He had to take me." The venom in his voice made her catch her breath.

"How you must have hated her."

He looked at her, startled. "I hated my grandfather. He was the one who sent her away. I used to pray she was dead so she had an excuse not to care about me. Then I decided it must be my fault."

"Yours? How could any of it be your fault?"

"If she hadn't gotten pregnant, she'd have been home where she belonged. My grandfather told me over and over that I was the 'fruit of her sin.'''

Taylor went down on her knees beside his chair, wrapped her arms around him and pressed her head against his chest. "It's a miracle you're the man that you are."

He stroked her hair. "I guess my gram loved me enough to keep me straight. And the old man did teach me to build and carve. He worked twelve—fourteen hours a day. He was a genius in his way."

She looked up at him, her eyes bright with tears. "Nick, if my mother had abandoned me that way, I wouldn't love carousels, I'd spend the rest of my life blowing the damn things up.''

"I did hate them. Then right after I graduated from high school Gram gave me a shoe box. Every year on my birthday until I was sixteen my mother had sent me a birthday card and a carousel horse—sometimes only a picture, mostly just Christmas tree ornaments, but something that showed she remembered and loved me. My grandfather told my gram to destroy them. Gram was afraid to give them to me at the time, but she hid them for me until then. But she paid for it,'' he said dryly.

"He found out?''

"Oh, yeah. When Gram gave me the shoe box, I went out and got drunk. I stayed out all night. I must have read those letters a thousand times. Before I went home I gave the box to my best friend to keep. Knew I'd get a beating, but I was mad enough to kill my grandfather.''

"You told him you had the things?''

"Gram already had. When I walked up the back steps that morning I heard him yelling at her. I was still a little drunk. He was a big man, and strong. She'd been serving him breakfast at the kitchen table. He didn't even look at her, just lashed out and knocked her against the refrigerator. The dish went flying. I still remember the sound it made when it broke on the floor.''

Taylor stared at his profile. His voice had dropped to a whisper.

"I was eighteen, with a bad hangover and mad as hell.'' He blinked and turned to stare into her eyes.

"I kicked the chair out from under him, yanked him up off the floor and slugged him. I pinned him against the wall with my hands around his throat. I could hear Gram screaming and feel her beating on my back, begging me to stop. I told him that if he ever raised a hand to either of us again, I'd kill him.''

"My God, what did he do?"

"He called me a spawn of the devil, said he'd have me locked up, said he'd beat the skin off my back, said he'd call the police, said he should have strangled me and let the dogs eat me."

"Did he have you arrested?"

"Hell, no. I told him if there were any police to be called I'd be the one calling them, and then I'd call his preacher and tell the whole congregation what a hypocritical wife-beating monster he really was and how he made his money faking antiques. I think that scared him, but not nearly as much as when I started laughing at him. He thought I'd gone nuts."

"So how did it end?"

"I walked out, joined the army and didn't go home for four years. He wouldn't even let me come back for Gram's funeral two years later. God, I still miss her."

"Did you ever see him again?"

"I wound up taking care of him until he had to go into a nursing home, taking over the business—running it honest, for a change—to pay his bills in the nursing home until he died."

"Did you ever forgive him?"

"We forgave each other. I guess in his way he really loved me, as much as he was capable of love. Hate eats you alive, Taylor. Gram tried to teach me that."

"Did you ever find your mother?"

"Gram said she died when I was sixteen—that's why the cards and presents stopped."

Taylor still knelt at his feet. "How can you be so calm about all this?"

He smiled at her. "It's not new to me, babe. Tell a story often enough and you get some distance, get to see things a little clearer. Most people try to do the best they can. Even my poor mother."

"Do you know what happened to her?"

"She married. Never had any other kids. I hope she found some peace. My granddad and I did finally. And I came back to the carousel."

He put his hands under her arms and stood up with her against him. She clung to him and felt the tears running down her cheeks.

He stroked her hair. "Hey, it's okay." He held her away from him. "That why I love carousels, Taylor. Nobody ever gets lost on a carousel—they just go around the curve and out of sight for a while, then they come back with music and bright lights."

"Why are you telling me this now?"

"Because last night wasn't any one-night stand, at least not for me. I want you to know about me, about what makes me tick—maybe warn you."

She stepped away. "Warn me? About what?"

"You told me about your dad and about Paul and Vollmer. I saw you with your brother, remember? I know how you feel about violence. I guess I'm about the mildest human being this side of Caspar Milquetoast most of the time, but there's violence in me too. I know it, I feel it. It scares the hell out of me."

"You forgave your family, Nick. And you're still making allowances for the friends who betray you. But there's one other person who truly deserves your forgiveness."

"Who?"

"You, yourself. There's violence in all of us. In me too. All we can do is fight it or channel it. I wanted to kill Paul. Three teenagers did it for me."

"But you didn't hit him before he left."

"If I'd hit him, it would have been with an iron skillet or a brass lamp. I had enough sense not to want to spend the next seven to ten years in jail for manslaughter, but the desire was there. My mother thinks I sold everything, moved to the country, cut my hair, changed my lifestyle, even went to work for Mel all because of grief.'' She shook her head. ''I never was the child my parents thought I was. This is me. Abrasive, difficult, nervy, opinionated, bad-tempered—''

''—beautiful, passionate, tender, empathetic.'' He grinned at her. ''Opinionated and nervy I'll buy.''

''Thank you very much. But we were talking about you. Don't you think it's time you let go of your guilt over your grandfather?''

He shook his head. ''There's worse.''

''What could be worse?''

''I learned what my grandfather taught me because I loved the wood, but I was a troublemaker. I'm lucky I graduated. I spent more time in the principal's office than I did in class.''

''So? Hardly surprising, given your background.''

''Today they'd say I had an attention deficit disorder. Then they just said I was stupid. My grades were lousy. Except in shop. There was this shop teacher, a little scrawny guy named Mr. Archer. He took an interest, let me stay after school and work with him. I betrayed him, Taylor. I stole a Skil saw from the lab.''

Taylor exhaled. ''Did he find out?''

''Oh, yeah. I already outweighed the guy by fifty or sixty pounds and was maybe five or six inches taller, but he lit into me with everything he had. Then he sat me down and told me all about honor. I brought back the Skil saw two hours later. I've tried to live up to Mr. Archer's standards ever since.''

''I wonder if he knows?''

''He knows all right. He retired about six years ago. I still go over there for barbecues in the summer, and his grandchildren have their own private carousel horse to play with. Thing is, Taylor, I stole from my friend, and I beat up my grandfather. I work with my hands in a business that barely makes ends meet, and I create—as you told me the first day we met—stupid toys. I've got you mixed up in murder and put your life on the line right along with mine. If you've got any sense, you'd pick up your satchel and go home to Elmo before you get hurt. And if I had any sense, I'd damn well make you.''

"Don't try it, buster," Taylor said. She shoved him into the chair and wriggled into his lap. "You're a good, decent man and a hell of a craftsman. You also do certain other things moderately well.''

He grinned and ran his hand up her back.

"I refuse to allow you to drown in self-pity or wind up in bankruptcy court because you feel that's what you deserve.''

"Where do we go from here?''

She stood and took his empty plate and her own to the sink, rinsed them and stuck them in the dishwasher. "I have the feeling we know more than we think we do," she said thoughtfully.

He watched her.

"What time is it?" she asked suddenly.

"Nine-twenty. Why?''

"Because I just got an idea. If it pans out, we're on our way.''

She picked up the telephone book on the side table, checked a number and dialed it.

"Good morning," she said brightly. "To whom am I speaking?" She listened, covered the mouthpiece and motioned Nick towards the extension in the bedroom. He went in and picked it up, careful not to make any noise.

"Thank you so much, Mrs. Oliphant. I have a problem I hope you can help me with.''

"Ma'am?" A thickly accented southern voice came down the line.

"My accountant is trying to do my end-of-the-year tax statement, and he's ready to kill me. I cannot for the life of me find the receipt for my county taxes this year. I keep thinking I must have paid in August when I paid the city taxes, but without the receipt I just don't know. Could you look them up for me?"

Nick heard a sigh. "Yes, ma'am," the voice said wearily. It was obviously not an unusual request. "Name?"

"Fields. Clara Fields." Taylor crossed her fingers and held her breath.

After a moment the voice came back. "Yes ma'am, you paid both of 'em. Which one?"

Taylor's eyes widened. She'd thought they might have one storage location, not two. "Uh—better give me both." She hesitated a moment. "Maybe I didn't get the receipt because the address is wrong or something. What addresses do you have for me?"

The bored voice answered at once. "Forty-eight sixty-two Park Lane Terrace."

"Yes, that's correct." Taylor stuck the telephone between her ear and shoulder and scribbled on the front of the telephone book.

"And thirty-three fifty-five Newcomb."

"What zip code?"

A deep sigh. "Three-eight-one-four-six."

Taylor wrote. "Thank you so much, Mrs. Oliphant," she trilled.

"Y'all want me to send copies of those receipts?"

"That would be wonderful. What address are you sending them to?"

The voice suddenly sounded sharp. "We've been sending them to Mississippi. Is that correct?" Suspicion began to eddy down the line.

"Wonderful. Thanks so much." Taylor hung up the phone and shouted.

Nick came out of the bedroom grinning. Taylor was dancing around the room like a madwoman.

"At last! A decent piece of luck."

Nick leaned against the doorjamb. "I am impressed."

Taylor winked at him. "Well, you should be." She sobered. "Now, all we have to do is figure out which one has the animals."

"No telling."

"So we start with the closest one." Taylor picked up her satchel. "Come on, we can call Mel from the car and you can tell him what a brilliant investigator I turned out to be."

"WHA—?" MAX SAID SLEEPILY, as he opened the door.

A stubble of white beard gleamed on his cheeks. His eyes looked sunken, the whites unhealthily yellow and webbed with red veins. He seemed to have shrunk.

Veda gave him one stern glance and pushed past him. He followed her to the kitchen. She nodded approvingly at the full coffee pot, pulled down a couple of mugs from the shelf beside the sink and poured each of them a cup. Then she handed Max his, and sat down at the kitchen table.

"Sit," she ordered.

He obeyed, warily.

"Maximillian Jefferson Beaumont, you are not a jerk, you're an idiot," Veda said.

He drew himself up. "Now wait just a damn minute, Veda—"

She held up her hand. "You could have confided in any of us about your grandson. We'd have helped you even if we had to stand on Main Street with tin cups. You chose to steal. You slapped every one of us in the face, starting with Nick, whom you profess to love. If that's your idea of love and honor, I pity the men you led into battle."

"Now, hold on. I protest—"

"We, you and I, are going to fix things now, today."

Max stared at Veda as though he'd never seen her before.

Veda waved her hand around her. "How many square feet do you have in this place?"

Max stammered. "About five thousand." Then he rallied. "Hell, Veda, I will not live anywhere but this house."

"You'll be sharing a six-by-ten cell with three very large and possibly amorous men if you don't listen up," Veda continued. "I'm not asking you to sell this house. I'm asking to share it with you."

Max gaped at her. "But, but…"

She waved a hand. "I'm not going to move in with you. Frankly, at the moment I'd rather sleep with an armadillo. The place is going to kill you before you're old enough to collect social security. You only use the downstairs. You did have sense enough to set up a master suite down here so that when you can't get up the stairs any longer you won't have to go into a nursing home. That was about the most sensible thing you've done lately."

"Thank you, I think." Max attempted a smile.

"My son is an architect," Veda said. "My suggestion is that you turn this place into a duplex. Downstairs for you, upstairs for me."

"Don't be ridiculous," Max snapped. Veda merely looked at him, her head cocked to one side like a bird's. "Besides, I don't have twenty-thousand to reimburse the amusement park, so where would we get the twenty or thirty grand to finish the upstairs? And what happens when you can no longer climb the stairs?"

"We put in an elevator or one of those stair-climbing things," Veda said. She leaned forward. "I have the money, Max. My townhouse was bought for cash and I am a relatively rich woman. I also desperately need more room and I like the neighborhood, but most of these old places are too big and too expensive for me. Half of this place would be perfect. We put in a separate entrance and a verandah across the back.'' She pointed. ''The neighborhood is zoned for multiple-family dwellings. You could even redo the carriage house and rent it out.''

Max shook his head. ''This is all going too fast for me.''

''I'm sure it is. But I'm fed to my back teeth with all this nonsense about money. Are you aware that Nick is on the hook to buy back Pete Marley's hippocampus for thirty-five thousand dollars at the end of next week?''

''What? That's crazy!''

''Of course it is, but his sense of morality and ethics demands it. Those are, I might add, concepts completely foreign to your makeup.''

''Now wait just a minute, Veda. I never thought anyone would be hurt by what I did. I told Nick I'd do it again in the same circumstances.''

''Proves my point. Nick wouldn't, even if it meant he had to sell a kidney. So, do we proceed?''

''With what?''

''I intend to fax my son copies of the blueprints of this house as soon as I leave here. If it is feasible, we can go condo.''

Max gulped. ''It's...uh...worth pursuing.''

''Fine. As earnest money I'd put up twenty thousand dollars cash immediately.''

Max exhaled deeply. ''To pay for the stolen carousel horse.''

''Precisely. Deal?''

Max nodded slowly. ''It's something to think about.''

Veda stuck out her hand. ''Deal?'' She realized that Max looked as though he'd just had a minor stroke. His eyes were unfocused and his mouth hung slack.

After a moment he broke into a wan smile. ''Deal.''

''Good.'' Veda took their cups to the pot and refilled them. She brought Max's back and set it in front of him.

He made no move to take it. Veda waved her hand over hers and blew into it a moment, then took a tentative sip.

She set it down in front of her. "Next problem."

"I beg your pardon?"

"Nick needs thirty-five thousand dollars by the end of next week. He may be able to get it eventually by suing Eberhardt's estate, but not in that length of time. I, for one, do not intend to have Rounders go bankrupt. I propose to call Marcus this morning and tell him I want a hundred thousand dollars available to hand over to Nick before the end of next week, just in case he discovers more than one horse has been sold."

"You think he'll do it?"

"He'll do it, all right. It's chicken feed to Marcus. The problem is getting Nick to accept it."

"Never happen."

"We have to make it happen. And I think I know how. I'm going to make him feel so guilty about the possibility of having to close Rounders over this, and abandon the carvers and everything we've all worked for, that he'll positively beg to let Marcus Cato bail him out."

Max curled his lip, but said nothing.

"I'll bet you dinner that if it comes to a choice between accepting help from Marcus and shutting down Rounders, Nick will bite the bullet and accept." She stuck out her hand. "Deal?"

Max shrugged and smiled. "Yeah. Deal." He took her hand.

"Good. Now find me those plans."

Max bit his lip uncertainly. "Veda, I'm still not sure this is the way to go."

"The alternative is to sell the Rounders building to some developer."

Max ran a thumb across the stubble on his chin. "We'd

all make a hefty profit. Rounders could always move some-place else.''

Veda looked at him appraisingly. "You had offers?"

Max raised his eyebrows, drank his coffee and leaned back expansively. The chair wobbled precariously beneath him. "Couple. Real estate agent called me a week ago with a very nice offer."

Veda leaned forward eagerly. "Who was the client?"

Max shook his head. "Some developer, I assume. That property was worth squat when we took it, but what with all the fancy houses going up on the bluff and all the loft apartments, it's gotten valuable again."

"Max, I want the name of that agent."

Max looked around. "Probably got it somewhere. Is it important?"

Veda nodded. "It could be. I need to use your phone while you hunt for that number and those plans."

She waited until Max left the room, then dialed Mel Bor-man and told him about her conversation. He seemed eager to talk to her in a way that Max never would be.

"I'll give you the agent's name and number as soon as Max hunts it up. Mel, do you think it's possible the murders and all the rest of what's been happening could have some-thing to do with a real estate deal?"

"Anything's possible. Veda, you doing anything for lunch today?"

Veda felt herself blushing. "I've got errands, then I'm going to Rounders and carve on Harvey."

"I'll pick you up at Rounders about twelve-thirty."

"I'll be grungy."

Mel's laugh rumbled down the phone line. "You'll be beautiful."

Veda hung up the phone and took her pulse. Definitely racing. Nobody had called her beautiful since Bill died. Things were looking up.

CHAPTER FIFTEEN

NICK OPENED ROUNDERS and left Taylor crowing to Mel on the phone about their progress. Mel, in turn, brought her up to date about the real estate offer for the Rounders warehouse.

"I'm calling the agent, Taylor. Interesting if the offer comes from somebody we know."

"Why kill the Eberhardts unless the animals are the motive?"

"No idea. Vollmer called me this morning trying to locate you."

"Stall him. I don't have time to talk to him today."

Mel laughed. "Sooner or later he's bound to discover you're with Kendall. He's going to hate that."

"Tough." Taylor took a deep breath. "Mel, I don't know why I feel we're on the homestretch. We seem to have more possibilities, not fewer."

Mel laughed. "You've got a nose, Ms. Hunt. Right when you think everything's screwed up like a ball of yarn the cat dragged in, that's when you find the single strand, and all of a sudden it unrolls smooth as silk."

"You feel that way too?"

"Nope. But then I'm not that close to it. You be careful."

"Eugene only stalks by night."

"Don't count on it."

Taylor hung up, grabbed her satchel and headed downstairs.

Veda was there, along with a pair of heavyset, fortyish

women who looked as though they could manhandle the engine out of an eighteen-wheeler. Nick introduced them as Corinne and Sally.

Corinne smiled perfunctorily and went back to sanding a haunch. Sally wriggled her fingers and turned back to carving a giraffe's head.

"Veda's in charge until I get back," Nick said. All three women nodded without looking up from their work. "Okay, we're outa here," Nick said and took Taylor's arm. "We better take the Rounders truck. We might have some animals to bring back."

"Even if we find them, Danny Vollmer will want them for evidence."

Nick checked. "I suppose he will. Damn!"

THE HOUSE ON NEWCOMB was a vintage nineteen-seventies ranch-style house set well back from a winding street in a neighborhood on its way down. But the yards on either side were neatly trimmed; in one a few late yellow roses held on. It was obvious that no one had attended to the Eberhardt yard in several weeks.

The neighborhood seemed deserted. Families at work. A perfect setting for the Eberhardts.

Taylor rang the bell. After a full minute she dug her lock pick out of her satchel and went to work. She could feel Nick's amusement at her obvious lack of coordination. Three minutes later the lock clicked, and Taylor wiped the film of sweat off her lip, stood and brushed off the knees of her jeans. "There," she said with obvious pride. Nick applauded silently, then leaned down and kissed her.

"Whoa," she gasped. "This is office hours. You promised."

She handed Nick another pair of surgical gloves, crossed her fingers and held them under Nick's nose, then opened the door.

The house smelled unused and dank. Nick clicked the light switch and a dim bulb lit in the hall.

"It's empty!" Taylor wailed. "Nobody's been here for months!"

"Maybe it was rental property they hadn't had time to get ready to rent after the last tenants left."

Taylor nodded. "You're probably right." She looked out in the backyard. "There's a storage shed out behind the carport," she said.

"I'll check it. You look in the storage room in the carport."

"Meet you back at the car."

A few minutes later she climbed into the passenger side of the Rounders truck. "Major waste of time," she said.

"Now *you* sound depressed," Nick told her. He reached over and ran his hand down her cheek. She covered his hand with hers.

"Sorry. I was so positive we'd find the animals."

"We will. At the other house."

The other house lay down a back road thirty miles away on the edge of the old section of Ellendale. After three tries, they finally located the mailbox canting crazily on the edge of a steep roadside ditch.

Nick turned into the narrow gravel driveway that wound back through a thick stand of old oak and locust trees thickly grown with poison ivy and lovevine. The trees flamed with autumn colors among the pines and scrub spruces. There was no lawn to be mowed, only several acres of thick forest and underbrush.

"This can't be right." Even Taylor's whisper sounded loud in the oppressive silence under the trees.

The truck inched around a final curve. The house was a prewar bungalow built of dark red brick the color of dried blood. Gravel created a turnaround in front that would handle relatively large vehicles. Behind the house they could glimpse a metal building that looked like the twin of the shop in Oxford.

Taylor felt the flow of adrenaline and drew a deep breath. She was almost afraid of what they'd find.

Nick turned off the ignition and then turned to her. "Ready?" he said, and smiled.

She nodded and climbed out of the truck.

"Let's try the house first," she said and walked up onto the concrete front porch. She tried to peer into the front windows, but there were heavy drapes across them. She raised her electric pick in salute and went to work on the front door.

After only a minute the lock clicked. Taylor closed her eyes and put the pick back in her satchel.

Nick wrapped his arms around her, and she leaned against him gratefully. "Whatever we find inside, remember, you found these houses." He held her chin in his hand and raised her face to kiss her gently. "That's my girl," he whispered.

Taylor wanted to stay in his arms forever. She didn't want to open the door to another empty house.

But this one wasn't empty.

It was like walking into a Chinese palace hidden behind the walls of a tenement. They wandered from room to room, flicking on the lights in Venetian chandeliers as they went. Oriental rugs lay two and three deep against stained pine floors. Only the living room and one bedroom were furnished, but they were opulent. The drapes were maroon damask heavy with gold bullion fringe.

The bedroom was furnished with a circular king-size bed covered by a real fur throw.

"Oh, my," Taylor said.

"I'll bet this is where Clara planned to spend the night."

"Some hideaway. I wonder whether Clara and Helmut used it together or separately with other lovers."

"We'll probably never know," Nick said. He picked up

a heavy gilt picture frame. "I never saw Helmut, but this is sure Clara." He held it out.

"Has to be Helmut. He just looks like a Helmut, doesn't he? White hair, white beard, that square Germanic face." She set the picture down again and leaned against Nick. "I've been thinking of them as thieves, pure and simple. But they were people, Nick. They must have loved each other. They didn't deserve to die the way they did."

He slid his arm around her waist and kissed the top of her head. "No, they didn't."

"No carousel animals. I was so sure." Then she brightened. "Attic? Basement?"

Nick shook his head. "From the pitch of the roof I'd say there might be enough attic space to store the Christmas lights."

"Damn!" Taylor said.

"The animals are in the workshop," Nick said with complete composure. "You know they are, I know they are. Come on. We've held off long enough."

They walked around the side of the house towards the workshop. Doors wide and high enough to accommodate a big truck opened onto the gravel turnaround. Beside them stood a single steel entry door. It was padlocked.

Taylor picked the lock up in her hand. "Piece o' cake," she said with more bravado than she felt. But she had it open in less than a minute, removed it from its hasp and opened the door.

The workshop lay in total darkness. The scents of paint, solvent and kerosene mingled with the odor of old dirt and new wood. Nick felt for the light switch without success.

"Don't move," he said and inched along the wall. "Here we go."

The only lights were a string of fluorescent work lights along the ridge beam that left the edges of the room in shadow. Taylor yelped. She stood nose to nose with an angry stallion.

"Nick! Nick, darling Nick, the animals! They're here!"

The animals were reflected in ornately carved pier mirrors that stood seven feet tall. They leaned against bow-front secretaries and block-fronted chest-on-chests. Taylor saw a lovely old sleigh bed against the far wall with what looked like its original rope mattress still intact. Pedestal tables stood at the back with matching dining chairs stacked on top of them.

Nick began to caress the burled walnut of an exquisite plantation desk only a foot from the light switch. "These didn't come from nineteen-twenty," he said softly. "These are real."

Taylor heard the awe in his voice. His own animals were forgotten. She watched him move among the pieces like a blind man, caressing the wood the way he had last night caressed her body. She wrapped her arms around herself, not only because the room was as cold as the November day, but because she suddenly saw the bright carousel animals and the other lovely old pieces as prisoners walled up in an evil dungeon by pitiless wardens.

She went to Nick, grateful for the warmth of his body.

He felt her nearness and turned to take her in his arms. "My God, Taylor, it's all stolen. Got to be." His voice broke. "These things ought to be in climate-controlled environments. Hell, in museums! Not rotting in a godforsaken backwoods barn."

"We've got to call Mel and Danny Vollmer," Taylor said and was horrified to discover her voice was shaking. "I hate this place."

"Well, Lordy, Lordy, lookie here!"

Taylor jumped.

Eugene Lewis lounged in the doorway. He pointed a revolver at them. "Y'all come on out here where I can see you.'' He smiled at Taylor. ''Drop that purse, honey lamb, right there and move away from it, or I'll drop you right where you stand.''

Nick moved so that his body covered Taylor's. ''Put the gun down, Eugene. You can't get both of us.''

''Hell, yes I can, and you know it.'' Eugene sounded remarkably cheerful. Taylor wondered whether he'd been drinking, and decided that it probably wouldn't matter. ''I said put the satchel down. Now.''

Taylor eased her satchel to the floor without taking her eyes off Eugene.

She wondered if she dared dive behind one of the chests, and decided against it. Eugene would merely shoot Nick and then come for her.

''Step away from it.'' Eugene waggled the gun.

They stepped.

Eugene looked around him, shook his head and chortled. ''I never thought y'all'd find this stuff. I been looking ever since that old fart Eberhardt got fried.''

''You didn't know where it was?'' Taylor asked.

''Hell, no. Why you think I been after you? Clara and Helmut moved them damn animals the minute I took my eyes off 'em and didn't tell nobody where they'd got to. His eyes darted around the room. ''Damn! Look at all this.''

''Eugene, this isn't going to work,'' Nick said reasonably. ''Plenty of people know where we are.''

''They do not. Now you and the little lady turn around and assume the position.''

He's going to kill us, Taylor thought. She looked at Nick. His jaw was set, his eyes hard. *Please God,* she prayed, *I don't want to die just when I've found Nick.*

''Do it,'' Eugene said conversationally. They did. Side by side they leaned their hands onto the top of a block-front chest.

Taylor heard Eugene's shuffling steps behind them, then a movement of air.

The gun came down on the back of Nick's head.

Taylor screamed.

Nick dropped to his knees in the aisle. Taylor tried to kneel beside him, but Eugene pulled her away. "Uh-uh, sweet thang," he said. "You and me's got some unfinished business." He dragged her backward away from Nick, who knelt on his hands and knees shaking his head. A thin trickle of blood seeped from his scalp.

"Please, I've got to help him," Taylor begged.

"Oh, yes, ma'am, let's hear those pleases some more," Eugene said. "Hey, Kendall, this time the lady's not gonna get away from me the way she did when I grabbed her Thursday night, and you ain't gonna be there for her to run to."

Nick put his hand against the back of his neck and raised his head. His eyes were glazed with pain and something else. He looked from Eugene to Taylor.

She shook her head in silent entreaty.

"Woman's got her a kick like a mule." Eugene laughed. "Ain't no woman ever kicked the stew out of me before. We was gonna have us a fine time, weren't we, sweet thang?"

Taylor felt his hot breath against her ear and smelled the stench of him. His grip tightened. He held her with one arm, but she felt the cold steel of the gun against her other side. He could shoot her in an instant and still kill Nick.

"Well, dang," Eugene said. "She didn't tell you, did she?"

Nick stared at Taylor.

"I thought sure she'd run right on up them stairs and tell you how her and me had us a little prayer meeting outside the front door." He pulled Taylor roughly against him. "I owe her one. Now, you get to watch me teach her some

manners," Eugene said. "And after that y'all are gonna find
them records, and after that I may just let you go."

"What records?" Taylor squeaked.

"Why, sweet thang, the records of what all the ol' man
stole, who it got stole from, and what it's worth." He began
to laugh. "Dang! Here I thought that was what you was
looking for all this time."

Taylor was having trouble breathing.

She felt the same rush of terrible heat she'd felt outside
Rounders, but this was worse, much worse. She should have
told Nick. She'd promised herself Eugene wouldn't get her
again. Mel had warned her.

Everybody had warned her.

"Maybe we better start by getting nekkid," Eugene said.
"Hey, sweet thang?" He sneered at Nick. "Hear that? Her
and me's gonna get nekkid." He scraped his cheek down
Taylor's. "I'm gonna get me into some places she ain't
never felt no man before."

Nick growled. Eugene snapped to attention and swung the
gun in his direction. "Uh-uh. Stay down there on your
knees. Put your hands behind your head. You gonna get to
watch your woman on her knees real soon."

Eugene's arm tightened around her. Today his feet were
splayed wide. She couldn't stamp him. She didn't know
what to do except stand here and take it.

He whispered to her, but loud enough so that Nick could
hear. "Anybody ever take a piece of baling wire to your
tail, sweet thang?" He caressed her breast with the barrel
of the gun. "Tell you how it works. First I tie you face
down to that old bedstead over there, then I strip you nekkid,
and I beat the crap out of you. I can make a real pretty
pattern all the way from your neck to your knees. They tell
me after a while it just feels hot, but I'm gonna feel hotter.
You gonna be beggin' to do every little thing I want you
to."

Taylor's eyes begged Nick to stay still. If this hideous thing happened to her, she'd endure it so long as Eugene didn't kill them both. Maybe after Eugene had taken his fill of her, she could catch him off guard.

She prayed Eugene was too dumb to realize that if he did, indeed, beat and rape her, he'd better kill Nick, because Nick would certainly kill him—even if it took the rest of his life.

"First off, we need us some rope," Eugene said.

CHAPTER SIXTEEN

"YOU, FACE DOWN ON THE FLOOR, lock your hands behind
your neck," Eugene told Nick. He kept his gun pressed
under Taylor's breast.

Nick sank to his knees, then stretched out on his face and
locked his hands. Taylor could see even in this dim light
that his knuckles were white. Blood from his scalp dripped
onto the concrete. His respiration was fast and strong, but
he might have a serious concussion or a brain hemorrhage.
She whimpered. Nick tried to raise his head.

"You want me to blow the back of your head in?" Eugene snarled. "That'll keep you down there, all right."

He dragged Taylor over Nick's prostrate form. Taylor
tried to kneel beside him, but Eugene dug his fingers into
her arm. She realized she was losing the feeling in the fingers of her right hand.

Eugene couldn't afford to leave either of them alive. The
only decision he had left to make was when to kill them—
before or after he raped and tortured Taylor. Well, she
planned to stay alive as long as she could. She'd beaten him
once, she would again.

Step by wary step he backed her towards the front of the
room.

She forced herself to concentrate on something other than
Eugene. All along she'd been sure that Eugene had the Eberhardt's records and the remaining carousel animals. Now it
seemed she'd been wrong about that too. Her gaze darted

around the shadowy room. Plenty of drawers to hide papers in.

Even if Helmut had only paid off his contact for the sale of Marley's hippocampus, that name would be listed. They'd know who had set Rounders up for the theft. How many animals were left unsold?

Eugene's face against hers kept her from seeing more than half the room. She counted six horses. There might be others behind larger pieces of furniture.

"Hey, here we go," Eugene said cheerfully. He nodded at a thick roll of duct tape on the concrete floor by the front door. "Now ain't that lucky. Lot harder to break tape. No knots to come aloose." He pulled her down with him. "Pick it up. I only got two hands."

Taylor picked up the roll of tape.

"Now let's us get your friend taped up." He said to Nick, "Hey, you get on up slow and easy and come on down here."

Nick stood, but swayed uncertainly.

"Did I tell you to drop them hands?" Eugene snarled. "Nossir, you turn around real slow and march on down here. Yeah." For a moment Taylor felt the steel gun barrel leave her side. She tensed. Maybe she could throw her weight against Eugene, knock him off balance long enough to dislodge the gun.

"Not this time." Eugene pulled her back against him roughly. "Fool me once—shame on you. Fool me twice—shame on me."

Nick gave her a barely perceptible shake of his head. His lips were set in a thin hard line. The blood had begun to dry in his hair.

Eugene's broad head swiveled on its thick neck as he searched for a place strong enough to hold Nick. "Okay. Even you can't break one of them steel uprights. Tape you up to one of them real pretty and then I can take all the time

I want taping this pretty lady here to that bed. Got to pick a place where you can see everything, though. Wouldn't want you to miss nothing.'' He snickered.

Nick had not spoken since Eugene hit him. Now, he complied silently. Only his eyes and the set of his jaw betrayed his fury.

Taylor guessed that Eugene was too high on adrenaline to read that look. Maybe he was too sure of his position to care. ''Thought you was a tough guy,'' Eugene said. ''Could be I was wrong about you and this sweet thang here. Could be you gonna like watching.''

''Nick,'' Taylor whispered. She longed to tell him that she loved him, but she couldn't bear to have Eugene's filthy ears hear the words.

Nick's eyes held hers. He didn't even blink. She saw the pulse leap at the side of his throat, the cords standing out in his arms and hands. He stood with his back to the beam and crossed his wrists behind it.

''Now, honey chile, you do the honors.'' Eugene grinned. ''Don't think you can fake it, 'cause I'm gonna check it after you get through.'' He handed the roll of tape to Taylor and stepped away from her. His gun did not waver.

She loosened the end of the tape and began to roll it around Nick's wrists. It caught the dark hair on his forearms, and she thought for a crazy moment how much it would hurt when he pulled it off, then knew she was one giggle away from hysteria. What did chafed wrists matter when you were lying dead with a bullet in your brain? She bit her lip until she could taste blood.

''That's enough. Don't take much,'' Eugene said. The roll of tape hung from Nick's bound wrists. ''Don't want to waste it. You and me's going to need it. Well, damn. What the Sam Hill am I going to cut it with?'' Eugene sighed and peered into the gloom. ''Hell, nothing ever works right.'' He clicked his tongue against his teeth.

He turned to Taylor. "Bite it."

She stared at him blankly.

"You know, bend down and bite across it, then you can tear it."

Taylor bent. After she bit the tape she let her lips linger for a moment on the palm of Nick's hand. His fingers curled gently to caress her cheek.

She staggered and caught herself one-handed against the concrete.

Eugene stayed outside Nick's kicking area, grabbed Taylor's upper arm and pulled her up and away. He winked at Nick. "Might oughta gag you, but you'll probably want to yell. Ain't nobody gonna hear you except this sweet thang here, and she's gonna be doing her own yelling. What the hell. Yell away."

Now it was Taylor's turn. Eugene shoved her before him toward the sleigh bed. The frame was constructed of a simple wooden rectangle with heavy hemp rope stretched top to bottom and side to side like the weft and warp of a weaver's loom.

She'd have no chance once she lay spread-eagled on her face, wrists and arms taped to the rope. Better to take a bullet now. She might only be wounded, might be able to wrestle the pistol from him if she surprised him.

He hit her hard in the small of the back. She stumbled and fell face down onto the bed.

Before she could react he was on her, his knee in the small of her back, his weight pressing her down. He captured her wrists in both his hands. What had he done with the gun? She struggled and screamed. The rope bit into her face, her breasts and stomach.

She heard the tape rip and felt it around her wrists. She kicked back at him, but he only laughed. He wound the tape around the rope in front of the headboard. She bucked against him frantically.

He grabbed her right ankle and taped it to the right corner of the bed. She kicked at him ineffectually, and he reached around and swatted her across her bottom. "Now, you just behave yourself, missy."

Then he taped her other ankle to the other side of the bed.

She lay spread like a butterfly on a board. "Damn you!" she snarled. "Damn you to hell!"

He cuffed her across the back of her head hard enough to bounce her face off the taut ropes. "Ain't that a nice way to talk? What would your momma say?"

He shifted his weight and stood up. She could turn her head only far enough to see his legs in their dirty jeans.

"Yeah," he whispered. "Oh, yeah."

He pulled her sweater up to her armpits. She felt the rush of cold air against her bare back and began to shiver. She gritted her teeth to keep them from chattering.

She wanted to shut her eyes, her mind and spirit away in some secret place that Eugene couldn't reach. She wanted to faint, but she'd never been able to do that, not even when Daddy came at her with his belt, not even when Paul used his psychological terror tactics on her. She'd be fully aware of what happened to her every moment, no matter how terrible. She swallowed convulsively. Her mouth was so dry she couldn't even lick her lips.

"Please," she begged. "Please don't do this."

"Why the hell not?" he said. His voice sounded thick and hoarse. The rope protested as he knelt over her, one leg on either side of her thighs. He ran one finger down her spine.

"You ain't ready yet, sweet thang," he said. He bent and kissed the nape of her neck gently. "I don't take no woman before her time." He laughed. "Just like one of them wine commercials."

Taylor was afraid she was going to be sick.

"Leave her alone, you bastard," Nick snarled. His voice

rasped with anger as though his hatred choked him with his own bile. "Do whatever you want with me, but leave her alone."

Eugene left her. His footsteps moved away on the concrete, then Nick's breath exploded. He began to cough.

"Nick!" she cried.

"Shut up, bitch," Eugene said. "He's fine. Man don't talk too good with a fist in his gut." He tittered. "Now what the hell would I want with you when I got her?"

Taylor heard another blow and screamed in impotent fury.

"I'm a real man," Eugene said with obvious pride.

Taylor took a deep breath and snarled, "You're no man. No woman would have you unless you tied her up and beat her first."

Taylor heard Nick's quick intake of breath. "Taylor, shut up."

It was like baiting a bull using a red cape. She and Nick, each trying to take the heat off the other. She pictured Eugene's heavy head swinging from Nick to her.

"That ain't at all a nice thing to say," Eugene whined. His footsteps came back. She waited for him to hit her, perhaps kick her. She tensed her body and clenched her teeth.

Nothing happened. She opened her eyes and saw his legs beside her again. He was doing something with his hands, but she couldn't tell what.

Then he showed her.

"I can't find me no baling wire in this place," he said conversationally, "but I done found this wire coat hanger. My daddy used to whip me with one of them when I was a kid. Hurts like hell." He giggled. "I'm good with it. Before I get through you gonna look like somebody's been playing tic-tac-toe on you."

Taylor moaned. Tears spilled over the rims of her eyes. Her nose started to run; she couldn't even wipe it. She struggled against her bonds, frantic, powerless, unable to endure what she couldn't escape.

"You say when, pretty lady," Eugene crooned. "You got all the power. All you got to do is beg me to quit. Tell me you'll do anything I want if I'll just stop. But you got to come up with some fine ideas. I got plenty of good ones myself, but I bet you can come up with something real interesting if you try real hard."

"I'll give you some ideas, you bastard," she shrieked. "You want to know what I'd like to do to you?"

She expected him to hit her. Instead he laughed. "Bet you just can. Hey, you over there. Me and her gonna teach you a few things." His voice dropped to a whisper. "Don't you give over too soon, though, you hear? I like this part a lot."

She braced herself.

Suddenly, she heard a thud and felt the bed spring under her. Out of the corner of her eye she caught a glimpse of Eugene. He seemed to be flying. Something was wrong with his mouth.

He screamed and scrabbled backward. Something heavy dove across the bed.

She twisted her head, but saw only a flurry of arms and legs, heard only Eugene's scream.

The steel door opened and shut, then opened again.

She heard three short pops. Shots.

Dear God, she prayed, *let Nick live.*

The door slammed once more. Hands tore the tape loose from her ankles, then her wrists. Someone turned her over, gathered her up, held her.

"Nick," she sobbed.

"I didn't kill him, Taylor," he snarled. "Damnation. I missed him in the trees." He rocked her like a mother with a new baby. "I've got to kill him."

She began to shake. "I'm going to throw up," she said.

She pulled away from him, scrambled to her feet and got to the door, but Nick put his hand on it.

"He might still be out there."

Taylor clapped a hand over her mouth and shook her head. If Eugene waited, he waited. She opened the door, stumbled towards the undergrowth and fell on her hands and knees on the edge of the gravel. Nick stood guard over her with Eugene's pistol in his hand.

She threw up until she thought her stomach would come up through her esophagus. Finally she struggled to her feet.

Darkness had fallen. Night creatures rustled through the leaves.

Nick held the door open for her. Taylor walked in calmly. She wanted to sit down, but the only place close was that damned bed. She wouldn't sit on that if her life depended on it.

Nick shut the door behind them and dropped the inside bolt into place.

His wrists still wore bits of tape. Bloody tape.

"Oh, God, Nick. How did you get free?" She reached out to him.

"There was a burr on the side of that beam." He held out his bloody wrists and his voice broke. "I'm so sorry it took me so long."

She went into his arms. They held each other silently and hard.

"Please, Nick, please take me out of here," she whispered. "Take me someplace clean."

"I'm taking you to the hospital," he said.

She shook her head. "No! I don't want a hospital. I want a shower and some clean clothes and a place where people aren't crazy."

"But—"

"We've got to find a phone and call Mel. I also want my Glock," she said grimly. "For all the good it did me." She squared her shoulders and turned to him with a flash of her old grit. "You don't get to shoot him. I do."

Outside she leaned against the metal wall of the building while Nick locked the padlock.

Two miles down the road Nick spotted a pay phone in the parking area in front of a small grocery store. He pulled in. "I'll call Borman. He can call Vollmer."

"Nick? Please don't tell what happened to me. I couldn't bear it."

She saw his jaw set.

"Mel needs to know."

"That Eugene was there, yes. But not the rest of it, please, Nick."

"He has to know."

"Not the details. We both had a bad time, but there's no real damage done. Thanks to you, we're alive. Mel warned me Eugene might not wait for dark."

"He must have been following us all afternoon. I never spotted him. It's my fault."

"No! It's Eugene's fault and whoever hired him in the first place!" Taylor banged her fist down on the console. "I won't let the son of a bitch beat me."

BY THE TIME MEL DROVE UP to Taylor's cabin, she was asleep, curled like a child on her bed in the loft. Her hair was still damp, her body shiny from the scrubbing she'd given it. Her arms were bruised, the rope had burned her cheek, and her wrists and ankles were raw, but that was the extent of her physical damage. The psychological damage had yet to surface.

She had not asked Nick to join her in the shower. He hadn't offered.

Perhaps he never would. Last night might be the only time they'd have together. They'd crossed a terrible line. Nick wasn't to blame—he'd rescued her. But not before he'd seen Eugene put his hands on her, seen her lashed to that bed. He might not admit it, but she'd be a constant reminder to him of his own impotence.

She'd gotten them into it. She should have realized that Eugene was trailing them, should have told Mel where they'd be and what they hoped to find. She'd been so sure that she could locate the animals, solve the puzzle alone, and prove to Mel and Nick what a marvelous detective she was that she'd damn near gotten both of them killed.

"Hell of a team player you are," she'd told her reflection in the steamy mirror. "Mel was right. You belong at a computer terminal or handing out subpoenas." Her lip began to quiver. "Oh, God, I want my mother." Even as she said the words, she knew she could never tell Irene Maxwell about tonight, about Eugene, about any of it. Her life had turned into one long secret.

She pulled on her oldest sweats, ran a comb through her hair, took a deep breath and opened the bathroom door.

Nick stood by the front window. Eugene's thirty-eight and her Glock lay on the computer desk beside him.

"Nick, I'm not much good with first aid," she said. "Don't you think you ought to go to the hospital? You might have a concussion, and those gashes on your wrists could get infected."

He shook his head. "Veda's coming out. She'll fix me up."

"I can't face anyone." She felt tears spill over the rims of her eyes. "I'm so tired."

"Taylor, why didn't you tell me Eugene attacked you?"

"Not now, Nick, please."

His voice sounded grim. "Yes, now." He loomed in front of her. "He could have killed you."

She turned away, hugging herself. "I knew you'd act like this."

"What way am I supposed to react? Say, 'hey, go to it, babe,' and walk away?"

"Yes! You sound like my mother. Maybe I made the wrong decision, but it was my decision to make, not yours. And the last thing I need right now is for you to tell me what an incompetent idiot I am." She heard the tears in her voice and hated herself because of them.

"I didn't mean—"

"The hell you didn't."

He started to reach out to her, then let his arms drop to his sides. "I need to take you in my arms and make it all go away, but I don't know whether that's what you want."

She wrapped her arms across her body. "I'm okay." She tried to keep her tone light. "A good night's sleep and I'll be fine." She sighed. "I'm going to bed. You all do whatever you want down here. I guarantee I won't hear you." She crossed to the ladder.

"Taylor," he said softly, "I can't make it go away, but we'll get through this. I don't know how, but I promise you we will."

She smiled sadly, then turned to climb the ladder.

Nick settled by the door with both guns. Elmo jumped onto his lap.

Only eight-thirty.

Last night he and Taylor had made wonderful love. This morning they'd shared their first breakfast together. In another lifetime.

His stomach lurched, and he remembered that neither one of them had eaten anything since that breakfast. Taylor had thrown that up. She'd be starving before morning. He couldn't manage to feed her, much less protect her.

The cabin lay completely silent. He couldn't even hear Taylor breathe.

She was right. If she'd told him Eugene had attacked her

she'd have been off the case in five minutes. And he'd never have had the chance to know her, to make love with her.

To fall in love with her.

He loved her so much that he had tried to kill a man for her. She deserved a better kind of love than that. While he'd worked to slice through the tape that bound his wrists, Nick had refused to think about Eugene with Taylor. Anger might make him stupid. He had to stay cool, uninvolved, careful. If Eugene raped her before he could break free, they could deal with the consequences of that together. All that mattered at that moment had been to keep her alive.

But all his careful plans had evaporated in atavistic rage the moment he felt the last strand of duct tape part. He simply dove at Eugene and bashed him in the face.

Eugene must have realized that without his gun he didn't stand a chance against Nick's fury. Eugene had been smart to run.

Nick had shot at him as he ran. In the gathering darkness he'd missed, but that didn't change anything. Nick knew he wasn't shooting to save his own life or even the life of his woman. He'd left Taylor lashed face down to that bed while he'd tried to kill another human being. The worst part was that he knew he'd do the same thing again.

For the sake of his own immortal soul, he prayed Eugene was long gone.

MEL BROUGHT VEDA WITH HIM. "Taylor's truck was still at Veda's, so she drove it out. I carry a set of Taylor's keys and she has mine. Sometimes we have to walk away from our cars."

Veda eyed Nick's wrists and asked, "When was your last tetanus shot?"

"Two years ago," he said. "It was a ten-year shot."

When she spotted the blood in his hair and on his collar she demanded that he go to the hospital for X rays.

"I'm not leaving Taylor," he said stubbornly. "I had my chimes rung but I never lost consciousness. I've got a head like one of those statues on Easter Island. Leave me be."

"Come into the bathroom," Veda ordered.

Mel followed them and stood outside the open bathroom door. "I called Vollmer. Gave him the address of that place. Told him Lewis tried to murder you both. He was going to send a squad car over here and drag you both downtown."

Veda smiled. "Mel told him if he came anywhere near either of you tonight we'd sic Rico on him. Officially you're both too ill to talk to the police."

"Vollmer must have loved that."

"He didn't. But he's agreed to hold off for a bit."

Mel jerked a thumb overhead towards the loft. "Tell me what happened."

Nick left out the grimmer details, but he could see from Mel's expression, and the way that Veda's nimble fingers stopped while he described the scene, that they guessed.

"I'm staying," Nick said. "Eugene could come back to finish the job."

"She may wake up screaming. I'm staying too," Veda told them both defiantly.

"Makes three of us," Mel said. "Anything to eat in this place?" He rummaged in the refrigerator. "Cat food, cat food, cat food and something that probably didn't start out green. I'll go get some burgers." He pointed a thumb over his head again and raised his eyebrows. "Get something for her or not?"

Nick said, "Who knows? Get an extra burger. She can always feed it to Elmo tomorrow."

Veda patted Nick's bandaged wrist. "Very minor damage. I've seen you do worse with a chisel. You'll be fine." She glanced up at him. "That was a stupid thing to say. You're not fine, you're terrible."

"I'll be fine when Eugene Lewis is dead."

CHAPTER SEVENTEEN

VEDA CLEARED AWAY THE BURGER MESS and fell asleep curled like a hedgehog at the far end of the sofa. Mel nodded beside her. His right hand rested lightly on her calf. Nick stretched in the wing chair, feet propped on the coffee table. The two pistols lay on the end table beside him.

At midnight Nick whispered, "Take her home." He pointed to Veda. "Nothing's going to happen tonight."

Mel ran his hand down his face, shook Veda awake and aimed her towards the front door. "We'll bring breakfast," he whispered. "About eight. You going to bed?"

Nick shook his head. "I'll sleep in the chair." He ran his hand down his cheek and felt the rasp of dark beard. "If this keeps up I might as well carry my razor with me every time I leave Rounders."

Veda yawned and patted his arm. "We'll stop by and get you some clean clothes on our way, dear. I've got the keys."

As soon as their car drove out, Nick settled himself and once again Elmo found a comfortable spot on Nick's lap.

He'd fire Taylor after breakfast while Veda and Mel were there to back him up. Officially he'd be firing Mel, not Taylor, but that was only a polite fiction.

Taylor kept telling anyone who'd listen how mundane being a detective was. In the few days he'd known her they'd found a corpse and been shot at twice. She'd been attacked outside Rounders, discovered a cache of stolen furniture, been tortured and nearly raped.

He should have gone with his gut instinct and not hired

her in the first place. What did it matter if he went bankrupt or spent the rest of his life suspecting his friends and partners if it meant Taylor stayed alive, healthy, and a part of his life?

That was the problem. She wouldn't be part of his life—not after he fired her. She probably wouldn't even speak to him. Trouble was, he could no longer visualize life without her.

Sooner or later he'd have to deal with that. He'd started out merely wanting to feel those long legs of hers wrapped around his waist. Along the line his feelings had grown and mutated. Oh, there was desire, all right. But it was more than that. He wanted to trace the line of her square jaw, see the flash in her eyes. All her moods, her fierce need for independence, her drive to be good at her job had become important to him because they mattered so deeply to her. How could he fire her if he loved her? And if he wanted to keep her healthy, how could he not?

He shifted uncomfortably in his chair. He could climb that ladder and slip back into bed with her. It was what he wanted. But was it what she needed after Eugene? She might not want another man's hands on her for quite a while.

Could he endure that?

Hell, he'd have to if he loved her. Unfortunately, he admitted, he did love her, though God knew how it had happened. He hadn't planned to fall in love with her. Maybe he was doomed the minute she stalked into his life like Wyatt Earp at the O.K. Corral.

But he'd walk away from her before he'd let her get hurt again. He'd proved he couldn't protect her. Intellectually, he knew he wasn't to blame any more than she was, but that didn't help his masculine pride any.

Killing Eugene seemed a reasonable response at the time. But he didn't want to shoot the bastard. He wanted to work him over from the top of his pointed thick skull to the soles of his undoubtedly flat feet.

Elmo protested. Nick realized he'd tightened his grip on the cat's soft fur. He relaxed and scratched Elmo under the chin. The cat began to purr. "Sorry, Elmo," Nick whispered. He settled back so that he could see both the door and the ladder to the loft.

It was going to be a long night.

"I KEEP TELLING YOU I'm perfectly fine," Taylor said as she bit into her third blueberry muffin.

Veda raised her eyebrows, and Mel shook his head.

Taylor laid her hand on Mel's arm. "Listen, what happened with Eugene is a one-in-a-million chance. How many guys are willing to take off their cervical collars to beat me up when it means their disability payments will be cut off?" She buttered the second half of her muffin. "Besides, we found most of the stuff—that's half of our assignment."

"That's all of your assignment," Nick said quietly.

"What?" Taylor asked.

"As of this moment the Borman Detective Agency and its operatives are no longer on the case." He turned to Mel. "Get your expense report together and send me a bill."

"Now, just a minute," Taylor said.

Nick turned to her. "I mean it, Taylor. This time I'm firing you for real."

"Just like that?"

"You've done a good job—a great job. But this is murder and you're in the line of fire. I can't take the responsibility."

"Who *asked* you to take the responsibility?" Taylor slid her chair back and stood up. She stuck her finger against her breastbone. "Me. My responsibility. My job! You can't fire me now when it's all over—bar the shouting."

"What do you mean?"

She strode around the room like a caged tiger. "Mel, tell

this nincompoop that the only danger I'm going to be in is from computer burnout or repetitive strain syndrome.''

Mel rumbled. ''Taylor, he's got a point. You should have told me you got attacked outside Rounders.''

Taylor threw up her hands. ''So he could fire me before we found the animals?'' She took a deep breath. ''Nick,'' she said reasonably, ''Eugene is either already in custody or will be before the day is out. He's got three police forces looking for him.''

''That doesn't get us any closer to the Rounders connection.''

''Of *course* it does. Once Vollmer starts throwing charges at him, Eugene will roll over on his contact so fast he'll start an earthquake. I saw six animals in that storeroom. There may have been more, but worst-case scenario is that you have all but four back. Marley bought one. One may well have burned up in the arson in Oxford, but even if it didn't, that leaves only three animals left to trace and identify.'' She threw up her hands. ''Don't you see? Once Eugene spills his guts, the police either decide he's an accessory or that he did the killings himself, but it won't matter. He and his contact will fall all over themselves blaming each other. All we have left to do is find out what Eberhardt did with the remaining animals. That's legwork and computer work. It's about as dangerous as feeding the ducks in Audubon Park. And I am very, very good at it.''

''After last night—''

She flipped a hand. ''Last night won't happen again. I'm shamed and embarrassed but I'll get over it. Could have happened in the grocery parking lot. It's a fact of life— women get attacked. Housewives and bank executives and corporate lawyers are just as much at risk. Are you saying they ought to enter your friendly neighborhood cloistered nunnery?'' She considered. ''Cloisters aren't safe either these days.''

"The risk is much higher when you're out stalking some-one who's already killed two people," Veda said.

Taylor turned on her. "Don't you start. You're supposed to be on my side."

"I'm not on anybody's side. You had a bad experience. Acknowledge it."

"I *do* acknowledge it! But don't you see, if I quit now or if Nick fires me, Eugene wins! The murderer wins! He controls what we do and how we think." She drew herself up. "Nobody controls me. Nobody. Never again."

Nick found himself wavering. His head told him that she made sense, that she needed to keep on, to fight back over what had been done to her. His heart told him to keep her safe—and to hell with her self-esteem.

The gate alarm buzzed. "Oh, damn!" Taylor said and went to the intercom.

"Taylor. It's Danny. Open up."

"That's all we need," Taylor said and punched the buzzer. She turned to the three people at the table. "If I have to tell Danny every dirty detail of yesterday, I will. But for pity's sake, don't help!"

She opened the door and went outside to wait for him.

"She's right," Mel said and poured himself another cup of coffee. "Mr. Lewis will tell the police everything he knows. His actions do not speak of a man who is willing to keep a vow of silence when faced with prison."

They listened to the murmur of Taylor and Vollmer's voices outside the door. Nick closed his eyes. He wasn't certain he could put up with Vollmer's attitude. Whether Vollmer said the words or not, they'd be implied. Nick had done a lousy job of protecting his woman.

Taylor opened the door and came in with Vollmer. Nick was afraid she was going to faint. She shook her head at him and closed her eyes for a moment. "I was wrong," she said. "It's not over."

Vollmer walked in with the authority of a banty-rooster and a grin without a trace of merriment. "Well, well, well," he said. "Have I interrupted a party? Fancy brunch at the country house?"

Taylor stood by the door with her hand on the knob. Nick went towards her, but Vollmer neatly sidestepped to block his way. He looked up at Nick but spoke to the group. "At one-thirty this morning the charred remains of a stolen blue four-door Mercury sedan were found in a ditch in the county. Upon investigation of said remains, the partially charred body of a male was found in the front seat. Said body's butt wasn't sufficiently charred to destroy his wallet, which bore a Mississippi driver's license in the name of one Eugene P. Lewis late of Oxford."

Veda moaned.

"One more thing. Said Eugene P. Lewis's body had no smoke in its lungs largely because said body had taken a slug sometime before the fire started."

Taylor leaned against the door frame. Her face was gray.

"How long had he been dead?" Mel asked.

"Won't know until the autopsy. Won't know about the slug either." Vollmer stared belligerently at Nick. "You like to tell me where you were from seven last evening until two this morning?"

"Nick," Veda said, "you don't have to answer any of this man's questions."

"He and I were together from late yesterday morning until you got here," Taylor said.

Vollmer glanced at Taylor and then back at Nick. His eyes narrowed, and Nick saw his fingers flex. "You sleep in the same bed?"

"What do you think?" Taylor asked. She glared at Mel and Veda as though daring them to contradict her.

"Mel and Veda were here until midnight," Nick said. "After that I didn't leave the house."

"You went to sleep sometime, didn't you?" Vollmer asked, turning to Taylor. "I seem to recall you sleep real hard after you make love. If it's been good, that is."

Nick drew in his breath. He knew Vollmer was baiting him, trying to make him do something stupid.

"How would you know?" Taylor asked sweetly.

Veda covered her snicker with a cough.

"I didn't sleep hard enough for Nick to slip away from me long enough to go to the bathroom or to find another condom." Taylor arched her eyebrows prettily at Vollmer.

Nick watched the blood rush up the man's neck and suffuse his face. Oh, yeah, he still wanted Taylor all right. And now he had real reason to want Nick in prison for a long stretch.

"Of course," Taylor said, "there's another reason I know he didn't go anywhere."

"Yeah?"

"He doesn't know the gate code." She smiled triumphantly. "He could drive out, but he couldn't get back in unless he knocked the gates off their hinges." She turned to Mel.

Mel relaxed, leaned back in his chair and nodded at Vollmer. "You didn't notice anything amiss, did you, Detective, when Taylor buzzed you in?"

Vollmer didn't give up easily. "Maybe Eugene picked him up and he climbed back over the fence."

"Oh, Danny, get real."

"Maybe he hitchhiked."

"Sure. Would you pick up somebody his size at two in the morning on a country road beside a burning car?" Taylor laughed.

Nick smiled. He could take care of himself, but Taylor needed this confrontation.

"Smart-ass," Vollmer said with forced amiability, then turned grim. "Smart enough to get that pretty little tail in a crack you can't get it out of one of these days." To Nick he said, "Once the autopsy comes in, you and I are going to have a little talk without your mouthpiece over there."

"I'll bring my other mouthpiece instead—the one with the Boston accent."

Vollmer gave a strangled snarl, turned on his heel and stalked out.

Nick knew Taylor's pattern now. Smart-mouth the authority figure, stand up to the bully, and then the moment the danger was over, collapse into heart palpitations and nausea.

He took her in his arms without a thought for Veda and Mel. He could feel her heart beating frantically against him and hear her breath coming in short, shallow gasps.

He relished the feel of her against him and knew it might be the last time. Eugene died because Nick Kendall had shot him as he ran away from the Eberhardt warehouse. Sooner or later Nick would have to tell Vollmer. Maybe they'd call it self-defense, maybe voluntary manslaughter. In any case he needed to talk to Rico Cabrizzo first.

He had to stay out of jail long enough to make certain that Taylor was safe. That meant she had to stay as far from him as possible.

Taylor slipped out of his arms quickly and went to stand behind Mel. "So, we're still on the job, right?"

Nick shook his head. "Wrong." He spoke to Mel and pointedly ignored Taylor. "I meant what I said."

"How about if Mel takes over?" Taylor asked. Nick heard the edge of desperation in her voice.

Again he shook his head. "You couldn't stay out of it."

Mel nodded. "He's right." He patted Taylor's hand. "The Paradise Café thing is hotting up. I can use you to check some credit references for me."

"No!" Taylor turned to Veda. "You tell them."

Veda shook her head. "Leave me out of it." She raised

her eyebrows at Mel and went to the door. Mel followed. "Whatever personal is going on between you, work it out without us."

Taylor followed. "He may still be in danger. After all, he can identify the animals."

Mel kept his tone even. "The remaining animals are off the market, the killer has nothing to fear from either of you. All he has to do is keep his head down and write the whole thing off as an investment that went bad."

"Meanwhile Nick pays thirty-five thousand dollars to Pete Marley."

"That was always a possibility," Nick said quietly.

"We're already working on that little problem," Veda said. She touched Taylor's arm. "Don't worry, dear. It'll all work out."

"Take a couple of days off," Mel said. "Then come back raring to work." He leaned over and kissed her on the cheek, something he had never done before.

She flinched.

He gave Veda a baffled glance. She shook her head, stood on tiptoes to kiss Nick on the cheek, and dragged Mel to his car.

Nick closed the door behind them. Taylor wouldn't give up without a fight. She stood with her back to him, her arms wrapped around her body.

He could tell she was battling for control.

"It's no thanks to me either of us is alive," she said.

"Not true."

"Don't be kind and don't condescend." She whirled to face him. The tears in her eyes shone like stars.

He longed to go to her and kiss those tears away, heal her bruised ego and her wounded spirit. But he stayed where he was and tried to keep the anguish out of his voice. "I'm not condescending. You found the animals. That was something."

"Thank you very much. I didn't, however, find the thief. I seem to recall that was my assignment, wasn't it? I've cost you thirty-five thousand dollars and possibly Rounders." She pointed at the side table. "I'm always telling my mother I carry a gun, but it hasn't been much help, has it? It's either not available or I get the stupid thing taken away from me. What good is it? Come to think of it, what good am I?"

"You're damn good. You weren't supposed to fall over a dead body the first day."

"Really? You warned me this could be dangerous, but did I listen? Nooo." She turned away from him. "I didn't tell Mel about Eberhardt or Eugene." She took a deep breath. "I am not a team player."

"Everybody makes lousy decisions sometimes. Hey, you can play on my team any day."

"Can I really? Even with Eugene's handprints on my ass?" Suddenly all the spirit seemed to drain out of her. "I understand what this is really about. You're dealing with it intellectually like a nice, intelligent modern man who doesn't believe women ask to get assaulted, being supportive and thoughtful and all the rest of the psychological buzzwords. The reality is that the thought of taking me to bed after what went on yesterday probably revolts the hell out of you. Every time you look at me you see me on that bed with Eugene's hands on me, and you remember that you couldn't do a goddamn thing about it."

"Taylor!" He went to her then, grabbed her arms, spun her around and held her at arm's length. "It's eating me alive that I couldn't protect you, but that doesn't mean I don't want you every bit as much as I ever did. Goddammit, I want you alive! The first day we met, you said if things got tough you'd run like hell and let the police handle it. Do it!"

She pulled away from him. "Fine. You're right, Mel's right, Veda's right, and I'm whining like a kid whose lollipop got stolen. I agree. I'm not rational. I'm mad as hell about this. I have a score to settle. But it's your call, buster, and you've called it. Now get out of my house and out of my life until I come to terms with my failure." She spun away. "Shouldn't take long. I've had plenty of experience."

"Taylor, baby—"

"Get out, please. Right now. I cannot take one more minute of this."

He knew the instant he walked out the door that she'd slam it behind him and fall apart. But this time he'd lost his privilege to hold her while she retched.

His plan had worked, oh yeah, it had worked all too well. She'd be safe away from him.

Somehow when this mess was over, he vowed, he'd get her back.

That is, if he wasn't sitting in jail convicted of murder.

This time he felt as though he were the one who was going to throw up. "I'll call you tomorrow," he said and opened the door.

"Don't."

CHAPTER EIGHTEEN

"MOTHER, IT'S TAYLOR."

"Oh, Taysie, darling, I've been so worried, but at least I haven't seen anything else about you in the papers. Bradley was terribly upset. I do think you owe him an apology."

Elmo climbed up to Taylor's shoulder and tried to stick his nose between the telephone and her hand. Taylor shoved him off. He stalked away grumbling. "Wrong way round. He owes me one."

"You're always so hard on him."

"Maybe that's because you're always so easy."

"Taysie, you know your father didn't believe any woman should ever correct a man—even her own son."

"And look how he's turned out."

"He's turned out very well." Irene sounded as though she were trying to convince herself as much as her daughter.

"Mother, he's been up on disciplinary charges by the bar association twice, he is a dangerously unfaithful husband who may one day bring home more than the bacon to his wife, and he—like his father before him—beats both his wife and his children."

"Taysie, how can you say things like that?"

"Because I'm tired, miserable, wallowing in self-pity and sick to death of secrets. Not that they're secrets from you."

"Bradley has promised me—"

"Mother, I didn't call to talk about Bradley."

"No, of course you didn't, Taysie." There was a silence

before her mother asked, "Why are you tired and miserable?"

"Long story. I wanted to hear your voice, reassure you."

"I wish your uncle Mark had never left you that place! What was he thinking, leaving his hunting cabin to a woman!"

"He gave me sanctuary."

"What a strange thing to say. Paul's death ruined your life."

Taylor took a deep breath. Maybe it was time to give her mother a little reality therapy. "If he hadn't been killed, he'd probably have been divorced citing the secretary whose apartment he paid for." The moment the words left her mouth Taylor regretted them.

"Taylor Hunt, only a very weak woman divorces a man over mistresses. We Maxwell women have never been weak."

"I beg your pardon?"

"Your father kept every secretary he had until his prostate gave out, and he slapped me every bit as often as he took after you and Bradley. Any southern woman knows that sort of thing is the price one pays for a fine home and a decent life."

"A *decent life*?"

"Of course. All my furs and jewelry are out of guilt."

"Mother," Taylor said with wonder, "you and I are on different planets, but God help me, I'm your child. I put up with it from Paul for six years."

"And would have continued for the sake of your children, just as I did."

"No, mother, I would not." Taylor leaned her head back against the chair and checked the clock. Nine-thirty in the morning. The day already seemed a millennium long. She took a deep breath. Maybe secrets were better in the long run.

"Look," she said, "let's not quarrel. You bought me lunch, how about I buy you lunch to reciprocate?"

"Oh, Taysie darling, I can't, not today. But I'll tell you what, meet me about four and we'll have a gooey desert, just the way we used to."

Taylor laughed. "Sure. Yes, I'd like that. Life may let you down, but chocolate hangs in there."

"Oh, good. I'll be at CeCe Washburn's new shop in Germantown."

Sandbagged again. Taylor dropped her head into her hand and acknowledged defeat. "All right, CeCe Washburn's it is. But I'm still not taking that job."

She hung up the phone, leaned back in the leather chair, then nestled her cheek against the leather. It still smelled like Nick—fresh-cut wood and pine straw. Her heart lurched. She missed him already.

Before she lost her nerve, she picked up the phone again and dialed Mel's number. When he answered she said without preamble, "Consider this my two weeks' notice, Mel. That should give you time to find another investigator."

"Taylor? Don't be silly, girl. This is only one case."

"No, Mel, it was *my* case. I wanted to show off how great I was, and I screwed up every step of the way including going to bed with the client and almost getting us both killed. But I'm not going back to sitting in front of a computer screen staring at little green letters until my eyes cross."

"Nobody says you have to."

"At the moment it's all I'm good for. My worst mistake was putting Nick in jeopardy. And I fell in love with him. I had no right to do that."

"Taylor, honey—"

"Please, listen. Consider me off the clock for the next two days, then I'll give you ten working days on the Paradise Café thing. If by the end of that time the police haven't caught Nick's thief, then I'm going to do their jobs for them—free, gratis, no client.''

Mel sighed. ''Take your two days. Get your head straight. But I'm not letting you go without a fight.''

''Fight away. You can't win until I do.''

She longed to go straight back to bed, pull the covers over her head and sleep for the whole two days. Not possible. Mel said somebody always knew the truth. She dragged out her tape recorder, turned on her computer, set up her files and began to transcribe her notes.

The moment she heard Nick on the tape, she hit the ''stop'' button. The sound of his voice enveloped her in warm honey. She closed her eyes and leaned her head on her computer desk, then raised it with a jerk when she realized she'd deposited three lines of Ks across the screen.

''Deal with Nick later,'' she told herself sternly, fast-forwarded and began to transcribe Estelle Grierson's discussion of Clara's wild days at Ole Miss.

Two hours later she got up to go to the bathroom, eased her aching back, shook out her shoulders and arms. She was too stupid to see what must be there. So she called Danny Vollmer and asked him to lunch.

''What for?'' he asked suspiciously. ''Don't give me any garbage about just wanting to see me again either.''

''Maybe it's time to mend fences. Whether we like it or not, we got history.''

''And you want to pick my brain.''

''Partly. Partly I want to give you some of the information I may have that you don't.''

He asked suspiciously, ''What do I have to do in return?''

''Eat and don't pay the bill.''

He thought a moment, and then said, ''Okay, but I won't have much time. I'll meet you. Say where and when, and make it someplace in the neighborhood.''

Taylor wore her good wool blazer and slacks. Her mother

didn't have to know that once again she'd dressed up for someone else.

"I'M INTERROGATING KENDALL this afternoon," Danny said the moment they sat down.

Taylor took a deep breath and toyed with her spoon as though the prospect of Nick in Vollmer's hands didn't scare the bejesus out of her. "I know you don't really think he killed anyone."

Vollmer leaned over. "There's something going on. His lawyer—that Cabrizzo guy—called me to make the appointment. When lawyers do that, it's because their clients have confessed something to them and want to make the best deal they can."

"Nick doesn't have anything to confess."

"Yeah, right." Vollmer concentrated on his menu.

"Are there any preliminary findings on Eugene's autopsy?"

"Come on, Taylor," he said. "You're here to tell me, not to pump me, remember?"

"I will tell you. Answer the question."

Vollmer clicked his tongue against his teeth in annoyance. "One thirty-eight slug killed him."

Taylor went hot remembering the three shots Nick fired after Eugene.

She formed her question cautiously, almost afraid to hear the answer. "Was Eugene shot in the back?"

Vollmer glanced up from his menu and saw her face. He lowered the card slowly and narrowed his eyes at her. "Why?"

"Please, Danny, it's important."

"Okay. He was shot from the side at close range. The bullet tore the hell out of his right lung and punctured his left one before lodging in a rib."

"Could he have driven for any distance after he was shot?"

Danny snorted. "He was dead in minutes, and probably unconscious instantly."

Taylor sank back in her chair. "I know why Nick's coming to see you."

"Yeah?"

"He thinks he killed Eugene. Yesterday when Eugene ran away, Nick fired three shots after him with Eugene's own thirty-eight. He thinks one of those shots connected, and that Eugene drove around with a slug in him until he ran off the road and died."

"Damn," Danny said softly. He ran his hand across his mouth and drank half his iced tea in one gulp. "Was he really with you last night?"

Taylor nodded.

"God! I hate mysteries," Danny said. "I wanted him for Eugene's killing. Really wanted him." He looked straight into her eyes. "Mistake to let personal feelings interfere with the job."

Taylor couldn't have agreed more.

"At any rate, he's got his animals back," Danny said. "No sense in keeping them for evidence." He laughed. "I can just see the evidence man if we tried to bring in a bunch of huge carousel animals. We dusted them for fingerprints and told Kendall to come pick them up. He should have them back safe and sound at that warehouse by now."

"How many did you find?"

"Eight."

Taylor let out a sigh of relief. "If we assume one burned up at Eberhardt's, that leaves them all accounted for. That means Nick is safe. Thank God." Then she realized the return of the animals severed her last connection with Rounders. "Have you started trying to locate the owners of all that other stuff? I suppose it was all stolen."

"Some of it came from museums, some from auctions and private houses. Some of it we may never trace."

"What about the records? The Eberhardts couldn't keep that much information in their heads."

Danny shook his head. "We've been over both houses and that warehouse with a fine-tooth comb. No records. It's possible they burned up in the fire at the shop, but we can't count on that. We're checking to see if they rented any safety deposit boxes in local banks under either 'Eberhardt' or 'Fields'. If they used a fake name, we may never find the records."

"Eugene swore there were records, but even *he* didn't know where, exactly."

"He sure can't tell us now." Their food arrived. Danny tucked into his goulash; Taylor suddenly found that she had no appetite. She pulled her chicken salad apart and picked at it with her fork.

Danny didn't register that she wasn't eating until his own lunch was half gone. Then he glanced up at her and asked, "So, you in love with this guy or what?"

Taylor caught her breath. "He's a client."

"Bull. This morning when I went for Kendall you tore into me like a banshee. You're like a damn mother hen. I hope he appreciates it."

"Nope. He fired me this morning. Whatever we had is definitely over."

"Sure. Right." Danny buttered a popover and bit into it greedily. He spoke with his mouth full. "So, your turn."

Taylor reached for her satchel. "I brought you Eugene's thirty-eight with three shots fired."

Vollmer choked. "You what?" He wiped his mouth and leaned across the table. "Are you crazy? You should never have picked up the damn gun."

Taylor hunched her shoulders. "Neither of us was thinking very clearly. I'm sorry."

"Hang on to it until we're in the parking lot. These old biddies would probably have strokes if you handed me a gun."

"It's got Nick's fingerprints on it."

Vollmer nodded.

"But it won't be the gun that shot Eugene."

"Yeah, okay, but shooting off a firearm in the city is against the law."

Taylor raised her hands and laughed. "Get a grip. I'll swear it was self-defense. No prosecutor in his right mind would go to the grand jury."

"Maybe. I'm still going to use every bit of leverage to wring Kendall so dry he'll think he's been microwaved."

"You just said personal animosity does not mix with good police work."

"This is different—" he reached across the table and touched her hand "—this is you."

She pulled away, but smiled to take some of the sting out of her words. "I owe you a lot, Danny. You single-handedly picked my self-esteem out of the mud. I hope you'll always be my friend."

"But no more than a friend." Danny shrugged and leaned back in his chair. "Just for that—I get dessert."

Taylor laughed.

"And then you start at the beginning of this mess and tell me everything you know, think, or even suspect. Got that?"

"Yessir, Mr. Policeman, sir." Taylor threw him a salute.

She'd tell him no more than she wanted him to know. She'd always been able to con Danny, and she had no intention of turning over a new leaf now.

"HELLO, CECE," Taylor said. "My mother here yet?"

"Taylor, how nice." CeCe stood behind a glass case full of antique jewelry with a large spray bottle of glass cleaner and a wad of paper towels. "Come to help out? I still haven't hired anyone."

"Ask me again in a couple of weeks. I'm going to need a job."

CeCe raised her eyebrows. "Well, I just might do that little thing."

"Obviously, my mother's late as usual." The shop was not yet fully organized, but opulence overflowed in every direction. "CeCe, I need a favor." She told CeCe about Estelle Grierson. She expected CeCe to respond grudgingly, but instead the woman seemed elated at the prospect of digging through the ruins of Eberhardt's shop.

"I'm so glad you asked me," CeCe said, rubbing her hands together. "A lot of it may be junk but there's bound to be some marvelous things left."

Taylor gave her Estelle's telephone number and breathed a sigh of relief. She owed Estelle Grierson.

"I can see why mother loves this place," she said. "She's crazy about antique jewelry." Taylor ran her eye casually over the cloisonné necklaces, old jade amulets, and soft baroque pearls. She leaned forward and pointed at a gold necklace and pendant at the end of the case. "Could I see that thing? I know somebody who's got one."

CeCe opened the case and pulled out the necklace. "Lovely piece. A lady's gold pencil from about nineteen-hundred." She handed the necklace to Taylor. "Not expensive. The chain is, of course. But the pencil's only a hundred and fifty dollars—and it's twenty-four-carat gold."

Taylor touched it and felt an almost electrical tingle run from it up her arms. "It's a pencil? It's only four inches long."

CeCe laughed throatily. "Here, dear." She took off the top of the pencil and spread it like a telescope, then put the top back on. The pencil was now a respectable ten inches long. "See," she said, "you put the lead into the end and it feeds down through the hole at the bottom in that little narrow part.''

"I thought it was an old-fashioned hypodermic needle." Taylor handed it back. "Are they rare?"

"I'd say so. Not unique, certainly, but quite rare. I've never seen another one like it, and I've been in the business for forty years."

Taylor picked up her satchel and threaded her way to the door. "Would you tell my mother I had an emergency? I'll call her tonight."

Irene was climbing out of her car outside.

"Taysie, darling, I'm sorry I'm late."

Taylor kissed her cheek on the fly. "Sorry, Mother, something came up. I'll call you." She ran to her truck and climbed in. As she backed out, she saw Irene staring after her openmouthed.

No grateful hospital board had given Margery Chessman a fancy antique hypodermic needle.

One lady's gold pencil, circa 1904 had been missing from the inventory of Helmut's store after the robbery. Taylor had assumed that it had been destroyed, but this was too much of a coincidence to be ignored. Unless there were three pencils kicking around—highly unlikely given the rarity of the thing—that pencil around Margery's neck came from Helmut Eberhardt's store. And it had been listed on his inventory when he died.

So unless Margery or Josh Chessman drove to Oxford the day of his death and bought the thing—and both of them denied having been out of town that day—that pencil was taken either just before or just after Eberhardt was killed. Margery surely had no reason to kill Eberhardt. That left good ol' Josh.

Taylor could imagine his eyes lighting on it in Helmut's display case as he made his way out the front door and away from the flames that lapped Helmut's body. A gold pencil would appeal to an academic, surely. But why on earth would he be crazy enough to give it to his wife? Unless she found it and thought it was a present for her. Josh would hardly deny that under the circumstances. Nobody was likely to connect it with Eberhardt, after all. Perfectly safe for Margery to walk around with it hanging among her other baubles.

Taylor knew she ought to call Vollmer, but if she guessed correctly, he'd still be interrogating Nick. A lousy little pencil was not hard evidence. She dialed Mel and got the Borman Agency answering machine. She called information for Veda's number and got an answering machine there too. She called Rounders on the assumption that Veda—or at least some of the carvers—would be there.

Another damn answering machine! The world was being run by robots who couldn't even talk to one another.

In desperation she called Max Beaumont. No answer, no machine. She couldn't call Josh Chessman. What would she say to Margery? Margery had sworn Josh had been in his office at seven-thirty on Monday night while Clara Eberhardt was being stabbed to death.

Chessman had sworn he'd been duking it out with his latest abandoned mistress. They'd accepted his story. Margery could be lying, or the mistress might still be very much in love with Josh and happy to lie for him. Maybe Josh had paid her off.

Finally, Josh might have had his calls forwarded to his car phone. He might have been answering Margery's call as he tried to avoid sideswiping Taylor coming out of the Rounders alleyway Monday evening.

He had opportunity to steal. He had keys to Rounders. He knew Clara Eberhardt well. He even owed her—or she might have felt that he did.

Maybe Josh wanted enough of his own money to be able to dump Margery. She was the one with ambition. Josh seemed more likely to want a nubile young wife, a cushy tenured job and plenty of free time to play at Rounders.

If all the animals in Rounders had been sold, he stood to make in the neighborhood of three-hundred thousand dollars in nontaxable income that he could hide in a safety deposit box and dole out in such small amounts that the I.R.S. wouldn't be suspicious.

But one gold pencil didn't make a case.

Taylor needed the Eberhardts' records right now! She needed to be able to tie Chessman to the stolen animals.

She called Chessman's number. If she were going on a fishing expedition, she didn't want to run into the resident shark. Margery answered and told her that Josh had office hours tonight until eight. He wouldn't be available to talk to her until the following morning.

"Are you going to be home? Can you give him a message?" Taylor asked.

"I have a board meeting and a dinner engagement. I will be home very late."

Taylor decided that counted as a 'no.' She thanked Margery and hung up. So Josh was safely out of the picture. So was everyone else including Nick. She had the next two hours to find those records.

She pulled into the nearest parking lot and cut her engine. She had a feeling that if she put her mind to it, she could figure out where those blasted records had to be. If they were on computer disks, they'd make up a fairly small package. The police had searched Eberhardt's house, shop, rental property and warehouse, and had come up empty. Policemen knew how to search. They got plenty of practice going after drugs.

So either the records did not exist, or they were in a truly weird place.

But Eugene swore they existed. The killer thought they

existed. Taylor had to believe they existed. Otherwise, why would the killer continue to target her and Nick?

Where was there left to search? The police would have found records or lockbox keys or disks even if they were taped to the bottoms of drawers or the backs of picture frames.

And chances were that Helmut and Clara would have wanted to keep their records accessible, able to be updated fairly quickly. They wouldn't have used the local bank.

She leaned her head against the back of her seat. She was developing a major pain behind her right eye. She longed to stop worrying about the records…and Nick…and Vollmer…and these murders… It almost made her wish she had one of those crystal glasses full of single-malt whiskey that Marcus Cato had thrust at her from the belly of his fancy armored horse.

Suddenly her eyes widened. Oh, yeah. She knew one place she'd bet the police had not searched. And it was just weird enough to be the right place. She grinned and started her truck.

CHAPTER NINETEEN

"YOU DO KNOW FIRING A GUN is against the law?" Vollmer said for the sixth time.

Cabrizzo came to attention. "My client was in fear for his life."

"Hell, Cabrizzo," Detective Harrison said, "the guy was running away."

"For all my client knew, he was running to his vehicle for another weapon. Did you find another weapon in his car?"

"None of your business."

"Certainly it's my business. Do you have any reason to believe that any of the shots he fired after this retreating criminal could have caused said criminal's death?" Then, when nobody answered, "Come on, Vollmer, give already."

Vollmer shrugged. "Okay. Eugene Lewis was shot once at close range while he was sitting in the front seat of his car fifty miles from that place the Eberhardts were using. He died almost instantly."

Nick surged to his feet.

Harrison and Vollmer did the same thing so quickly that their chairs fell over backwards.

"Vollmer, you bastard, you put me through hell for three hours when you knew I didn't shoot Eugene!"

Rico grabbed Nick's arm. "Sit down."

Rico gathered up his notes and opened his briefcase. He

said cheerfully, "Okay, you guys, we're outa here. You want to talk to my client again, you get a warrant. Okay?"

"Wait a minute," Harrison said, "we're not through."

"Sure you are," Rico said.

Nick laid a hand on Rico's arm and spoke to Vollmer. "If I were you, Detective, I'd stop letting my personal feelings interfere with my job and go looking for whoever set Helmut Eberhardt on fire, because the same person who did that stole my animals, killed Clara and Eugene, and, if you're not careful, could kill Taylor Hunt."

"Taylor's out of it," Vollmer said.

"The hell she is."

"I had lunch with her today. She's the one gave me the gun."

Nick looked confused.

"She said you were clear on Lewis and she'd testify for you. She's getting out of the P.I. racket."

"She said she was not going to be a P.I. any longer?" Nick asked. "Her precise words?"

"She said she'd given Borman two weeks' notice."

"Can we get out of here now?" Nick didn't believe that Taylor had simply given up. He wanted to know where she was and what she was up to, and he wanted to know immediately.

TAYLOR CALLED MARCUS FROM HER TRUCK. Better to confirm her theory before she wasted a lot of time. He picked up the phone himself.

"Child, how you doin'?" he asked.

"Fine, Marcus. Got a quick question for you."

"Sure."

"How hard is it to hollow out one of those animals to set up something like your bar?"

"Bodies are put together from a bunch of different pieces of wood. They're naturally hollow."

"So what you're telling me is that the bodies of all wooden carousel animals are at least partially empty?"

"Pretty much. Why?"

"Thank you, Marcus, thank you very much."

Computer disks would fit easily into the hollow belly of a carousel animal.

Twenty minutes later, Taylor stepped from her truck onto the dark loading dock of Rounders, held her penlight between her teeth, and went to work on the padlock that held the door to the back stairs. When and if Vollmer turned Nick loose, he'd see her truck parked in his spot in the alley and know that she was here. Just to be safe, she'd left word on his answering machine outlining her suspicions of Josh.

She'd already left word on Mel's. Wouldn't it be nice if somebody occasionally answered a telephone?

The lock clicked and she ran up the stairs, ignoring the eerie sound of her shoes against the metal treads. She pushed through the door to the storeroom and flicked on the overhead lights.

She figured that Nick's newly returned animals should be among those at the very back, closest to her. In ten, fifteen minutes max, she'd know whether the Eberhardts had stashed their records in the belly of one of Nick's stolen animals.

She tried to remember what the six animals she'd seen at the warehouse looked like, but she'd had eyes for nothing but Eugene and his gun. She'd have to start with the back row and try them all until she found the right one.

She tried tapping. They all sounded hollow. She tried looking for hinges. None. She tried looking for seam lines.

Finally she laid her satchel on the seat of one of the chariots and began to crawl around on her hands and knees. At this rate, it would take her not fifteen minutes, but several hours to test her theory.

Clara must have been crazy or unbelievably greedy to

leave the safety of The Peabody lobby to come bopping up here with the man who abandoned her in college.

Suddenly the note slid into Taylor's mind like an overhead being projected on a wall. It hadn't said "Meet *at* PB..." but "meet pb..."—lower case.

Maybe pb stood not for Peabody but for "prissy bitch." Which prissy bitch? Estelle had referred to all the sorority sisters as prissy bitches. A name popped into Taylor's mind. Margery Chessman! She'd been ex-president of the sorority.

Margery could have stolen the gold pencil herself and hired Eugene. She knew Rounders as well as Josh did and was at Ole Miss at the same time as Clara. If Margery had been Helmut's co-thief, Clara wouldn't have been afraid of her. Certainly not if Margery offered to keep the scam going.

And after Margery stuck a chisel into Clara, she could easily call Josh from her car phone and ask him when to put the lamb chops on. She'd know she had plenty of time to beat him home.

Taylor ducked under an ostrich.

"Two minds with but a single thought."

Taylor jumped, banged her head painfully on the ostrich's belly, and lifted her head.

Margery Chessman, impeccable as ever and wearing at least half a pound of antique gold around her neck, stood in the open doorway pointing a large black automatic at Taylor's breastbone.

CHAPTER TWENTY

"DAMN!" Margery snarled. "You are the most infuriating woman. I told you I have an important dinner engagement. I value punctuality."

Taylor cleared her throat. "The police are on their way." She tried to keep her eyes on Margery's face, rather than on the black hole at the end of that revolver. She could feel the sweat sliding down her spine.

Margery laughed. "No, they're not. Josh found out Nick fired you this morning. You're on your own."

"I called the police on my car phone."

"To say what? I am off to meet a killer at Rounders?" Margery laughed.

Taylor could see her satchel containing her Glock once again out of reach. If she got out of this alive she vowed to start wearing it in a holster and the heck with the fashion statement. At least this time the safety catch was off. If she could reach it before Margery shot her, she'd have a chance to shoot first.

Margery waggled her own gun. "Go on, dear. You were doing fine. You've eliminated all but two of the animals Helmut stole. Let's see, we've got Nick's ostrich and the pig left to check." She wrinkled her forehead. "Ostrich, I think."

Taylor turned to the ostrich. Margery's deep voice stopped her.

"On the other hand, the pig has a bigger belly." She grinned. "It would hold more."

"Which?" Taylor spread her hands. Margery seemed amenable to keeping her alive so long as she was the one doing the crawling around on the floor.

"The ostrich, I think. It's higher off the ground. Helmut was too lazy to bend down when he could do a job standing up."

Taylor turned to the ostrich.

"Ah-ah," Margery said. "Don't make any sudden moves or I'll splatter you all over the room and find the records myself."

"And then what?" Taylor asked. "Everyone else has alibis. You'll stick out like a sore thumb."

"It will look like one of those random things."

"Sure it will."

Margery tapped her toe impatiently. "Find the records, then I'll decide what to do with you. I will shoot you if I have to, but if you're good, maybe there's another way."

Of course there was. On Mars in a parallel universe. Taylor had to get to that satchel. She moved towards the ostrich's midsection as slowly as she could. She tried to slide around the far side so that she could put the animal between her and Margery, but Margery stopped her with a gesture.

The ostrich leaned against the wall just under the master electrical panel. The door to the panel hung wide open. The master electrical switch lay just to the right of Taylor's shoulder.

With luck she could throw the switch with her shoulder and plunge the room into darkness, then dive for her satchel before Margery could react.

It wasn't much, but it was worth a try. "Did Josh tell you that Nick had discovered Marley's fake?"

Margery rolled her eyes. "Josh tells me everything. Otherwise I'd never have dared leave you people messing up my house exchanging information the other night. After Nick called from Seattle, I put enough sleeping pills in

Josh's martini to knock him out, then I drove to Oxford to get rid of Eberhardt.'' She snickered. ''I toasted his cold feet for him.''

Taylor gulped. ''Why kill Clara?''

Margery snorted. ''Stupid woman wanted to dump the remaining animals on the market at one time and then see if there were any really extraordinary ones left here that we could steal. Even in college she had no sense of proportion. If she'd tried to pledge my sorority, I'd have blackballed her myself.''

''With so much history, she wasn't worried about coming down here with you?''

''When I first sounded Helmut out about stealing the horses, I think she gloried in the discovery that I was not Miss Goody Two-shoes.'' Margery laughed and shrugged. ''I never was, of course. I just covered my little peccadilloes up better than she did.''

''And when you came at her with a wood chisel?''

''She never saw it. The velvet throw protected my clothes, although I'd had the good sense to wear my raincoat.'' Margery sighed. ''Very expensive, too. I dropped it in a Dumpster outside the theater arts building. It's long buried in a landfill somewhere. Pity. I liked that coat.''

Taylor began to feel along the ostrich's belly.

''Well?'' Margery asked.

Taylor felt a slit and dug her fingernails into it. She pushed harder. ''Got to be a catch here somewhere.''

''Be careful. Don't break it.''

As though it mattered. Taylor continued to press and pull against the feathers, the wings, the saddle pad. Nothing moved or clicked. She heard Margery shifting restlessly behind her and decided she'd better keep talking. ''Okay, so you hired Eugene. Why'd you kill him?''

''I blame you for that,'' Margery said. ''He couldn't seem to kill you, and I knew if he got caught he'd talk. You and

Nick have been an incredible nuisance. I merely wanted the animals and the records before you got them. I have been acting in self-defense from the start. People menaced me. I removed them. I don't know why the police have to be called into what is essentially a private matter."

Taylor gaped at her.

Margery continued reasonably. "All I wanted was money to entertain enough bigwigs to get Josh that job. These stupid toys…" Margery waved the gun at the animals, but not quite far enough from Taylor's midsection to make diving for the light switch practicable. Not yet.

Taylor remembered thinking they were "stupid toys." Now they were the friendliest things in the room.

"…were sitting here waiting for a museum that will never open," Margery continued. "Might as well do me some good. When Nick discovered the fake at Marley's and went ballistic, I had to protect myself. I have a reputation in this town."

"Three deaths to protect your reputation?"

"Certainly. I do resent having to kill Eugene. We shared some very, very happy times together."

Taylor felt the skin on her arms begin to tingle and the hair along the nape of her neck stand to attention. She turned her head under the ostrich's wing so that she could see Margery's face.

Her eyes held a faraway look that curdled Taylor's blood.

"Eugene had the brains of a newt, but the sexual stamina of a Brahma bull." She grinned at Taylor kittenishly. "He told me what he had planned for you just before I shot him. I'm sorry for your sake you never experienced his prowess firsthand."

"I'm not."

Margery continued as though Taylor had not spoken. "I killed Eugene over your interference. I resent that."

"Gee, sorry," Taylor said.

Margery stole a quick glance at her slim gold wristwatch. "Either get that thing open or try the pig," she said. "Josh and I have an informal dinner with the chairman of the department of arts and sciences in a little over an hour."

Taylor was about to move to the pig when she pulled on the final feather and heard a tinny click. Without warning, a panel opened in the ostrich's belly and a gray box of computer disks fell to the floor.

Taylor jumped, Margery jumped. Taylor reached up, threw the master switch and dove for the floor as far from Margery and as close to her satchel as she could.

Taylor saw the spurt of flame from the barrel before the sound of Margery's shot echoed off the brick walls.

WHEN NICK COULDN'T reach Taylor from his truck, he'd dialed Mel.

"How the hell do I know where she is?" Mel swore. "She said she knew where to find the evidence to prove Josh Chessman was a killer."

"Josh? That's nuts. You didn't try to stop her?"

"It was a message, Kendall, on my answering machine. A message. I've been calling everybody I know since trying to locate her."

"Damn!"

Nick saw Margery's Cadillac parked by the front door. Margery never came near Rounders. How had she gotten in?

Of course! Josh's keys. With a sense of foreboding, Nick cut his engine and leapt for the front door.

He saw a sliver of light under the door to the carving room. He went up softly and opened the door as the lights went out.

A second later he heard the shot.

TAYLOR SAW the door to the carving room start to open.

"Taylor? Margery? What the hell's going on?"

Oh, God, it was Nick! In another second he'd be silhouetted against the moonlight from the windows. A perfect target.

"No!" Taylor shoved the ostrich with all her might.

Margery screamed and fell against the wall.

Her second shot went high.

Taylor grabbed her satchel and hit the master switch again.

"Bitch!" Margery snarled, and blinked as the light came on. Taylor swung the satchel at Margery's gun hand.

The gun flew wide, and Taylor hit Margery as hard as she could with a solid right cross.

She heard the crunch, saw Margery's eyes cross, and felt a jolt of pain all the way to her shoulder. The room began to spin as waves of nausea washed over her.

She saw Nick's face, felt him swing her into his arms, smiled up at him blearily, and said, "Told you I could take care of myself."

TAYLOR WOKE TO FIND her right hand in a cast halfway up her forearm. Her hand throbbed with the urgent push-pull of a catgut bow on an untuned violin.

"You're awake," someone said.

"I'm thirsty," Taylor croaked. Someone held her head while she sipped cold water. She looked up into Veda's face.

"Do I live or what?" Taylor asked.

Veda smiled and let her head fall back gently against the pillows. "You live in a cast for six weeks, then do therapy for a month. It will not be a picnic."

"That witch did break my hand. I could kill her!"

"No, dear, you nearly broke *her* jaw. You only cracked three bones in your hand. Quite a punch."

"Nick?"

"He's been here all evening. I sent him home to bathe

and shave. He smelled like a goat. He should be back momentarily.''

''What happened to Margery?''

''She's upstairs screaming because she's in the prison ward rather than a fancy private room in a private hospital.''

''Poor Josh.''

''Poor Josh, my foot. He swears he didn't know what Margery was up to. I don't buy it. He didn't want to see is all.'' Veda plumped up Taylor's pillows. ''Vollmer's lurking outside. He's very angry at you.''

''Let him lurk.''

''Mel's outside as well. He's even angrier than Danny.''

''Are you angry?''

''Not at you.''

''Good. My throat hurts.'' She swallowed. ''How long have I been here?''

''Four hours or so. They doped you up in the ambulance.''

''Veda. I'm so hungry! I never get anything to eat anymore.''

''Nick's bringing burgers.''

Taylor sat up suddenly, then yelped as pain shot up her left arm. ''Oh, God, does my mother know?''

''Ask Mel. I'll get him.''

A moment later Mel came in. Taylor caught a glimpse of Veda backing Danny Vollmer away from the door.

Taylor took one look at the set of Mel's jaw and burst into tears. He patted her good shoulder awkwardly.

''I was so scared,'' she sobbed.

''You were so dumb.''

''No, I wasn't, either. I left you a message. I thought it was Josh, and I made sure he was occupied and wouldn't walk in on me. I only figured out it was Margery a minute before she got there. I thought I was safe.''

''At least you figured it out. Nobody else did.''

"Have you called my mother?"

"Well, about that, Taylor, I wanted to see how long you were going to be here..."

"You haven't! Thank God." She tried to take his hand but winced. "Promise me you won't tell her."

"Taylor, there's Vollmer, and the newspapers—"

"Lie! Say I had an accident. Anything. She must not find out."

"Taylor, you're wearing a cast."

"I'll make something up. Please. I couldn't take it, and I sure couldn't take Bradley bitching at me."

"Taylor, about your two weeks' notice."

"Can I take it back?" She gave him her most appealing smile. "I know I can't use the computer for a while, but there's got to be something I can do."

"You still want to go on with this after what happened last night?"

"Of course. It won't happen again."

"Woman, get out of my way or I will remove you." Danny Vollmer shoved the door open and pushed past Veda. "Are you out of your mind?"

"I'm glad to see you too, Detective Vollmer," Taylor muttered.

"I need a statement from you."

"Did you find the computer disks?" Taylor asked. Now that the fog in her brain was lifting, she remembered the reason she went to Rounders in the first place.

"Yeah. Eberhardt kept great records. Almost all inside jobs. A lot of people are going to be very unhappy when they get arrested for complicity in grand theft."

"Margery?" Taylor asked.

"Josh called Cabrizzo, but he had a conflict of interest because he represents Nick. He got another hotshot lawyer off the fourteenth tee. When Margery told him to plead self-defense, I thought he'd have a coronary right there. She's regaling everybody including the orderlies with how smart she is."

"She's crazy."

"Tell me about it."

She lay back against the pillows. "Danny, I'm very tired and I hurt a lot. Can you come back tomorrow?"

"Doctor says you can go home in the morning."

"Then come see me at the cabin tomorrow. With Margery in custody, there's no rush, is there?"

Vollmer grinned and shrugged. "Sure, kid." He leaned over and kissed her cheek. "I'm glad you're alive and if you ever pull a stunt like this again, I'll kill you myself. Clear?"

She nodded. Even that effort made her head ache.

"Come on, Mel, you talk to me," Vollmer said. The two men left the room together.

Veda sat in the visitor's chair and cleared her throat. "Taylor, we have to talk."

"Not you too."

"Ever since I met you I've heard nothing but what an ordinary job you do. In one week you've been shot at twice, attacked twice and mauled once, faced down a killer, and broken your hand. That does not sound like the job description for a bank teller."

"It's never happened before."

"You have also fallen madly in love with your client."

"I'll get over it."

"You were down there looking for some way to clear this up to save Nick."

Taylor flushed. "I'm a professional."

"Professional my Aunt Fanny. Nick brought you into Emergency and stayed right with you the whole time. You should see the way he looks at you. He's so much in love with you he's downright sickening."

"I won't let him run my life. That lovesick man fired me, remember?"

"He's terrified of losing you the way he lost his mother and his grandmother."

"That's *his* problem."

"Is your precious independence so great? Isn't it just lonely?"

"Get off my case, Veda."

"Not until you admit you love him."

"All right, I am in love with Nick Kendall. Now, are you satisfied?"

"I don't know how you and Nick plan to work it out, but you'd better try because the years can be very lonely with nothing but your cat for company."

"I don't know that we can."

"Try. For Veda. Please."

"Yes, Veda, I'll try."

"Good, because you are sadly lacking one element you told me was essential for a good P.I."

"What?"

Veda pointed down her arm from her bandaged shoulder to the cast on her hand. "You, Taylor Hunt, are not a fast healer."

SHE DRIFTED INTO FITFUL SLEEP. She wanted to go home to Elmo, to hide behind her gates and lick her wounds.

She woke to see Nick holding a paper bag in one hand and a bouquet of roses in the other. The bag smelled better than the roses. She couldn't eat roses.

"You're going to need some help for a couple of days," he said.

"I'll manage." She reached for the bag.

"I'm volunteering. Elmo may run out of cat food. You can't drive for a week at least."

"What about Rounders?"

"Veda and Max can fill in. Josh—" he shook his head "—Josh has other commitments at the moment."

She closed her eyes. "I didn't know I was taking chances, Nick. I didn't do anything intrinsically stupid."

"Dammit! I almost lost you!"

"And you almost walked into an ambush! It cuts both ways, buster." She dug in the bag, unwrapped a burger and took a big bite. "Nobody's safe. I may walk out of here this afternoon and get run over by an eighteen-wheeler. You could plunge off a cliff on your motorcycle."

"You put yourself in harm's way."

"It was a fluke." She raised her hand, cast and all, and tried to stroke his cheek. She misjudged the distance and clunked him soundly on the nose. "Oh, Nick, darling," she wailed. "I'm sorry."

He blinked, rubbed his nose and took her plaster paw in both his hands. "Look, Taylor, I love you. I sure as hell didn't plan on it, and I wish to God it hadn't happened. I don't have a damn thing to offer you but debts and dust. But I'd rather see what you're up to than worry about what trouble you're getting into behind my back."

"We're going to fight about this a lot," she said softly.

"We can make up afterwards. He tilted her chin so that she looked into his eyes. "Marry me."

"You want to marry me—broken hand, cast and all?"

He reached for her other hand and held it to his lips. "Your left hand's not broken. My grandmother's ring should fit just fine."

"Do you know what you're getting yourself into?" Taylor asked.

He rubbed his bruised nose, then leaned down and kissed her gently. "I've got a pretty good idea. A lifetime of love."

EPILOGUE

"TAYLOR KENDALL, GET DOWN off that chair this instant!"
Veda stood in the entrance to the new Rounders building
with her hands on her hips. She wore a jonquil-yellow linen
dress and matching mid-heel pumps. "If Nick catches you
up there, he'll kill *me*." She reached up and took Taylor's
arm.

Taylor descended laboriously. "I'm pregnant, Veda, not
disabled."

"You're nearly seven *months* pregnant, you ninny. What
were you doing up there anyway?"

"Somebody hung the elf sign crooked. Can't have that.
I've become rather fond of that sign."

"If Max can't keep that grandson of his from climbing
on top of every animal in the museum I'm going to put in
a call to the elves to come get him. When I left to go change
clothes he was trying to climb up the band organ to get to
the rounding boards."

"He seems a nice enough little boy. Max is so proud to
have him here visiting."

"He's got Max's devilishness in his eyes. And entirely
too much energy. You wait until you're chasing young
Whatsit—" she pointed to Taylor's burgeoning belly "—all
over those acres of yours."

"I've got two o'clock feedings to get through first." She
ticked off her fingers. "Plus, the contractors out at the cottage still haven't finished the second bathroom, the baby's
room needs wallpaper, and Nick has been so busy moving

Rounders into the new building and setting up this museum that he hasn't varnished the library bookshelves. The man is a master woodworker! It's a classic case of shoemakers' children having no shoes."

The double doors from the foyer to the main part of the building swung open. Charlene Cato stuck her elegant head out. "Veda, where have you been? The caterers didn't bring enough ice buckets for the champagne, so I called Marcus and told him to bring some of ours, but as usual, he was due here a half hour ago. I swear, one of these days I will murder that man." Her eyes opened wide and she glanced at Taylor. "Oh, dear, that wasn't a very politic thing to say under the circumstances, was it?"

Taylor shrugged. "Life goes on. Even for Margery who, according to the doctors, is so far in la-la-land at this point that she will probably never come to trial."

"Good thing for Josh. Now that he's back to just being a professor, he seems so much happier," Charlene said.

"Nick says Josh promised to come to the opening today, even though he's no longer technically a partner. At least he came up with the money for Marley," Taylor said.

"That was the least he could do under the circumstances." Veda sniffed. "Well, Charlene, I'm here now. What do you want me to do?"

Charlene took a deep breath, then glanced back over her shoulder. "Nick Kendall, don't you dare move that rabbit one inch! It's right where it belongs." The doors swung shut behind her.

Veda burst out laughing. "Charlene has always avoided this place like the plague. Now she's acting as if she were the one who bought out Josh's share, instead of Marcus."

"I think she enjoys managing. You must admit, she's been a godsend setting up the museum. I certainly haven't been much help."

"Neither have I, what with moving into my new duplex.

I have already warned Max I will not baby-sit for his grandson when he visits.'' She grinned. ''Well, not often, at any rate.''

''You don't have much free time anyway—with Mel hanging around. Come on, Veda. Rounders is supposed to open for the public in...'' She glanced at the slim gold watch on her wrist. ''Oh, good grief! Ten minutes.''

The scene that met them was organized chaos. At least Taylor hoped it was organized. Caterers in white jackets scurried back and forth from the small galley kitchen at the back of the room. Waving a pencil over her head, Charlene chased one of the waiters, who held a tray loaded with champagne glasses.

''The place looks great,'' Taylor said. ''I can't believe you got all this done so quickly.''

Nick had borrowed a miniature carousel from one of his old friends. It revolved slowly in the middle of the banquet table on which platters of hors d'oeuvres sat waiting to be attacked the moment the doors opened. There was punch, and waiters would circulate with trays of filled champagne flutes. Charlene Cato believed in doing things right or not at all, and since Marcus had volunteered to pay for everything, the rest of the Rounders crew agreed wholeheartedly.

Nick had turned off the sound on the miniature carousel's music box so that it would not compete with the big band organ in the corner. As soon as they were ready to open the doors, he'd crank up the organ to play real carousel music.

The room was spacious and airy. No dust motes here, although Taylor did miss the skylights at the old Rounders that had let in the starlight at night. Here the walls shone crisply white and were hung with painted rounding boards from the tops of carousels. Beneath the rounding boards hung restored black-and-white photographs of great old carousels, workshops and master craftsmen.

The carousel animals posed and pranced around the room.

Taylor wondered how on earth she could ever have thought they were silly.

But then, that was before she discovered Nick. And love.

Nick must be in the workroom behind the museum space. That would be open to the public as well today. The sharp instruments were locked away, but the works currently being carved sat on their tables so visitors could see the process of creation from start to finish.

"Sit down before you fall down," Veda said, and shoved Taylor toward one of the rented chairs along the wall. "I'll bring you some fruit punch. No champagne for you. You really should put your feet up while you have a chance. Once everybody else gets here, including all the media people, you'll be run off your feet being a good hostess."

Taylor nodded gratefully. She sat quietly in her corner. As usual, once she relaxed, the baby danced the rhumba.

She loved being pregnant with Nick's baby, although the timing could have been better. After they had announced to Irene that they were getting married as soon as they could get a license, and to heck with Taylor's broken hand and with convention, they had planned to finish expanding and updating Taylor's cottage, move Rounders to its new suburban location, and get the museum up and running. And all that before they even thought of starting a family. Whatsit, however, had other ideas.

Probably just as well. Taylor would be thirty-five when Whatsit saw the light of day, and Nick would be forty-three. She leaned her head against the wall and closed her eyes a moment.

For the last few months she had been like a cat, content to search out the nearest sunbeam to snooze in.

"Darling, you do look lovely."

Taylor opened her eyes. "Hello, Mother. And no, I look like a beached walrus."

"I've just been telling that darling Nick of yours that

CeCe Washburn wants at least two more of his animals for her shop. They're selling like mad."

"Good thing, the way we're spending money on Rounders and the house."

"Oh, darling—"

She patted her mother's knee. "I'm kidding. We've got more students than we can handle these days, and with all the publicity about opening the museum, we should pick up even more."

"Well." Irene sniffed. "At least one of my children is happy. Poor Brad! His divorce is about to kill him."

"He should have thought of that earlier."

"Now Taysie..." She glanced up. "Oh, here's Nick." She whispered to Taylor, "Can't you make him put on a tie for a few hours?"

"Never happen." She reached up a hand. Nick took it in his large one and pulled her to her feet and into his arms. "I convinced him to wear new jeans. That's something."

"I should never have listened to you," Nick said. "These need at least a dozen washes to feel comfortable." He nuzzled her neck. "You, however, feel extremely comfortable."

"Well, I'm not. I can barely reach your mouth over this shelf I'm carrying around in front of me."

Nick kissed her. "I'll always figure out a way to kiss you." He stroked her belly gently. "Hey, Whatsit seems to have calmed down."

"Waiting for a ride on one of your horses." She linked her arm with his and leaned her head against his shoulder. "I'm so glad the amusement park decided to leave your horse on the carousel. I can hardly wait to put Whatsit on top of her father's contribution to the world of antique carousels."

Marcus Cato erupted through the double doors. He held a pair of silver champagne buckets in his left hand and another in his right. "Where's that demanding wife of mine?"

"Marcus, where *have* you been?" Charlene grabbed the buckets and strode away.

Marcus grinned and sauntered over to Nick and Taylor. He nodded down at Irene. "Hello, Mrs. Maxwell."

Irene extended her hand and allowed herself to be pulled to her feet. She simpered. "Dr. Cato. How nice to see you."

"And you, pretty thing," he said to Taylor, "you sure you don't have triplets in there?"

"I hope not, for all our sakes."

Max Beaumont wandered up. "Nick will have to give up riding his Harley once he's a father." He held the hand of a small boy with mischievous eyes—his grandfather's eyes.

"Nobody's giving up anything," Taylor said. "The minute I'm over looking like the Michelin man, I am going back to work, but only on the computer from home, at least for the moment. I can't see dragging young Whatsit here along on surveillance, at least for a couple of months."

"Darling, you're not serious!" Irene Maxwell said.

"Of course not, Mother." Taylor smiled up at Nick. "Nick's going to bring her to Rounders if and when I start going out on jobs again. That child is going to have so many nannies she won't be able to keep them straight."

"Don't forget uncles," Max said. "It'll have quite a few of those as well. How does Borman feel about your going back to work?"

"Borman is delighted," Mel said from behind him. "Here, Taylor, Veda said to bring you this punch."

"Thanks." She drank it greedily. "Now, all of you scat. I need a few minutes' peace before we open the doors. You too, Nick."

"I'd rather stay here with you and Whatsit."

"Nick!" Veda called from across the room. "I have no idea how to turn on this band organ contraption."

"Damn! Be right there." He caressed Taylor's hair. "You okay?"

"I'll probably race the guests to the hors d'oeuvres. Other than that, I'm fine."

"And beautiful." He bent to kiss her. "Be right back, love. We can greet the public together."

He glanced over his shoulder at her as he went to find Veda. Taylor kept saying she felt enormous, but in his eyes she looked downright glorious. More beautiful with every passing day.

At first he'd feared that pregnancy would leave her discontented, but she had wandered through the spring and summer languidly, paying little attention to anything except Nick and the baby growing inside her. That might change, but he doubted it. No matter how crazy their lives seemed to be these days, the moment they were together they felt wrapped in a cocoon of peace.

He'd wondered that first November night what a commitment from Taylor Hunt might do to his life. He'd never considered what *his* commitment to *her* might do. She fitted as sweetly into the empty spaces in his soul as he fitted into her body. She was his love, his world, his family. He watched her and vowed to be the kind of father to Whatsit that he and Taylor had never known.

"Here, Veda, all you do is flip this switch." Suddenly the *oom-pah* and *tweedle-dee* of the band organ filled the room.

"Turn it down!" Veda yelled with her fingers in her ears.

He nodded, lowered the sound to background level, then sought out his wife once more.

Laughing at the noise, she came into his arms. "Look at them!" she said, her eyes sweeping across the multicolored carousel animals. "They're begging to dance." She touched her tummy. "Like Whatsit. I don't think we'll ever be able to sell her to the elves, dear heart."

"Fine with me, love. The sign reads, 'unaccompanied

children' and since I intend to hold tight to both of you for the rest of our lives, it doesn't apply.'' He held her a moment and kissed her gently. ''Now, let's open the doors and let the party begin.''

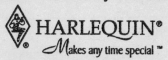

MEN at WORK

All work and no play?
Not these men!

July 1998

MACKENZIE'S LADY by Dallas Schulze

Undercover agent Mackenzie Donahue's
lazy smile and deep blue eyes were his best
weapons. But after rescuing—and kissing!—
damsel in distress Holly Reynolds, how could
he betray her by spying on her brother?

August 1998

MISS LIZ'S PASSION by Sherryl Woods

Todd Lewis could put up a building with ease,
but quailed at the sight of a classroom! Still,
Liz Gentry, his son's teacher, was no battle-ax,
and soon Todd started planning some
extracurricular activities of his own....

September 1998

A CLASSIC ENCOUNTER
by Emilie Richards

Doctor Chris Matthews was intelligent, sexy
and *very* good with his hands—which made
him all the more dangerous to single mom
Lizette St. Hilaire. So how long could she
resist Chris's special brand of TLC?

Available at your favorite retail outlet!

MEN AT WORK™

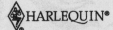 HARLEQUIN®  Silhouette®

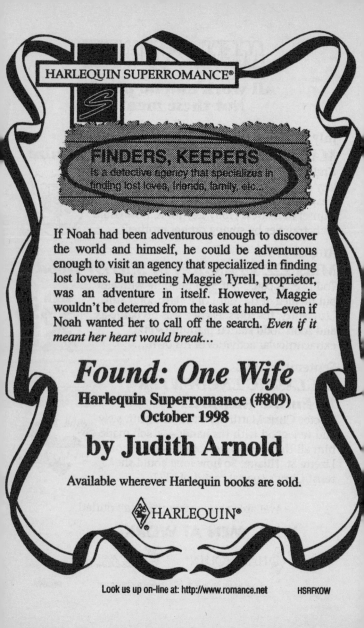

HARLEQUIN SUPERROMANCE®

FINDERS, KEEPERS

Is a detective agency that specializes in finding lost loves, friends, family, etc...

If Noah had been adventurous enough to discover the world and himself, he could be adventurous enough to visit an agency that specialized in finding lost lovers. But meeting Maggie Tyrell, proprietor, was an adventure in itself. However, Maggie wouldn't be deterred from the task at hand—even if Noah wanted her to call off the search. *Even if it meant her heart would break...*

Found: One Wife

Harlequin Superromance (#809)
October 1998

by Judith Arnold

Available wherever Harlequin books are sold.

HARLEQUIN®

HARLEQUIN SUPERROMANCE®

DEBORAH'S SON

by award-winning author
Rebecca Winters

Deborah's pregnant. The man she loves—the baby's
father—doesn't know. He's withdrawn from her for reasons
she doesn't understand. But she has to tell him. *Wants* to tell
him. She wants them to be a family.

Available in October
wherever Harlequin books are sold.

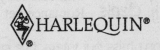

HSR9ML

![Harlequin Superromance logo] **HARLEQUIN SUPERROMANCE®**

COMING NEXT MONTH